COUSINS

TALANOA

Contemporary Pacific Literature

Vilsoni Hereniko, General Editor

Patricia Grace

COUSINS

University of Hawai'i Press
HONOLULU

First published by Penguin Books 1992

Published in North America by University of Hawai'i Press 1998

Printed in the United States of America

98 99 00 01 02 03   5 4 3 2 1

Library of Congress Cataloging-in-Publication Data

Grace, Patricia, 1937–

    Cousins / Patricia Grace.

      p. cm. — (Talanoa)

    ISBN 0–8248–2074–6 (paper)

    1. Maori (New Zealand people)—Fiction. 2. Women,

Maori—New Zealand—Fiction. I. Title. II. Series.

PR9639.3.G7C68   1998

823—dc21   98–10574

                                             CIP

University of Hawai'i Press books are printed on acid-free paper
and meet the guidelines for permanence and durability of the
Council on Library Resources

To the descendants of
Te Kakakura and Unaiki Whareangiangi

acknowledgements

I would like to acknowledge the assistance of the Literature Committee of the Queen Elizabeth II Arts Council while writing *Cousins.*

For conversation and information, my love and thanks to Joyce Gunson, Frances Warren, Harata Solomon, Dick Grace, Edie Tipuna, Mihipeka Edwards, Mary Mataira, Tungia Baker, Irihapeti Ramsden, Jensen Parata, Paparangi Reid, Rosemary Parker and Phyllis Grace.

editor's note

Cousins is the eleventh title in the *Talanoa* series. Established in 1993 by the University of Hawai'i Press in order to make the best writing by Pacific Islanders readily available to American and European readers, *Talanoa* is dominated primarily by Polynesian male authors. This reflects the historical reality of western education in the Pacific in which Polynesia and Polynesian males had a head start over their regional and female counterparts. Patricia Grace's introduction to the literary world through her first collection of short stories—*Waiariki* (1975)—was a first for Pacific women.

The preceding "cousins" of this novel by Grace are *Mutuwhenua: The Moon Sleeps* (1978) and *Potiki* (1986). Themes familiar to Grace's followers—conflicts between Maori and *Pakeha* (white New Zealanders), tradition and modernity, land rights and claims, and the role of women in contemporary society—are explored in greater depth in this novel. Grace offers her readers rare and detailed portraits of three Maori women who share a common heritage but whose personal journeys into the emotional, cultural, and political worlds that inform and circumscribe their actions are as different as their names. Mata, Makareta, and Missy may begin the same, but the responses of each to the attractions and dangers of urban life where old and new worlds collide are always personal and unique.

Patricia Grace has said on more than one occasion that character is central to her fiction. Character therefore becomes the pivotal point around which her novel is constructed. The result of this approach to storytelling is a narrative that is circular or spiral in form. This departure from the linear mode is reinforced by Grace's characters, who struggle constantly to reconcile tradition with modern progress. Rather than embracing change as inevitable forward movement, or abandoning the past as irrelevant in the present, Grace offers her readers an alternative worldview through the character of Makareta: "It's not sticking to the old ways that's important—but it's us being us. Using all the new knowledge our way. Everything new belongs to us." The indigenization of western institutions and systems as advocated here, illuminated and reinforced by the novel's structure, is one of Grace's most important contributions to Pacific literature.

Cousins is Grace's most ambitious work to date. Its keenly observed exploration of the female psyche of three Maori women in contemporary New Zealand is a most welcome and important addition to the chorus of voices that make up the Talanoa series.

Vilsoni Hereniko

MATA

one

Walked enough, and didn't know how she had come to be in the middle of the road. Couldn't remember leaving the footpaths where she'd walked this afternoon, this morning, earlier, before, when?

Middle of the road, not moving. One foot not placing itself in front of the other. Hands not paddling — this side, that side — helping her forward. Eyes not looking out but looking down instead, at two feet. At two big-toe toenails cracked, grooved, blacked, crusted and hoofed. Rusty saws. And at the next-toe toenails fluted and humpy, hooked and clawed, scratch-picking at the tarry middle of the road. Middle-toe toenails? Left one gone, right one worn down, nearly gone. It was a grey, sick-skin colour, like part of a nerveless tooth, gaudy like a bruise, like a battering, like a tatter, like a ripped scrap. Next-toe toenails, left and right were underfolded beneath the middle ones, joint bones poking up white, the two bone lumps propping up dirty skin. Then the little-toe toenails had ingrown, biting the toe skin, the toe flesh. There was blood and dirt. One could be the other, dirt or blood. Some of the dirt was tar from middle-of-the-road walking. Didn't remember leaving the footpaths to walk the middle of the road.

All day walking the footpaths. At first not on the cracks, but after that, anywhere where her feet placed themselves, one down, one forward, then the down one forward. Hands had paddled her — one hand and then the other — trapping air and thrusting it back. Her handful of air, then not hers, paddling back to wherever it would go.

Foot dust too. A puff of dust from under one foot shuffling backwards. Hers, not hers. Then from under the other, back and gone. Unowned. Nothing owned nothing owed as she'd made her way, spoken to only by signs which said: Cross, Wait, Switch Go Slow, Keep Clear, King Bun, Red Hot Specials, Neon Tops,

Book Exchange, Open, Natural Health, Sticky Filth, Vacancy, Family Planning, Showing Daily 6 and 8 p.m., Travel Rarotonga Hawaii, Apply Within, Way Down Sale, Sorry We Are Closed, Stow It Don't Throw It, Greenstone, Shark Teeth, To Clear, Caution Fire Engine, Natural Health, Take A Closer Look, Cafe Paradiso, B.Y.O., One Hour Photos, Conjugal Rights, Unauthorised Vehicles will be Towed Away. And breath, hers, not hers. Out of breath.

Now she stood in the middle of the night, in the middle of the tarry road. No one, only herself. No shoppers now, no workers or kids on skateboards, no joggers, movie-goers or night walkers. The doorways, over-ramps and parks had taken in the pale old men and the dark children who were the street people. No cars, no trucks or vans, no boy on a bike, no girl running — no woman watching, turning her head, staring from the window of a late bus going by.

Back there somewhere she had left the bad-luck cracks under the shop verandahs where she'd stepped past windows of shoes, skirts, dresses, nighties, lingerie, pantyhose and scarves. Past sweatsuits on racks, T-shirts on carousels, jackets and jeans, singlets and underpants, socks, pyjamas and ties. Silk flowers, gauze butterflies, masks and mirrors, Mickey and Donald, good-luck crockery, brass plates, water sets, fruit imitations, crystal balls and bowls and plastic chandeliers. Past hairdressers, photographers, jewellers, preachers, singers, sniffers and paper sellers. Hot bread, Chicken Spot, fruit and vegetables, fish and chips, buns, cakes, bread, pasties and pies, fish steaks, paua fritters, fillets of fish, crayfish, octopus, mussels in brine.

All day. But now in the middle of the tarry road she sat, pitchy-footed, feet and ankles specked with spotchy tar, breathing in and out, huffs and whiffs of breath going to wherever they would go. Sitting. Middle of the tarry road. Middle of the undark night, which was orange coloured, lit by the orange street lights and the spiky stars.

Down, tar. Up, stars. Tar stars. Stars, stares. After everyone had gone there'd been one bus, one late bus. Running girl gone, boy on a bike gone. The lost kids and lost old men had stepped into doorways, alleys, schoolyards, parks, and gone. There was just herself on the street side, walking, and from the passing bus a woman had looked out, staring in surprise from the bus's window. And now, once more, there was just herself, sitting, tar-gazing — her own black self, one dress and one saggy coat with big pockets, one shoe in each pocket, heels on the shoes worn down and two round holes in two soles. In one of the pockets there was a photograph in a frame. Somewhere back there, after the push and hustle, the fast cars and the buses rushing, she had bent, taken off one shoe and then the other and pocketed them.

When?

After that she'd walked again, and her feet, not her shoes, had flat-stepped over the already-gone footsteps of the people gone — over today's and yesterday's footprints of people striding, dawd-ling, staggering, dodging, zigging and zagging. Many footprints of many people. Her own wide feet had walked over them, foot over foot.

Then at the edge of the footpath she'd waited, back there in the undark dark, waited with a shoe in each pocket while the late-night bus bussed through over the recently tarred road, through the middle of the night-time.

The face she'd seen was a face like her own, wide and dark, with a thick frame of hair turning white, and there'd been surprise in the eyes that met hers. The bus beat its way onward and their eyes had held until the bus became a shape, a dimmer and dimmer light on the long road.

She'd stepped off the footpath then, out from under the shop verandahs with her pocketed shoes, to walk the middle of the road, still churning words through her mind, words to do with shops and goods, signs and messages — from hairdressers and supermarkets, laundrettes, fishmongers, butchers, coffee shops, florists, dentists, photographers, jewellers and pharmacists. To do with home-goers, park and doorway sleepers, light and stars, dark and walking, a woman turning, feet and faces, steps and stepping. She had crisscrossed her mind with words that were not thoughts, words that would not become thinking. Then she'd stopped.

Where? Didn't want to ask where or why, or to have thoughts that lead to thinking. Only wanted hands in shoes in pockets and just herself, her own ugly self, with her own big feet and big hands, her own wide face, her own bad hair, which was turning white, springing out round her big head. One coat, one dress. Shoes on their last legs or last feet or in their last pockets, a photo in a frame, and her name.

She wanted what up to now she'd tried not to have — just herself, which was what she'd always had. Just herself and her name, Mata Pairama.

Mata Pairama sitting on the road, breathing in and out, having thoughts but not thinking. Having thoughts that sometimes coiled, hunched against themselves waiting for a forgetful moment when they would become the thinking, become the questioning — the where, the why, the what — become once again the beginning of the answer search, the beginning once again of waiting.

But there would be no more waiting, no more seeking answers to questions thready already from fingering, because she knew now that there were no answers, unless the answers were 'Nowhere' 'No reason' 'Nothing' 'No one'.

Nothing and no one, only herself and her name, a dress, a coat, hands in shoes in pockets. Mata Pairama. There was a photo in a frame and two feet to walk her. She was her own self, ugly.

two

'Uglee. Uglee.'
 The kids sang it through the spaces in the boards, softly enough so that she could pretend not to hear. An eye moved behind a knot hole and she turned her head so as not to see it, turned on the stool, turned her back.

The woman in the thready dress, swinging the knob on the chimney, was her aunty. She had a pretty face, smiling with gappy teeth, smooth as though she could be young, younger than her dress.

Frown.

'Get in here, you kids, and stop getting smart. Bring wood, Chumchum. Missy, bring that baby and get the washing, get her a jersey too.' Aunty moved a pot over to the side of the range and shifted a tin across.

The boy came in, put wood on the hearth and stood brushing himself, swivelling his eyes and turning his mouth down at her. 'Stop that,' his mother said, clipping the side of his head with her hand.

'Only me been looking after Bubba,' the girl behind him said, 'Bubba done mimi, Bubba done tutae,' and Aunty stamped her foot, sending the girl out to the clothesline.

'Give Bubba to Mata,' she said.

The baby stank, and her name wasn't Mata. Why did her aunty keep calling her Mata, which didn't sound like a name at all — sounded like a noise instead, or butter. She didn't like people making up names who had cheeky brats for children and a stinken baby, but she was too shy to say anything about her name.

Now Aunty was smiling again, 'There, Bubba, your cousin Mata, see.'

'It's May.'

'What is?'

'My name. Like on my bag,' she said, showing the label, 'May Parker.'

'I saw, but I thought . . . So that's your name?'

'Yes.'

'My sister called you Mata.'

Stinken was a bad word and if kids were heard saying it at the Home matron would put soap in their mouths, or they'd have to bend over with their bottoms bare and get whacked with the cane. At meal-time they'd have to read the Bible while the others had tea. While she was on holiday she wasn't to forget to read the Lord's word, to pray night and morning and to do the Lord's will always. She had new sandals, and a brown and white gingham dress that Mrs Parkinson had made, for her holiday. She'd darned her socks and fixed the cuffs of her cardigan and had two hankies with her name on them. It was all because she had grandparents, aunts and uncles and cousins who had sent for her. Jean had been jealous about the grandparents and the sandals.

She mightn't see Jean again, mightn't ever go back to the Home because her grandparents would want her and keep her. Then she'd have dresses and shoes like the School kids who came out of their own doors of their own houses every day, who walked along their own paths and out of their own gates every morning on their way to school. Their own curtains at their own windows would shift and the mothers' hands would wave. Sometimes a mother would pop a head out of the window and call, 'Don't forget to come straight home after school.' The girls had skipping ropes and pencil cases, the boys had threepences and marbles.

The girl, Missy, came in with the washing and took it through to the other room. The boy was behind her with water in a basin that had a little piece of yellow soap in it. 'Get this nappy, Miss, take it to the lav,' her aunty called, and Missy went running, running, somewhere.

Where? Because *she* wanted to go to the lav, hadn't been since she left the Home, not even in the train.

'Stay in your seat,' Mrs Parkinson had said, 'Don't talk to anyone and don't get off at all until you get to your station. Also don't forget that I have charge of you, May. I am the one allowing you to have this holiday and I expect you to be well behaved and obedient. Home children are brought up to love and fear the Lord. You must guard against sin while you are away and beware of bad companions. And beware of the devil, who will whisper evil into your ears and lead you into temptation so that the gates of hell will be open unto you.'

As the train moved off she'd looked out of the window at the shunting engines, the railway buildings, the factories and sheds and the crisscrossing railway lines. Smoke and soot had streamed back from the engine as the train picked up speed. Telephone poles and sooty houses had flicked by. Pole, house house, pole, house house, faster and faster.

After that there were large paddocks where sheep grazed, or smaller ones where cows were feeding amongst tufts of weed, banks of cutty grass, rushes, and old, leaning trees. But she'd watched out for houses because that was what she liked best, liked thinking about houses.

Inside houses were mothers, fathers and children, tables and chairs, cups and dishes in cupboards, curtains with flowers on them, floral wallpaper, patterned mats on floors, beds with shiny bedspreads, drawers and wardrobes full of clothes. There were toys and dolls. The dolls had dresses and pants and there were tins of beads that you could make bangles and necklaces with, threading the beads on cotton — green white red, green white red, all red, all green, any way you liked. When it was long enough you tied it round the doll's wrist or neck.

Then the mother came and chased you out because you weren't allowed. Betty wasn't allowed to bring dirty, black children into the house to make bangles and necklaces for dolls. Or Home kids. Betty was a naughty, naughty girl.

Jumping up. Beads spilling, dropping on the flowery mat, sprinkling over the patterned lino. Running out nearly peeing, squeezing her legs together. 'Who told you you could come here . . . Off . . . And don't you ever let me catch you in here again.'

Out of the gate, down the street, nearly wetting herself.

She'd been late home and had been sent into the bathroom to bare her bottom for the cane. After the caning she'd peed, so the stick had come hitting down again For, Being, A, Dirty, Girl, Now, Clean, Up, This, Mess.

'Piss pants, piss pants,' the kids had said as she went for the mop and bucket, whispering so they wouldn't have their teeth prised open and their mouths washed out, 'Piss pants, piss pants,' hissing.

She'd stayed in her seat on the train even though she'd wanted to go to the lavatory. Now she wanted to go urgently and didn't know whether she should ask her aunty's permission or just stand up and look for Missy, who had run somewhere to the lav.

At school, stretching an arm high for the teacher to see, you had to say, 'Please may I leave the room?' Sometimes, one at a time, you were allowed to go, but sometimes you weren't.

'Did you go at lunchtime?' Miss Bower had asked.

'Yes, Miss Bower.'

'Well then, you can wait until after school, can't you?' Eyes. Eyes on her. Eyes on her Home dress, her Home haircut, her black face. Homey, Homey. Blackie, Blackie. 'Can't you?'

'Yes, Miss Bower.'

'Sit down then.' She'd sat, pressing her legs together, squeezing the bones at the sides of her knees and the fat parts at the tops of her legs, unable to write or read or listen.

There was a boy standing in the doorway with a snake and she was going to pee. 'Good boy, Manny,' her aunty said.

'I find hees hole. I pull him out by the bank go down.'

'Out on the block outside and I bring a knife.'

She could see that her aunty was pleased as she took a knife from a hook by the stove. Aunty Who? If she knew her aunty's name she could say please, Aunty Betty, or Jean, or Mary, may I leave the room?

She'd stepped off the train with her bag and looked for someone who might be her grandmother or grandfather, but had seen only the woman, or girl, in a big coat and girl's shoes. 'I'm your aunty,' the woman had said as though she was shy, but hadn't said a name, 'Give your bag.'

They'd walked together along a white road, not speaking, until her aunty had stopped and said, 'We get through here,' and had held the fence wires apart for her, 'That little house, it's where we going.' The new sandals were covered in white dust and had begun to hurt.

Once through the fence they'd headed down a slope, stepped across a small stream then taken a track through rushes and trees. 'Your grandmother and grandfather come back the day after tomorrow,' her aunty had said as they came out into a little yard. The boy and girl were there with the baby. They'd looked about the same ages as the cry-baby Home kids that she and Jean had to look after, dress, help, pull and chase to school, get the blame for. The two kids had gone behind the house pulling the dirty baby. But it wasn't a real house.

'Silly,' her aunty had called to them. Then she'd said, 'Come inside, Mata. Sit and rest, Mata dear.' But her name wasn't Mata.

There'd been room for her to sit between the table and the wall and there was a little window high above her head. It was like being in the fort that the School boys had made once, out of boxes and boards. There was a stove with a pot and a kerosene tin on it, a basin and a row of tins on a bench and boxes nailed to the walls like cupboards without doors. In the boxes were tin plates and mugs, bowls and billies and knives. The walls were papered with old *Free Lance* and *Auckland Weekly* pages and there was a lamp hanging from the ceiling on a piece of S-shaped wire.

The School boys' fort had had little doorways and passages that you crawled along to get to a small room where you could sit with your knees pulled up hard, but it was bad. Kids had taken their pants off in there, then someone had told and they'd all been caned. After that, boxes had been forbidden and the bank had been made out of bounds.

'Aunty I want to . . .' She stood up holding Bubba, jigging, and her aunty stopped in the doorway, turned with the knife.

'Sorry Mata . . . May . . . Out here.' She took the baby and pointed the knife along a path that went through long grass, 'There, at the end you can see.'

The grass was cold against her ankles and she was scared of snakes, wanted to run but thought she might pee herself. Pee was a swearing word. She hurried, keeping her muscles tight until she came to a little tin shed with a door hanging open.

Dark inside. Stinken. She wet into a big hole where you could fall. Drown and choke in people's wee and poo. There was newspaper to wipe with. Flies, spiders — perhaps snakes. She pulled her pants up quickly, smoothed her dress, shoved the door. Wanted to go home, running along the grassy, snaky path.

Then she stopped running. She was ten years old, nearly eleven. She liked her aunty and there were grandparents who were returning the day after next to take her home with them. At her grandparents' place there'd be pretty chairs and cushions, curtains and bedspreads. They'd want to keep her and she'd have dresses, skirts, a dressing gown, slippers and dolls. The cousins were cheeky brats, but what did it matter?

Under the tank stand was a tin of water and a box with basins and scraps of soap on it. There were buckets of washing and an old tub, and on a crosspiece of the stand there was a piece of mirror, a cup with a razor and shaving brush in it, a wire hairbrush, a big green comb with missing teeth and a greasy jar. Two stringy towels hung over a piece of wire that stretched from corner to corner. Aunty had sent Missy to show her what to do. Missy, ginger and scabby. Ginger face, ginger stripy hair, ginger scabby arms and legs, raggy ginger dress. Skinny, toothy, scabby and ginger.

Ginger eyes, too, watching, ginger eyelashes flicking as she stood on one leg scraping her other ankle up and down it. 'Makareta been on a train. Got a pie and a raspberry drink,' she said, then turned and listened. Ran, calling, 'Dadda, Dadda.'

When May returned to the yard her aunty and cousins were there looking at the cut-up thing on the board, the snake, and there was a ginger man there with wire hair. 'See, Bobby, it's May,' her aunty said, and the man hugged her and kissed her cheek.

'I thought it's something else, her name?'

'Mata, but she said she's May.'

'May-bee, May-bee . . .' he sang.

'Shut up, Bobby, she's shy.' Her aunty's face was red and smiling as she sat herself down on the stump by the axe.

> *May-bee my girl,*
> *What are we waiting for now?*

He picked Bubba up and leapt about on the dirt yard with her, singing.

It wasn't a real house but it was warm inside, better than the School boys' fort because you could stand up in it. It smelled like a pot cupboard. Her Uncle Bobby had lit the lamp but it didn't make much light and she could see only the table spread with newspaper and the things on it — salt in a cup, butter on a saucer, jam in a jar, bread that looked old, like the Wednesday bread they had at the Home. Wanted some. It was a long time since she'd had breakfast, which she hadn't wanted to eat at all because she'd felt too excited at the thought of going on holiday. But she'd made herself eat the porridge and had taken one bite out of her piece of toast before sneaking it to Jean.

Her aunty was by the stove putting food out for them, standing to one side so that light could reach the pot. Potato, and not snake, but eel. She hadn't heard of eating eel but it must be all right because they all liked it, picking at it with their fingers because they didn't know their manners, wiping sticky hands on the newspaper tablecloth.

There was only a spoon to use so she broke the potato with it and scraped a piece of eel flesh from a row of bones skinnier than pins, remembered they hadn't said grace. Tasted it — worse than turnips and tripe.

Aunty and Uncle smoked. Earlier, when they were outside, Aunty had sat down on a stump with an axe struck into it while her uncle had gone hoppywalking to the tank stand for a wash. While he was away, Aunty had made two skinny cigarettes with tobacco from a blue tin and Manny had brought her a stick from the fire to light them with. The two of them had sat there without saying anything, just smoking. She'd say her own grace in her head if she could remember how it started.

Remember. Everything you've been told, May. Pray at the beginning and end of each day, before and after meals. The Lord is our shepherd, remember. Give thee thanks, Lord, for which that, or that which thee or thy has set here . . . Pulled more of the eel flesh away from the bones and chewed it with a piece of the bread, the way you could eat turnips and tripe. Hungry.

Her aunty was dipping eel water from the pot and putting a mug of it down by each of them. Her uncle and the kids dipped bread into theirs because they didn't know their manners, eating the sloppy bread as though it was nice. We don't let bad-mannered girls go for holidays, remember. Eel was pie, eely water was raspberry drink. That's what she was having, a pie and a raspberry drink, like the boy and girl in the train.

Wires looping from lamppost to lamppost, wires stretching from fencepost to fencepost. Leaning against the window, she'd seen the black engine with the thick white smoke streaming.

Across from her were a mother and father with their two children. They'd had bags and pillows and had changed one of the seat-backs over so that they could all face one another as they went on holiday together. Back where they'd come from would be their house with locked windows and doors, but if you could go in you would find a kitchen with blue walls, blue linoleum, daisy curtains and white cupboard doors. In the sitting room there'd be a carpet-square with flowers and leaves on it, flower-patterned wallpaper, lacy curtains, a fireplace surrounded by brown bricks, a brown sofa and two easy chairs.

The girl's bedroom would have pink curtains and brown blinds, a bed with a shiny bedspread and a floral eiderdown on it. There'd be a polished dressing table with a brush and comb set, cat doilies and a trinket box, and on the floor there'd be a fawn-coloured lino and a pink mat. The girl would have a dressing gown and slippers with pompoms on them.

In the boy's bedroom there'd be green lino and a stripy bed-spread with curtains to match. There'd be cream-coloured wall-paper and brown blinds. A set of drawers, painted green, would have boys things on top of it — a cap gun, a ball of silver paper, a cross with a nail in it, plasticine armies facing each other behind plasticine barricades. The boy would have brown slippers and a brown dressing gown.

The mother and father's bedroom? But no, you weren't allowed. Betty had said no, no, not allowed to turn the knob, push the door, look in.

Then she and Betty had sat on the pink mat and dressed the dolls, which had frocks, singlets, pants, hats and cardigans. They'd made bead bangles and necklaces for them, then Betty's angry mother had come in.

Beads, beads, pattering, tinkling, scattering on the linoleum. Jumping up nearly pissing, running out the door and down the path. Betty, you bad, bad girl.

Bad boy and girl in the train. He's kicking. I'm not. Look, look, Mum . . . We're stopping very soon for refreshments. 'Ten minutes for refreshments,' the guard had said, coming through.

'Be very good and we'll get you a pie and a raspberry drink,' the mother and father had said. 'Sit there and be good until we get back.' From the window she'd watched father running to the refreshments counter with mother following. The children had waited, waited, jumping up every now and then to look out of the window. Ten minutes. Five minutes now. Three or two. The train could . . . Coming.

Father had had plates stacked one on top of the other with

all the pies on the top plate, balancing all on one big hand. He'd had two red drinks in the other hand, the necks of the bottles gripped between his fingers, straws bobbing in the fizz. Mother had brought cups of tea, fat white cups on fat white saucers. She had smiled and smiled coming into the train, and Father had reached into his pocket, taking out knives and forks.

'Have some more soup, May, there's more.'

'No thank you.'

'Missy, take Bubba from Dadda so Dadda and me can have kai. Wipe your hands.'

'Come on, Bubba,' Missy said.

Her aunty lifted the middle ring from the stove and a flame shot up as she scraped the eel bones in. There was a hissing sound and a fishy stink and the ring clattered back over the hole.

'May I leave the table please?'

'Yes, May dear.'

'Got any tablecloths like this one, ha ha, at that place where you come from?' her uncle asked.

She didn't know what to say.

'Don't, Bobby, she's shy of you, silly,' her aunty said as she handed a plate of food across to him.

> *Ah, Maluna,*
> *I love my*
> *Silver-belly tuna.*

'Take no notice, May, he's silly.'

She didn't know what to say and didn't know what to do now that she'd stood to leave the table, because there was nowhere else to go. Missy was sitting on the floor with Bubba on her lap and Manny and Chumchum had gone outside. Bubba had stopped grizzling and looked as though she might go to sleep. It was quiet now except for the sound of her aunty and uncle sucking bones and an occasional crackle and a rumble from the stove. She'd never heard a quiet like it.

'Sit down again, May,' her aunty said, 'We clear the table after and get the lamp down.'

three

U ndark dark.
      Light enough to see the blisters by as she sat in the middle of the black road, turning each foot. She leaned on one hand and rolled to her knees, rocked back on to the balls of her feet, pushing to stand.

Walking again, to where? To the wherever, the nowhere, the no ever, the ever nowhere, away, away. The long road curved.

There were houses which were only shapes in the night light, layers of shapes on the hill slopes, angled, turreted, fluted, stacked and domed. She used to dream of houses.

Walking, from where?

From there. From the very centre of the kitchen floor, on the worn linoleum spot, where she had stood that morning looking down at her feet, saying to them, 'You are what I have and you can walk me. You can walk me to the wardrobe where I put on my coat, walk me to the stool by the bed where I pick up the photograph, walk me to the cupboard where I put you into two shoes, walk me to the door which I open, out onto the step, down the path to the street and away. You can walk me from street to street to street.'

Away.

So she'd walked through early morning when the first buses and trucks went by and the early workers hurried along the footpaths, when vans were loaded and unloaded, doors were slammed and engines started, when street lights went out and building lights came on.

In the early morning she had passed warehouses, spaces and places to let or lease, railyards, factories and mini-markets. She'd come to the shopping centres as the footpaths filled, as vacuum cleaners were manoeuvred about stacks and between rows, as windows were rearranged, signs put up, put out, taken down, changed.

At mid-morning she'd gone along a pink arcade into a video parlour where the machines had stood unattended while the rat-tatting sounds pitched and volleyed off the black-painted walls. On the screens red and blue machine people waged war, gunfire clattered down the streets of Crime City, stadium heroes flickered backwards and forwards over fields of violent green and red-mouthed dragons stormed down Monster Lane. Past Ax Battle, Robocop, Shinobi, Wonder Boy, Black Ray Boy, Swat, Secret Service, Winning Run, Sword of Fury she'd gone, before coming back down the pink alley and out again, blinking into hard light. There'd been food smells — coffee, new bread and fries.

The shoppers browsed and she'd made her way amongst them, at first not stepping on cracks, but after a while treading where each foot put itself, not asking herself 'Where to?' 'Where from?', but seeking the sights, the sounds, the words, the smells, that would keep her from asking.

At midday, past Bargain Bookcase, Unisex Fashion, Cut Price Wines, Discount Meats, Josie's Patisserie, Lion Brown — on a long street of yards where flags and streamers announced cars for sale, service for cars, car wash, parts and accessories for cars — joggers emerged in clothing that said Bali, Hawaii, Love Your Heart, U.S.A., Rheineck, Nike, Tauranga, Canada, Lion Brown, Petone, Poneke, Italia, Masterton, Sydney, New York, Rage Without Alcohol, Kiwi, Ultra, Railways, Don't Worry Be Happy, Aotearoa. She'd gathered the words to her to keep thoughts and thinking away, walking on to early afternoon, to late afternoon, to evening, to night, to the middle of the night, to the middle of the road, going nowhere — until her feet had stopped.

So she'd sat, a shoe in each pocket, on the new tar seal, where earlier a bus had gone by with a woman looking from a window. Sat until the thoughts came knocking, turning themselves into questions: What will happen Something or nothing Nothing or something. And then she'd stood.

Walked again, letting her blistery, dirty feet take her along the middle of the road where trams once went, between an avenue of poles from which orange light seeped down. Hungry.

Yes, but without longing. She felt neither sad nor glad and

wished not to examine feelings or have thoughts that lead to thinking, wanted only her hunger and herself.

Sooner or later she would have to sleep, one of the street people. There were the pale old men with whisky and wine to keep their torments away, there were the brown kids dazed by the glue and solvents they'd inhaled, and now there was herself — a woman of middle age with nothing in a bottle or a bag to comfort her, but who churned street words, street sights and smells and sounds through her head, to keep from thinking.

Now she wanted nothing more than what she'd always had, which was nothing. Nothing, and just to walk, foot in front of blistery foot, her paddle-hands paddling back hefts of undark night.

four

D ark.
   Her aunty, with Bubba hooked under one arm and a candle in her hand, led them through the dark doorway into the other room, which was like a box that had been joined on. There were three beds in the box and each had a grey blanket edged in red wool stitching spread over it.

'You sleep there, May, with Missy.'

'I want Bubba,' Missy said.

'Bubba sleeping with me and Dadda tonight.'

'Bubba.'

'Shut up and get changed. Manny, Chum, get changed out there.'

'Me . . . I wanoo-oo.'

'Missy, shut up.'

'Bubba-aa.'

Missy shot out of her dress, put on a shirt and got in under the blankets complaining and sook-sook, like sucky-thumb Margaret and cry-baby Colleen at the Home.

The Home was far away, across paddocks, down a long white road, back along miles and miles of railway track, down one street after another, through a gate, across a yard, up four steps to a big wooden door with an egg-shaped handle. Inside there were a long passage and big rooms, big windows. Taps and pipes, lights hanging by cords from the high ceilings. A real house. Not just boxes joined, newspaper walls, lavatory that was only a deep hole. Sometimes her cousins didn't even use the lavatory. Bad. Aunty had sent them out to do wee on the grass.

'Come out for a mimi,' her aunty had said, so she'd gone out with Aunty and the kids to see what it was, and the boys had hooked their diddles out from the legs of their shorts, Missy had taken her pants down and bobbed and they'd all peed in the long grass.

'Come on, May, don't be shy,' Aunty had said, putting the lamp down and squatting. After a while she'd had to do it too because the lavatory was too far away in the dark. Her water had spurted into the grass smelling pissy and warm like Colleen and Margaret when they wet their beds.

Stinky, pissy. She and Jean would have to pull stinken Colleen and Margaret out of their beds, stand them on the floor and pull their damp nighties off them — naughty, grizzly, smelly crybabies, warm and sticky with snotty, bogey faces. Look, you wet your beds. They'd have to send Colleen and Margaret to take their sheets and nighties to the laundry then help them to bath and dress and have their breakfasts. Naughty wetty-pants girls who stank and sniffed and grizzled, pulling them to school.

Manny and Chumchum stepped over sook-sook Missy to get to their bed, and Bubba was already asleep in Aunty and Uncle's bed. So she had to get in with Missy because there was nowhere else to sleep. At the Home you weren't allowed in anyone else's bed. She thought it might be bad.

Her aunty went out taking the candle, and except for the little scrap of light that came from the kitchen, it was dark. The little fort house sat by itself, somewhere, on a dusty yard and there were no lit streets outside, no cars, trucks, trams going by. No door sounds, no water rushing in pipes or out of taps, along gutters and into the lavatory bowls. No dishes clacking in the sinks. No screaming, crying, sniffing, shifting, creaking. No whispering.

Whispering. 'I'm going to my grandparents.'

'They might want you and keep you and you might have dresses, brown shoes, new pencils in a box with a sliding lid that you can put a transfer of roses on.'

'There'll be flowers on wallpaper, curtains, floors.'

'Gloves for cold days. Ribbons . . .'

'Wardrobes.'

'Mirrors.'

'Dolls with dresses. I'll write to you.'

Whispering. Her aunty and uncle had gone out with the lamp. She could hear them outside whispering in the dark.

Shouting. She woke in the dark to shouting. A match flared and her aunty leaned over to light a candle, 'Wake up, wake up Bobby.' Her aunty sat up in bed, took Uncle by the shoulders and shook him. She sat him up and he leaned forward, putting his head in his hands.

'Give us a smoke, Glory,' he said.

five

It was still dark when she woke. There was a square of grey light high up, which was from a little window in the box that was a room. Bubba was crying in the kitchen and she could hear her uncle out under the tank stand snorting and blowing. Through the doorway she could see Aunty in the lamplight by the stove, scratching at the grate with a long poker, tumbling the wood, turning the damper, shifting the water tin.

After a while her aunty came into the bedroom with Bubba, laying her down with a bottle and going out again. Bubba sucked noisily, stopping occasionally to let the bubbles go because the teat had collapsed — just the way Baby Myra did at the Home. Suddenly Myra's eyes would close and she'd be asleep and even though you'd watched, kept your eyes fixed on her eyes, you didn't see it happen. Like Bubba now. Bubba was asleep.

Her uncle came back into the kitchen and she could hear Aunty telling him what to bring home, then he went out, his boots rattling the yard stones. How would she know when it was seven o'clock, time to be out and kneeling for morning prayers?

'Come and have a cup of tea, May,' her aunty said from by the door.

Then she didn't know what to do — there was no room between the beds to kneel for prayers and she couldn't get her clothes out of her bag without waking Missy. Anyway she didn't want to get dressed in a room where there were boys. Also she wasn't allowed tea.

But she wanted the tea.

The kids were still asleep. She hurried into the clothes she'd worn the day before that were supposed to be only for best. No brush and couldn't do her hair. Went into the kitchen.

'Tea, May, nice and hot. Milk in the billy, sugar in the jar.' Aunty was at the stove stirring porridge. In her other hand, clipped between her thumbnail and fingernail, she had a butt of cigarette which she put to her lips now and again, drawing her cheeks in, little threads of smoke coming from her nostrils. The milk had gone off and was floating in lumps on the tea. 'Have this before the kids wake up,' her aunty said as though she was pleased, ladling porridge into two plates and bringing them to the table, sitting, leaning into the light-circle, reaching, smiling. 'Bread on the board and golden syrup to put on.' May thought Aunty might like her.

'So, May, you nearly eleven?'

'Yes.'

'Like your cousin Makareta, our brother's daughter, the brother killed in the war.'

Telling her things as if she were grown up.

'Your mother was two years older than him, the oldest in the family. Our big sister. I'm the third one, then there's Aperehama.'

Her own mother's sister?

The realisation pierced her. This aunty was her own mother's sister, knew things about her own mother.

'We would've got you, May, if your father let us. Keita and Wi, your grandparents, they been trying to get you.'

Just then Chummy called out, Bubba started to grizzle and Aunty was swallowing the last of her tea and getting up. 'We have to take the washing down the creek,' she said. 'Have to have our wash down there too because the tank's low.'

Manny went through the kitchen and out the door and she heard him pissing in the grass. Piss was a bad word, you were supposed to say wee. Manny was doing a wee, fast and noisy — sounded more like pissing. God could read your thoughts and knew everything that was in your heart. He was everywhere, even in the spider lavatory. She wondered what a low tank was.

There was still a flame in the lamp but the circle of light had faded because daylight had come. Her aunty reached up and turned the wick down and a thin finger of smoke rose from the slot where it had gone.

My father didn't let them have me.

She went into the bedroom, slid her case from under the bed and changed into her pinafore, which was a faded green except where the hem had been let down and the darts opened out. Last year it had been Maggie's. She brushed her hair, pressing the springy curls down as best she could — bad curls that had to be cut, cut, cut, Matron snapping with the scissors, pulling down hard with the comb. Bad. She had to flatten her hair down with water every morning and slide her two long clips in to try and stop it from springing.

Betty Crosseyes had curls that her mother set in rags every night, that hung down loose and goldy when they were taken out in the mornings. Each curl was brushed round a finger with a slow twist of the brush. Betty had shown her how to do it on the doll. She had a white ribbon that tied in a bow at the top of her head, and clips with bluebirds on them that kept the ribbon from sliding.

When Matron had finished cutting her hair she would tell her to get the pan and brush and clean up the mess, so she'd sweep up all the bad curls and carry them down to the incinerator. One day James, the caretaker, had been down at the incinerator when she'd taken her hair to burn.

'Been shearing the black sheep, have they?' he'd said.

There was no water, no mirror. She combed her hair down as flat as she could and slid the clips in at each side. Bubba was watching her from Aunty's bed.

They took the path that went past the lav, through the cold grass, sourgrass and stinging nettles. The bag of washing that she carried over her shoulder kept slipping in her grip and every now and again she stopped and changed shoulders. The washing stank.

Her aunty, ahead of her, had Bubba tied to her back in a blanket and held a bundle of clothes in front of her as though she carried a big pumpkin with two tweaked leaves at the top of it. Manny was ahead with the water tins and Missy and Chummy, behind them, were stamping and grizzling with the billies and the bread.

Past the lavatory they went up to the top of a small hill where they rested. 'Down there,' her aunty said, and looking down May could see a small brown house with big trees around it. 'Your grandparents' place.'

Further on there were other houses, pretend houses, box houses, wood and tin, silver-looking, with worn tracks going here and there towards them through the grass and the trees. And in the distance was a house or a hall, triangle-shaped, that had high weeds growing all round it. They made their way down the slope, across a paddock and down a tree-covered bank to the creek. There was a clearing where the creek had been dammed.

Aunty took Bubba's clothes off and dropped them at the edge of the water. Missy and the boys stripped too, then went up along the bank rude. Aunty tucked her dress up and began undoing the bundles, sorting the washing into piles. Bubba, sitting beside her mother, slapped the water, laughing and screwing up her face.

She hadn't seen a creek before except from the window of the train. She thought of eels. 'Come down, May,' her aunty called, but she didn't. Instead she stood and watched Aunty soaping the clothes, rubbing and rinsing, then wringing them and tossing them into a tin behind her on the bank.

After a while her aunty called again, 'Come down, you can rinse, over in the running water by the stones. Kids can spread them on the bushes . . . Missy, Manny,' she called.

So May took her shoes off, went down the bank with the tin, stepped into the water thinking of eels.

'Tip them out, May, rinse, then chuck them back in the tin . . . Funny with only us home.'

Aunty had said the same thing that morning when she'd sent Manny with a billy somewhere to milk a cow — their grandparents' cow. Chummy had gone too, to feed chooks and a dog. He'd complained and cried about having to go, slapping his elbows against his sides as though he was pumping up tears. Aunty had given him porridge scraps and rotten milk for the chooks and two bits of old bread spread with fat, for the dog. 'What about *her*,' Chumchum had said with his feet planted, rocking his head in her direction. Aunty had had to smack him before he'd run off crying. 'Don't you eat that bread, for the dog,' Aunty had called after him. Then Aunty had turned back from the doorway and said, 'Funny with everyone gone.'

About an hour later Chummy had come back smiling, carrying a tin with five eggs in it. 'None broken,' he'd said. Manny was behind him walking carefully with the billy of milk.

Her aunty went up the bank with Bubba and began spreading the rinsed clothes over the bushes. May squeezed and wrung the last of the washing and went up to help, pleased to have her feet out of the water. 'That tree back of you,' her aunty said, 'that's where your cousin Makareta was born.' She looked at the tree but didn't understand what her aunty was talking about, hadn't heard of getting babies from trees. There was a hospital in the street next to her school where God left babies, but she hadn't heard of him leaving any in a tree. She was too shy to ask Aunty about it.

When they'd finished spreading the clothes Aunty sat Bubba on her hip, picked up a sack and they went together upstream where the ground was hard and stony in places, muddy and soft in others. Every now and again Aunty called, 'Manny, Missy, Chumchum,' and the kids answered from somewhere.

At a place where the creek was shallow and wide, her aunt gave Bubba to her to hold then stepped in and began picking handfuls of green plant that grew there. 'Growing good,' she said. Her dress was wet all round the hem.

Suddenly Manny was there with a tin which he poked close

to her face. 'Yaar,' he shouted. In the tin were insects, or something ugly, and he laughed when she jumped up squealing. He
reached in and took out one of the insects, thrusting it at her, and
the insect, close to her nose, waved its legs and its two big
pinchers. She left Bubba and ran into the water. 'Stop that,
Manny,' her aunty called. 'Missy, Chumchum, give you all a
hiding I come up there.' They were laughing as though they
might never stop. 'Koura, May, don't get scared. You kids . . .'
    But she *was* scared — of eels coming, of those pincher things.
She wanted to get out of the water, lifted one foot and then the
other, looking down at the stones wanting to hold on to Aunty's
dress. 'Wait till I get those kids . . .' They'd gone off through the
trees taking Bubba with them, laughing, naked and rude.
    The boys had their shorts on and Missy was wearing black
bloomers. They'd put a singlet on Bubba, who was lying in the
grass drinking from her bottle. She hoped they'd get a smack
from Aunty but they were keeping out of their mother's way.
The tin, with water in it, was sitting on two stones with dry grass
and sticks stuffed in between. The pinchers had been tipped out
onto the ground. Manny struck a match, lit the grass, and the
twigs crackled and flared. As the water began to boil her cousins
picked up the pinchers and dropped them in while her aunty cut
the bread into big slices with a butcher knife and spread them
with syrup.
    After a few minutes Manny moved the tin carefully with two
sticks, tilted it so that the water drained out, then tipped the
pinchers into the upside-down lid of a billy. They were dead.
They were red. 'See, May, you can eat . . .'
    But she wouldn't. The kids were picking them up, blowing,
tossing, pecking, getting little specks on their thumbnails which
they put into their mouths. Aunty poked little bits into Bubba's
mouth too and they all licked and sucked the shells, breaking off
the pinchers and sucking, looking at her to see if she would have
any but she wouldn't, even though she was hungry and the piece
of bread hadn't filled her up at all.
    Later, when the water tins were full and the washing had
been collected, Aunty and the kids went into the water and began
soaping themselves and bobbing up and down. Chumchum and

Missy were ginger, with ginger skins and ginger and yellow scraps of hair. Manny was black, with black hair sticking up like a brush, and Bubba was whitish with black curls on the top of her head. But on the back of her head she had no hair at all. Aunty had a light brown body, a dark brown face and dark brown arms and legs, black hair with bushy curls. Bad hair. Aunty passed Bubba to Manny while she soaped Missy's and Chumchum's hair and they ducked down under the water, leaving circles of soap on the surface, up again, blowing and spitting and popping their eyes.

At home she and Jean had to help Colleen and Margaret with their baths, washing their ears, necks, hair and helping them to dry themselves properly. Colleen and Margaret weren't sisters but they were twin-looking, skinny and white with wingy bones sticking out of their backs. Shivery, grizzly noises came out of their mouths as they were dried and helped on with their singlets. They were like scraggy, squeaky dolls.

'Is it paying day?' Missy asked as she dressed. Aunty was helping Manny to hitch the bundle of washing on his back and giving Chummy the billies to carry.

'Bring Bubba please, May,' she said. 'And if you can bring that bag . . . just pull it.'

So she picked up Bubba, resting her on one hip, and began dragging the bag of watercress. 'Is it paying day?' Missy asked again, and Manny and Chum stopped walking, stared hard at Aunty. 'Is it paying day?'

'Is it?'

'Paying day?'

'Yes.'

'Dadda coming?'

'How would I know?'

'When?'

'Keep quiet. Shut up about Dadda.' Aunty went ahead of them with the tin and the kids started hurrying after her with the billies and bundles.

She sat up late with Aunty drinking tea, just as if she were grown up. The kids were all asleep. There was a lamp in the middle of the table and her hands were in the circle of light holding a tin cup. Aunty's too. No faces. No ceiling, no walls, no floor. But there was a spot of red where the range was, from the last bit of fire in the stove.

She remembered she hadn't said prayers and hadn't read her scriptures since she'd been on holiday. Learning to be bad. After she'd finished her tea she thought she might get her scriptures from her bag and read them in the patch of light. On the other hand if she waited, made the tea last a long time, Aunty might say something — as she had yesterday and this morning — something important for her to know. She kept reminding herself that Aunty was her own mother's sister, her mother without a face. Aunty might say something about her mother's face.

And why she left me. And after that, why did she die?

There was a brown door, long ago, at the top of stairs that had a dark smell. The doorknob was high on the door, but she couldn't remember much of what was behind it except for a big window with six panes of glass and a brown couch where she would kneel and look out. The window looked down over roof tops, gorse banks, railings, lampposts, concrete steps and a zigzag path. Sometimes at night she had seen the searchlights looking for enemy planes, crisscrossing like knitting needles, knitting up black patches of sky.

Also in the room there was the shadow that was her mother and the shadow that was her father. She remembered having a schoolbag and a new dress because she was starting school. Her mother had put lunch and an apron into the bag and they'd walked together to school, holding hands. She remembered her mother's hand.

At school she'd hung the bag in the porch and her mother had bent down and kissed her, said goodbye and gone. There was her mother's hand turning the handle of the porch door — but she couldn't remember her mother's face. Couldn't remember her mother's voice, only that she'd spoken. In the classroom there were rows of desks and chairs and she'd sat still, wanting to be good, trying to know what to do.

When she'd gone to her bag at lunchtime there was no lunch in it. The teacher was very angry and knew who had taken the lunch and had smacked a boy hard on the legs with a ruler, afterwards had given her an orange.

After school her mother hadn't been there to meet her so she'd hurried on home, wanting to tell about the boy and the orange. But the brown door had been locked when she arrived and she'd waited at the top of the stairs until it was dark and her father came home. He'd rattled the door then gone downstairs and come back with a key and she'd gone inside and waited for her mother. When she woke in the morning her mother still hadn't come. Since then she'd waited every day.

Other people had come. A man and a woman came and talked to her father, then one day the woman packed her clothes in a bag and they'd gone in a bus to a big house where she thought her mother would be.

There were voices, men laughing. 'Hear that?' her aunty said. 'Your silly drunk uncle coming.' She listened. The voices came closer then she heard bottles clinking and footsteps coming across the yard.

'Hey, hey,' a voice called.

Her aunty slid the knife out of the door, it opened and her uncle stumbled in with an armload, 'Come in, Nonny.' The other man was bending, tugging at his bootlaces. He pulled his boots off and leaned for a moment in the doorway. 'How you, Gloria?'

'All right, Nonny.'

'How's the fire, Glory?' Her uncle went to the stove, dropped the grate door open and began putting wood in.

'What about your kids? What about a feed for them?' her aunty said.

'Wake them up.' He went towards the bedroom door. 'Wake up, kids. Dadda got chewing gum, Dadda got chocolate fish . . .'

'Shut up and leave them alone, too late now,' her aunty said, shifting the lamp onto its high hook as Bubba began to grizzle. 'See what you done.'

'Glor-ee-a . . .' he sang,

It's not Maree
It's Glo-ree-a
It's not Cherie
It's Glor-ee-a . . .

'You got tin milk and potatoes?'

'Tin milk, potatoes . . .' He began pulling potatoes from his pockets and putting them on the bench.

'Where's the rest, the sack?' Aunty Gloria asked.

'Fence, where they drop us off. And flap.' He unwrapped a wet parcel and began cutting the mutton flaps.

She's in my every dream . . .

'Get the beer in, Nonny, get my darling a beer.' He dropped the bones into a pot, began peeling potatoes and washing them in a scrap of water in a bowl, 'Get our niece some chocolate fish,' he said.

The fire was rumbling. She watched her uncle pull handfuls of watercress from the bag and put it in the pot. 'Not so smart 'cause Glo-ree-a is not in love with you . . . Hey hey, sing up, Glory, sing up, Nonny, drink up, ha ha.'

Her aunty and the man called Nonny were drinking beer out of tin cups. There was another parcel on the table and Aunty unwrapped milk powder, flour, comics, chocolate fish and chewing gum, putting the things away on the shelves made of boxes. The man called Nonny filled the cups again.

She watched as her uncle lifted the lid of the pot. Steam streamed upwards. He dropped the potatoes in and came and sat down beside her on the form taking the other cup, 'Yah ha, drink up, Glory . . .'

> *Wake up wake up,*
> *You sleepyhead,*
> *Get up get up,*
> *Get out of bed,*
> *Sing up sing up,*
> *Glor-oria,*
> *Live love laugh and be happy . . .*

Uncle, Aunty and the man called Nonny knew lots of songs which they sang on and on, joining each new song to the end of the one before. Some were in a language she didn't understand. Sitting up late as though she was grown up.

Marshmallow fish was really a chocolate fish, but she'd

picked the chocolate off bit by bit. She didn't know whether to eat the tail first or the head. Bit the head off and chewed. Aunty had given her the whole bagful but she was too shy to take another one even though she was hungry. Her uncle went into the bedroom and came out strumming a ukelele.

> *You like a ukelele lady*
> *Ukelele lady like-a you,*
> *You like to linger where it's shady*
> *Ukelele lady like-a too . . .*

He skipped and danced on the hearth and the stacked wood scattered. 'Sit down, Bobby, or you fall in the fire,' her aunty said.

> *Maybe she'll sigh*
> *And maybe not*
> *Maybe she'll cry*
> *And maybe not*
> *Maybe she'll find somebody else*
> *By and by . . .*

Uncle's fingers skipped on the strings of the uke and when he sat down again he hunched over it, occasionally tipping his head back to sing to the dark ceiling. The latest she'd ever been up, past midnight she thought.

They cleared the table and set it with bread and butter, salt and pepper and spoons and she was so hungry she felt sick with it as she watched her aunty put potatoes, watercress and meat on plates for them. Hoped she was going to like it. Her uncle had gone to sleep at one end of the table with his head on his arm.

He was called Bobby and her aunty was called Gloria. Aunty Gloria was her own mother's sister. The food was good and she tried to eat it slowly.

When she went into the other room to go to bed Bubba was asleep beside Missy and there was no room for her. Aunty Gloria came in, pulled her dress off and hung it on a nail. 'Come on, May, come and sleep with Aunty.'

Her aunty's voice sounded drunk and she thought her aunty must be very bad.

'Come on, my sister's baby, come and sleep with your aunty.'

So she got into bed beside Aunty, who moved her over close and cuddled her. She was shy to be cuddled but she liked it. Aunty had a beer smell, bad, but was warm and soft, mumbling and telling her things. 'Naughty Mummy and Daddy to leave their baby . . . And bloody Albert putting you in that place. Bad to my sister, Albert, only want her for a slave for him that's all. Didn't want any brown baby too.'

There were things for her to know which might not all be good things, but still she wanted to know. In the dark she was trying to remember her aunty's face, her mother's face, wanted Aunty Gloria to keep on talking. She reached out her arm, even though she wasn't used to it and put her arm round her own aunty, her own mother. 'Naughty sister not coming home, not bringing you. Keita . . .' She tried to keep her eyes open just in case Aunty Gloria talked some more, but after a while realised her aunty had gone to sleep. In the other room her uncle had woken and was starting to sing again.

six

She could hear bottles rattling in the other room and Aunty Gloria was talking. When she went out into the kitchen the man called Nonny was clearing bottles from the table and taking them outside. Aunty was putting wood in the stove while the kids grizzled round her. Uncle Bobby was asleep, stretched out on the form with his arms hanging backwards. 'Anyway, only time I get a decent sleep,' her aunty was saying. 'When he's full. Only time he's not yelling and crying in the middle of the night.'

'Off to get the spuds, Gloria,' Nonny said.

'Wake your mate up.'

'No, I'll get them.'

But her uncle was awake now too. He swung his legs and stood, staggered to the bedroom and got into bed. The kids were complaining about him. 'We don't like Dadda.'

'Yes we don't.'

'Nincompoop.'

'If he brought you chocolate fish and comics?' her aunty said as she dished food out of the pot for them.

'Where?'

'Where?'

'Behind the tin milk.'

Manny stood on the form and felt behind the tin of milk powder for the chocolate fish and comics. 'Give some to your cousin,' Aunty said. She wasn't allowed to read comics, only scriptures and school books, but she took the comic.

The kids sat at the table eating the chocolate fish, smiling and talking about them, 'Uncle Nonny, Uncle Nonny, we got a chogalafish,' Chummy said.

'Out here, Gloria?' Nonny called.

'And comics.'

'By the safe, by the tree,' her aunty called back. He moved out of sight then returned.

'Uncle Nonny, we got a chogalafish.'

'Catch them in the creek did yiz?' he said, which made the kids laugh. They began swimming their chocolate fish across the table.

'Mine's is a eel, mine's is a eel. Uncle Nonny, mine's is a eel.'

Then they bit off the heads and tails, pulled them apart and crammed their mouths full, chewing noisily. When they'd finished they began eating the food their mother had put out for them.

'Hope Win boxes your ears,' Aunty said to Nonny as he left, 'Hope she puts the butcher in the door and shuts you out.'

'Go on Gloria.'

'Well, bring her with you next time.'

Nonny went off down the bank laughing.

Outside, the kids sat cross-legged in the yard staring at the comics and when Aunty yelled at them telling them to get and have a wash they didn't look up or move. Uncle Bobby walked past with a towel round his neck. He spoke to them but they didn't hear, and when he came back from the tank stand he began jumping up and down and singing while little packets flew out of his pockets and his hands, landing on the ground. It was chewing gum. The kids left their comics and began diving about laughing and shouting. 'Ha ha, Dadda.'

'Juicy Fruit.'

'Spearmint, PK, Arrowmint.'

'Give some to your cousin,' Aunty said. So they gave her a Juicy Fruit, a Spearmint, a PK and an Arrowmint — four little packages, like four little presents, tiny parcels perfectly wrapped in waxed paper. There were four ridges in each of the parcels showing the outline of the oblongs of chewing gum inside. Paper labels fitted neatly round each packet telling which was Wrigley's PK, Wrigley's Spearmint, Wrigley's Arrowmint or Wrigley's Juicy Fruit. She undid the flap on one of the packets and thumbed a piece into her hand, little white pillow, put it into her mouth, sucking the sweet coating, wondering if she was bad.

Manny, Missy and Chumchum chewed noisily, opening their mouths wide and then cracking their teeth together, wide and crack, wide and crack. Aunty was yelling at them to go and have a wash because they were all going to Keita's, but it took them a long time to move. 'What about her, she haven't,' Missy said, pointing to her. 'Yeh, she haven't,' Chumchum said, screwing up his face and jumping in the air flicking his legs up behind him.

'Didn't yesterday too,' Missy said, 'She have no wash down the creek yesterday,' running along the path to the tank stand.

Aunty Gloria went inside and came out with a little bit of warm water in a tin, 'Come on, May,' she called. So then she had to go with Aunty Gloria even though she was shy of having a wash outside, didn't like those cheeky brats pulling faces and not liking her.

She waited until the boys had gone then began to wash herself with awful water, a raggy cloth, a piece of dirty soap. Missy was combing her hair and staring — at her face, at her dress, at her feet, 'Makareta got sandals,' Missy said, and just then Uncle Bobby went past calling, 'You got any bathroom like this in that place where you live, May? Got any long-drop dunny too?' He was on his way to the lavatory and he had a comic. He was silly.

Her grandparents' house was a real house with a glassed-in verandah. Inside there was a real kitchen with green-painted walls, a bench with a sink and tap and a big cupboard with a door on it. Missy and Chummy had been sent to feed the chooks and look for eggs, and Manny had gone to help his father catch a sheep, but she didn't know what for.

Through the door from the kitchen there was a sitting room with a fireplace, brown armchairs and a sofa with rugs on it. The walls were covered in a mottled yellow and brown wallpaper, and there were curtains made of patches that could have been pieces of dresses sewn together. There were photos in big frames of big, serious people who were all dressed up. On the floor there was a brown and orange mat and a rag rug curling at the corners. She carried Bubba to the sofa and put her down — runny-nosed, dribbly Bubba, asleep, sticky, floppy. Then she helped Aunty Gloria to drag the mats outside.

When they'd done that Aunty asked her to go and open the bedroom windows.

The windows were fastened by long rods, which she unclipped, lifted up and slid back through a square eye. The rods had holes that fitted nicely over little pegs to hold the windows open. There were three bedrooms, and as she was opening the windows of the third one Missy came in and opened the wardrobe doors, 'Makareta got four dress,' she said. 'Two in her bag and two here.'

'Get out of there Missy,' her mother called. 'Keep out your cousin's stuff.'

'Got slippers and shoes, a idledown and a pillow. Got a drawer with ribbon in it, long hair. Got Kui Hinemate for to wash her and for to do her hair.'

'Come out, Missy, leave your cousin's things. Get and bang the mats.'

Outside, her cousin skipped across the yard to a shed with a log for a step and a block swivelling on a nail that kept the door shut. Missy flicked the block and pushed the door open and inside there was a bath, two wooden tubs and a copper. Lined up against one wall were gumboots and big shoes. Baskets and old coats hung on nails high up. She and Missy banged the mats on the side of the shed and took them back in.

Aunty Gloria was rolling a big ball of dough on the table —

rolling, folding and pressing — and when they went out again, Uncle Bobby, Manny and Chum were coming across the paddock. Her uncle had an animal with no head and four feetless legs on his shoulder. Chummy was dawdling behind him with the animal head and Manny was running with knives. She watched her uncle push wire through the neck of the meat animal and hang it from the branch of a tree. He took a knife from Manny and began whipping it on a steel. 'Got any butcher shop like this where you come from, May?' and he laughed, drawing the knife down the pinkish flesh of the animal. She hurried inside.

The ball of dough was in a pot on the table and Aunty was tipping watercress into the sink. Chummy came in behind her, poking the animal head at her. 'Put it on the bench,' his mother said.

Hungry, and the food smelt good. The kids were all doing something, knew what to do — getting things, setting the table, bringing in wood, stoking the fire, wiping Bubba, sometimes sulking and stamping their feet on the boards because they were hungry. As they went by they snorted down their noses at her because she was standing there doing nothing and they didn't like her. Uncle Bobby was lighting the lamps and candles. In the yellow light he looked sad and serious.

Far away there were lights bobbing, of two torches. And going towards the two lights was another. It was Uncle Bobby with a lamp going out to help. His light jiggled as he hurried in the dark, getting closer to *them* — Uncle Bobby with a lamp, *them* with their torches. Him getting closer to *them*, *them* getting closer to him. All getting closer to each other. Then all of them together. There was a pause, then the three lights moved again, coming across the paddocks. Soon voices were heard, then footsteps and the heavy sounds of bundles, bags and shoes being put down. Aunty and the kids had gone out and left her there at the window with the candle. She was too shy to go out and thought it was silly to call grandparents Keita and Wi. Wi sounded like a bad word.

A young man and a young woman came in. The man was carrying a baby wrapped in a red blanket and he had the lantern, which he put on the bench. He was tall and thin, brown like shoes and doors. He had Aunty Gloria's face. He put the baby down on the sofa. The woman was thin too, fawn-coloured, and her eyes stuck out. She wore her hair long, kept back from her face with clips. The woman came over and kissed her, and when the man had put the baby down he came and kissed her too. She wasn't used to it and couldn't look at them.

A girl went through into a bedroom without noticing her, a girl with long plaits tied with white ribbons, wearing a blue coat and a white beret.

After the girl, a small woman, wearing a black suit and a black and white headscarf came in and stood just inside the doorway. She had a dark brown, round face and black-rimmed glasses. In the light of the lamp the glasses seemed to be her eyes. Behind her was an older woman, tall and yellowy with a coloured blanket wrapped about under her armpits. Her eyes were like two burnt holes.

The women turned towards her and began calling and making high crying sounds that terrified her so that she wanted to run.

'Come and greet your grandmothers, May,' Aunty Gloria said coming in behind the women. 'Your grandmothers Keita and Hinemate.' And the little woman held on to her, crying, wetting her, making strange noises. Didn't like it. Then the little woman let her go and the other woman took her by the shoulders and pushed her nose on to her nose, keeping it there while she wailed and cried. There were tears falling down all over her. She was wet and scared and wanted to go home.

At last the old woman released her and went towards the bedroom. Aunty Gloria came and sat her down and wiped her face. 'Don't worry, May,' she said.

When Keita came back into the kitchen she seemed a different person. She had changed her clothes and uncovered her hair, which was springy and black, and she moved briskly, taking up the lamp to stare at her. 'Huh, so they let you come . . . Well, Mata, not as good-looking as your mother but you got her eyes and her hair. Big like her too. Hope you're not stubborn like your mother.'

'Called May,' Aunty Gloria said. 'They call her May.'

'Called Mata, nothing else,' Keita said. 'That's just the father dipping his paddle in because he never wanted her to have her great-grandmother's name in the first place. Huh, even though he had no family to offer. But it's one thing my daughter was stubborn about, she gave her daughter my first mother's name. Do you hear that, Daughter's Daughter, it's Mata, nothing else. He didn't want any Maori name or any Maori daughter for that matter, or wife. Only wanted a slave for him and a prospect of land.'

Aunty Gloria was talking at the same time as Keita, in a quiet voice as though she wanted to cover what Keita was saying. 'Your own name from your great grandmother that died when Keita was born. Your real name. It's all right, Mata, when you get used to it.' Then as Keita finished speaking Aunty Gloria said, 'Help me, Mata dear, get their kai on the table.'

Uncle Bobby and a tall, wheezy man came in. 'Daughter,' the tall man said as Aunty Gloria went to greet him, then he said, 'Daughter's daughter?'

'Yes, it's Mata,' her aunty said.

'Come and kiss your grandfather, Mata Pairama.'

She didn't want to but she went to him and he held her close to him. He had a prickly face and a rough jacket. She wasn't used to it and wanted to pull away.

And wasn't used to people calling her Mata. It didn't sound like a real name at all, even though Aunty Gloria said it had already belonged to someone a long time ago. Now her grandfather had called her by a different last name as well, not Palmer. They were saying she wasn't May Palmer but Mata Something. She seemed to be changing into someone else, not being herself anymore, forgetting things. She hadn't read her scriptures and couldn't remember what she'd been told, couldn't remember what Jean, Margaret and Colleen looked like. At the Home she would've been talking to Jean and helping to bath Margaret and Colleen, whose faces she couldn't remember. She could remember something about them though — their bodies were white and shivery, and Margaret had hairy arms but Colleen didn't. They both had veiny wrists and were veiny and shivery behind the knees.

Aunty Gloria gave her a bowl of food to put on the table and the kids came in and sat up at the table by their grandfather, who was buttering bread for them. They were looking sideways at their mother, who pulled a funny, secret face at them. All the grown-ups had begun talking to each other in a strange language.

'Mata, your cousin Makareta,' Aunty Gloria said. The girl was there, a little taller than herself, wide body, fat face, dark brown skin, eyes brown and round. Her plaits had been brushed out and her hair fell in waves down to the backs of her knees. Pompom slippers and a blue dressing gown. The granny came in behind her, and her old, honeyish face, set with its two black eyes, was framed by thin white hair that had been done in two short plaits that rested forward of her shoulders. The girl Makareta leaned and kissed her as they were introduced but didn't say anything. Then the old woman turned Makareta away, talking to her in the different language. She didn't know if the girl had a mother, or if the mother had gone away or died. Makareta ate tidily while the granny talked on and on in a low voice.

That night she slept on the floor at one end of a mattress while Missy and Chumchum slept at the other end. They didn't want her there and they stayed awake for a time complaining.

At the Home she had a bed of her own next to Colleen, who slept under the blankets where she hid to suck her thumb. Next to Colleen was Margaret, who slept with her eyelids half open so you saw the whites of her eyes. White-eyes Margaret. There were little green birds with white rings in their eyes that came hanging and picking and flicking in the hedges sometimes, filling the hedges with tiny, white, moving eyes. Jean was in the corner bed where light came in through the cracks in the blinds — light from the street lamps, as well as sweeping light from the cars and trucks that went by. Last night Aunty Gloria had cuddled her to sleep and it was like having her own mother. She could hear Missy and Chumchum grinding their teeth in the dark.

seven

Manny came down the slope on the drum, his arms like two thin wings, flying. He leaned, and his feet beat faster and faster as the drum picked up speed over the holes and bumps. At the bottom of the hill he chose the moment, then threw himself sideways into the long grass before the drum hit the fence. After that it was someone else's turn — Missy's, Chumchum's, Alamein's, Jacko's or Billyboy's.

That morning all the aunties and uncles had come to see her and she'd had to greet each one while they cried over her and made strange sounds. She wasn't used to it.

Now all the cousins were having turns coming down the hill on a rolling drum, their feet running backwards, propelling it forward faster and faster, eyes sticking out like tops. Sometimes they could stay on until they reached the bottom, but sometimes the drum would leave them behind with their feet running in air and their bodies arching and falling. Nobody gave her a turn, but anyway she would've been too shy.

Nobody gave anybody a turn. If you wanted to ride the drum you had to get it yourself, had to wait and call as the drum came, rider flying, rider leaping and kicking a foot sideways, landing hard and springing out of the long grass. You had to guess where the drum was going to end up and be the first to put a hand on it calling, 'Mine's, mine's.' But she was too shy to call, or to grab the drum and push it up the hill. Too shy to run on it and probably wouldn't be able to do it anyway. If she could do it they might like her.

Looking back towards the house she could see Makareta watching from the step and wondered if her cousin was going to come and have a turn. That morning the old grandmother had helped Makareta make her bed and had laid out her clothes for her, peering and poking at each garment, smoothing them out on the bed with picky fingers. When Makareta was dressed, the

47

woman had sat her down on a stool and begun brushing her hair. Seen through the doorway from the kitchen where they were having breakfast, it was like looking through an opening to a room full of hair. After the brushing, the grandmother had made fat plaits, which became narrower and narrower down past the stool seat, almost to the floor, tying with bows as neat as butterflies.

Manny and Jacko were coming down the hill together now, their feet slap slapping. They leaned and straightened, leaned and straightened and their terrified faces jutted from their long, stretched necks. The other kids were dancing in the grass and yelling, 'Go, go, go,' and as it neared the bottom Alamein ran to claim it, calling Billyboy to be her partner. 'Mine's, mine's,' she called as Manny leapt off one side and Jacko off the other. The drum plunged forward and boomed against the fence.

Yes it was funny. It was fun. She wanted to dance in the grass too, run and shout, claim the drum and ride it down the hill, but she was too shy, too scared. She sat down and began scratching at the ground with a stick while Alamein and Billyboy pushed the drum back up the slope.

That was when she found the marble.

It looked like a perfectly round stone at first, but when she rubbed some of the dirt off she saw that it was a marble. She rubbed it in the grass until it was clean. Then she saw how beautiful it was. It was a big glass marble with blue, yellow, red and green ribbons swirling inside it. There were some mauve, smoky patches in it as well and some gold-brown speckles. It was as though there was a new little world right there inside the marble, and as though she was holding the new coloured world in her hand. She held it to her eye and to the sun's eye to let the light shine through, and it seemed she was in that new little world surrounded by whirling light and colour. Anyone could've found it, but she, Mata Pairama, was the one. She was Mata Pairama with a name of her own and she was the one who had found the marble.

She thought of showing it to someone, knowing that Jean would've liked it and wanted it. All of the Home kids would've wanted it and would've crowded round her trying to swap it for a half a piece of toast. The School kids would've wanted it too. They would have given her a pencil or a penny for it, or wanted to win it from her or fight her for it, even though they had marbles of their own. But none of their marbles had a four-colour ribbonning world, with a smoke sky and golden footsteps inside it. They would've called her names.

If Aunty Gloria was there she could've shown the marble to her, but Aunty Gloria, Uncle Bobby and Bubba had gone home. 'Goodbye, Mata,' Aunty Gloria had said. Then in a quiet voice she'd said, 'Keita might show you the photos if you ask.' She'd gone then, looking back and saying, 'Wave Bubba,' flapping Bubba's hand at her. She and Aunty Gloria could have talked about the world.

Back along the path she saw Makareta coming towards her and decided she'd show her the marble even though she felt shy and couldn't think of words to say. She waited until Makareta came close, then she held out the marble and said, 'I found this marble.' It was the first time she'd spoken to anyone since she'd come to her grandparent's place, 'Just there by the path.'

'Things come up out of the ground,' Makareta said. 'The old house used to be there.' It was the first time Makareta had spoken to her and she couldn't tell from Makareta's voice whether her cousin liked her or not, whether she liked the marble and wanted it, or not. 'Show it to them,' Makareta said.

The kids were resting, two of them sitting on the drum, the others lying in the grass. They were talking about bread and who should go to the house and get some for them.

'Missy.'

'No.'

'Jacko.'

'Not me, Keita be wild.'

'Chumchum, you and . . . Makareta, Makareta . . .'

'She found a marble,' Makareta said.

'Bread, Makareta, six bread.'

'Eight, eight bread.'

'Show them.' So she held the marble out for them to see and they became quiet, coming close to look at it. There was a circle of eyes looking into the little swirling world in her hand. Only that. No breathing, no sound — until the eyes shifted. Then the kids stood back, all their eyes on her face, and she felt shy of them. 'From the old house,' Makareta said. No one else spoke and she knew that they did like the marble. They wanted it or wanted to hold it, but no one spoke and they didn't shift their eyes from her face for a long time. At last they turned back to the drum. But she felt as if she had stolen something from them, or was to blame for something, but didn't know what.

Makareta went back to the house and Mata was by herself again, not talking to anybody, nobody talking to her. Didn't know if she could go inside or if she would get a growling from Keita, didn't know if she could go and see Aunty Gloria and show her the marble, talk about the world. Didn't know if she would sleep in Aunty Gloria's bed again with Aunty cuddling her as if she was her own daughter, telling her things as though she was a grown-up girl.

Soon afterwards Makareta returned with a pile of bread on her hand and the kids started shouting again. Makareta gave the the last piece to her. 'You've got to come and say goodbye,' she said.

Hungry, and the bread was good. She ate it slowly and noticed the others were eating slowly too, making their bread last a long time. They were all sitting except for Manny, who was jigging from foot to foot as he ate. He had fast feet and was the best drum rider of them all. All morning he'd been riding the cracks and bumps and hadn't been thrown off once. He was the first one to take the drum to the very top and was the longest stayer, never jumping off until the drum was almost hitting the fence. He was the one who should get the prize and she wasn't too shy to give it to him. She handed him the marble.

The kids all went quiet again and stared at her. Then Manny took his shirt off, wrapped the marble in it and put it on the ground, turned away and began rolling the drum. Missy climbed on to the fence wires and called to Makareta, who was on her way back to the house. 'Makareta, Makareta, she give it to Manny,' she called, the fence wires squealing. Makareta turned. 'She give it to Manny. She give Manny the marble.'

eight

Her first job at the factory was to wrap bundles of exercise books in brown wrapping, which she gummed down with strips of sticky paper. She would stack the wrapped bundles on the skid, glue on the labels, and when the skid was full Jerry would come with the trolley.

Jerry was a small man in a big overall and his hair was slicked back like two oiled wings above his white monkey face, bright monkey eyes. 'You'll get the hang of it in a day or two,' he'd said, eyeing the stack on her first day. Then he'd called to the other packer above the roll and rumble of the trolley as he trundled off to the store room, 'Back a winner on Saturday, didja?'

'No, did my dough, lost two pound five.'

'Same here, did my fiver.' Sometimes Jerry winked at her as he backed away and she thought he might like her.

Most of the women didn't. Stared at her clothes, her shoes, her bad hair, her black face, raised their eyebrows at each other, and at morning tea and lunchtimes didn't move over at the tables so she could sit down. They had smocks to put on over their dresses and flatties to put on in place of high heels, and in their handbags they had sticks of lipstick, powder compacts and jars of face cream. Just before the whistle went at four thirty they'd have turns at sneaking out to the wash room to cream and powder their faces and redden their lips before they went out on to the street, into the trams and buses, and home.

She liked listening to them talking about money, clothes, dances, parties, quarrels, earrings, stockings and make-up and many other things. Liked the hot-pie-and-smoke smell of the smoko room. The women all had husbands, boyfriends, children, friends to like or love, who liked or loved them — except perhaps for Ada, who had such a stern face and didn't talk much. She didn't know if Ada had anyone.

For some time she hadn't known Ada's name, but one day

Jerry had come in and called, 'That's the story, Ada. That's the story, Morning Glory,' as he'd swooped the trolley under the stack of paper she'd counted, and Ada had laughed, briefly, her face quickly becoming stern again. It was an old hard face with quick eyes. She had large brown hands that slid down the paper stacks with fingers scarcely moving — fanning and counting, fanning and counting. Mata didn't know if Ada liked her or not, but Ada was Maori too, which might mean that she *had* to like her. When they went into the smoko room Ada would move over on the seat to let her sit down.

A long time ago she had gone to her grandparent's place to stay. There were cousins and a lot of relatives there who had *had* to like her, had to kiss her and give her things. There was an aunty there who had cuddled her to sleep as if she were her own daughter and had talked to her and told her things as if she were grown up, as if she really did like her.

There was a grandmother called Keita, who was strict and crabby and had a stern face too. All the kids were scared of her, but Keita had bought her a coat and given her a photograph of her own mother. 'You look after it,' Keita had said. 'Put it in your bag. There's more for you when you're older . . . if you're a good girl.'

The photo was of a dark young woman with a wide, serious face and two thick plaits wound round her head. There was a little flowery hat sitting towards the back of her mother's head that couldn't be seen properly in the photo, and she was wearing a bridesmaid's dress and carrying flowers. She'd thought her mother was in heaven, but she'd found out she was really in the ground.

'It was at my mother and father's wedding,' Makareta had said about the photo. 'Your mother was a bridesmaid at my mother and father's wedding.'

'So where are they?'

'Who?'

'Your mother and father.'

'My father Rere was killed in the war. My mother Polly lives in Wellington,' Makareta had said in her exact way.

There were things that she had wanted to ask Makareta, but

most of her cousin's time was spent with Kui Hinemate and the other adults talking in another language, having her hair done, her clothes looked after, her food cooked for her. Then Makareta had said, 'My father has a memorial stone by where your mother is buried but he's not buried there, he's buried in Egypt.'

Makareta had gone then, led away to the garden by Kui Hinemate, who had a blanket for her to sit on and a sunhat for her to wear.

She hadn't known what Makareta was talking about, hadn't known why Makareta was talking about her mother, who had either died and come alive again as an angel in heaven, or was away somewhere and would come back to her one day. She'd thought Makareta was silly with her old creeping granny who treated her as though she was still a baby and talked to her in a silly language.

Mrs Parkinson had come to the Home to see her when her mother died and she'd had to put her school cardigan on, have her face and hands washed and her bad hair brushed down hard. Then she'd been shown into the visitor's room where Mrs Parkinson was waiting for her. 'It's about your mother, May,' Mrs Parkinson had said, and she'd thought she was going to be taken back to the room with the brown door where her mother would be. 'Two weeks ago your mother died and now she's gone to heaven to be with God. I've brought this for you, to help you,' and Mrs Parkinson had taken a book from her basket. 'It's the Lord's word, May. Read from it every day and the Lord will help you. Pray every day and the Good Father will hear you. Do you understand?'

'Yes.'

'What do you say then May?'

'Thank you.'

'And May, do you know who I am?'

'Mrs Parkinson.'

'Yes, but also I am your legal guardian, as arranged by your father after your mother left you. I am like a mother. I will visit you when I can.'

Mrs Parkinson stood as matron came in and the two women had talked in low voices for a while before Mrs Parkinson left.

'My mother died,' she'd said to Jean later. 'She's gone to live in heaven.'

'Mine too, when I was a baby.'

'What do they look like? What do our mothers look like?'

'Like angels in their nighties, with two big wings on their backs for them to fly,' Jean had said. So she'd made up an angel's face for her mother like the ones in the Sunday school pictures — a pale face with pink cheeks, blue eyes and long, gold hair. But even so she'd kept on waiting for her mother to come.

For a moment she'd stood watching silly Makareta follow her granny to the garden and then she'd started to run to Aunty Gloria's, calling along the track. 'Mata, what's wrong?' her aunty had said, coming out of the little house and putting her arms round her. 'What is it? Tell Aunty.'

'Aunty Gloria my mother's in heaven.'

'Yes . . .'

'Makareta said she's buried, in the ground.'

'At the urupa . . .'

'Makareta said . . . about my own mother.'

'We'll go there tomorrow.'

'Go?'

'To the urupa, to the cemetery, where your mother's buried.'

Then Aunty Gloria had cuddled her hard and said, 'Never mind, never mind. We tried to find you . . . Just remember you're our girl, our own girl with your own name just like Keita said.' Then Aunty had taken her inside and told her about her mother.

'We don't know how she met your father,' she'd said. 'He was round these parts keeping away from the cities because he was a seaman from England who ran off from his ship. Your Mummy was the big sister, the oldest, the one the old people had a special plan for. They watched her all the time, looked after her, so we don't know how she met Albert.

'One day she came home with him saying they were engaged to be married. Keita was angry, wouldn't allow it. She told Albert to get out and not come back. "He won't marry you," Keita told her. "You think he wants to marry a Maori girl? Of course not. And of course he won't do. We have better in mind for you."

'But two days later your mother left and there was nothing Keita could do. She wasn't their daughter any more, Keita said. This wasn't her home any more.

'Well, Albert wasn't good to her and she had to leave him. Had to leave you too because she had no money, no place to go. She went to find work so she could get some money and a place. When she got money she'd get you back somehow, that's what she thought. But she was already sick by then.

'She did get a job that first day, in a sewing factory. Worked there two days and on the third day collapsed over the machine and ended up in hospital. We didn't know she was sick. Didn't find out until a long time after when she wrote to us. We brought her home and all the time she talked about you, didn't know where you were. We tried to find you but your daddy was gone, already had a guardian for you and we didn't know who.'

At the cemetery there was a book made of white stone with words about her mother on its open pages. Some of the words she had been able to read: 'Died November 4th 1946 Aged 25 years. Always remembered.' But other words she couldn't read at all.

So everything was different from what she'd thought. Her mother was not an angel flying about the sky-heaven on gold-tipped wings, but was asleep in the ground instead with her angel's wings folded, her angel's face peaceful and her pale hands crossed on her angel chest. She'd helped Aunty Gloria to pull out weeds from her mother's grave and they'd put some flowers in a jar by the book which was called a stone.

Next to her mother's stone was another, not shaped like a book but like a slice of bread. It was the memorial stone for Makareta's father and she hadn't been able to read any of the words on it at all. Aunty Gloria had tidied round it and put some flowers there as well. 'These others here, they're all your relations too,' her aunty had said. 'No time to do them all today.' Then Aunty had shown her the different graves, saying who the people were.

It was then that Mata had realised something else. The words at the top of the stones were names, the names of the people buried there, because she could read some of them — Sarah,

Arthur, Mason, Henrietta, Bradford — in amongst other words that must have been names as well.

Her mother had a name.

Everything was different from what she'd thought. Other people knew that her mother had a name and that it was there on the stone — Anihera Keita Pairama — even though she couldn't read it. 'It's my mother's name,' she'd said, pointing to the stone.

'Yes.' But Aunty Gloria hadn't understood, had turned to go home.

'Aunty Gloria, Aunty Gloria, my mother's got a name.'

Then Aunty Gloria had cried and cuddled her and read the name out and helped her to say it. They'd gone home after that and Aunty Gloria had cried all the way down the track. They'd washed their hands in the tin of water at the bottom of the hill, and Aunty had washed her wet face and red eyes as well.

On the way home in the train she'd taken the photo out of her bag and held it to her chest. She'd thought about the next school holidays, when Keita would send for her, want her, tell her about her own mother and give her some of her mother's things. She'd thought about what the things might be, wondered about cups and saucers, china ornaments, a watch, a gold ring, a heart-shaped locket that hung from a gold chain, with a tiny ruby set into it and photos inside. Thinking about the locket and the ruby had made her remember the enormous ruby, the size of an orange, that had been stolen by an ugly thief from between the eyes of a handsome king's elephant. There was a story about it in the comic that she'd read to Missy and Chumchum while they'd waited on the station for the train.

Missy had liked her when she read the comics and when she'd read out the stories on the newspaper walls at Aunty Gloria's. They'd all liked her when she'd given Manny the marble. Keita had bought her a coat and given her a photo, and Aunty Gloria? Well, Aunty Gloria had cuddled her and talked to her and loved her, and told her she was their girl with her own name, belonging to them.

But now she knew that none of it was true. She wasn't their girl at all. She had waited every day but they hadn't sent for her. She'd never heard from any of them, never been there again.

So she thought it wouldn't be true about Ada liking her either, even though Ada was often kind.

She didn't know who there was to like or love her, or if there would ever be someone of her own to like or love.

She thought of the boy in the tram.

nine

Ada taught her how to count paper, showing her how to grip the bottom corner of a bundle with her right hand, turn her hand so that the sheets separated out at the top edge, then thumb down by twos with her other hand until she had counted twenty-four. She learned to shift each lot to form a fan, doing her best to keep a straight edge on the stack. 'Ha, getting the hang of it,' Ada said, coming to look over her shoulder after she'd been at it for a morning. 'Be counting in fours soon, then fives and sixes like me.' Ada straightened the stack for her. 'Like your job, do you?'

'Mm,' It was difficult to talk and count at the same time but she liked talking to Ada. She paused, thinking of something to say that would keep the conversation going. 'Mrs Parkinson got it for me,' she said.

'Mm?'

'Got me a place to board.'

'You like it . . . your place to board?'

'Yes.'

She turned back to her work thinking about some of the things she might tell Ada at some other time when she was practised enough to talk and count at once. She might tell her about Jean, who was married to Rick; Jean, who had saved up teatowels, sheets and pillowcases in a suitcase and become engaged to Rick, who had bought her a diamond ring; Jean with red bad hair. At night-time I tidy my room and write to Jean. I don't know if someone will like or love me.

But she didn't think she'd tell that last thing to Ada, or to anyone. It was Jean who used to talk about being liked and loved. Her fingers stopped counting and she said, 'I've got a photo of my mother in my room, of when she was a bridesmaid at a wedding.'

'Where's your mother?'

'Dead.'

'Where's your father?'

'Dead. Killed in the war in Egypt.' She didn't know what made her say it.

'My brother too,' Ada said.

'Killed?'

'Missing, they said, in action. Means they didn't find him. Means he's dead. And my husband come home with his hand blown off and a stomach full of bits and pieces . . . You got sisters, brothers?'

'No.'

'Grandparents, relations?'

'No.' She didn't know why she said it but in a way it was true. Ada turned to the door to call to Jerry and he came in whistling, rolling the trolley.

'You should get you a boyfriend,' Ada said.

There was someone ugly who waited at the tram stop every afternoon after work. He had a narrow head, a squashed neck, black lips and eyes, and a dark brown face. His shoulders were wide, his legs were shortish and as he walked he leaned from side to side as though he could be skating. He was Maori, like her, but she didn't know if that meant that he might like her.

In the afternoons, if she left work as soon as the bell went and hurried to the tram stop, he would be there and they'd both catch the same tram. He'd go to the middle compartment and she'd go to the front. She'd sit where she could see him, always disappointed that she had to get off the tram before he did. She didn't know if he was a boy or a man, but thought he might be ugly enough to like or love her.

One afternoon she decided to stay on the tram to see where the boyman got off and perhaps find out where he lived. She watched through the window to the open compartment where he sat smoking, leaning forward with his elbows on his knees. As the tram neared a stop that was two stops beyond hers, he stood and and went out on to the step, holding the outside handrail. He had one foot on the step and the other foot out ready to jump and he leapt out on to the road, throwing himself into a run alongside the slowing tram. Then he changed direction, running towards the footpath as people came swarming out from the stop, grabbing the handrails, climbing the steps and rushing for places to sit, straps to hold, windows to see out of, walls to lean against. She saw him run, dodging through the crowd into a doorway.

She didn't think she'd tell Ada about the boyman, and anyway it was too difficult to talk, get the counting right and keep the stack tidy. 'Got you a boyfriend yet?' Ada asked.

Getting better at counting, getting faster and able to keep her stack straight. She could count in fours. 'You don't say yes or no.' Ada's hands flowed down the stack counting and fanning.

'There's a boy . . . on the same tram as me going home.'

'What's his name?'

'I don't know.'

'Gives you the eye, does he?'

'No.'

'Good-looking, is he?'

'No.'

'Well . . . Well, got your eye on him, have you?'

'He nearly gets run over every afternoon jumping off the tram.'

'Running for the boozer?'

'The Central.'

'The Central hmm . . . Jerry . . . Hey, Jerry . . .' The trolley trundled in and Jerry steered it in under the stack. 'What you think, Jerry, this one here's got her eye on a fella rides on her tram.'

Jerry stepped on the lever to raise the skid. 'Ho, rides on her tram, does he?' The stack wobbled and steadied as he released the lever. 'Well now, Mata, you better watch yourself.' He rolled the trolley cleanly between the stacks past the staple machines. 'Hey what do you think, Mata's got herself a bloke rides on her tram,' he called to the women on the staplers.

The women smiled down on to the folded spines of note-books as they flicked the cardboard covers on top, slid the bundles through and worked the pedals. The staples hammered down. Some of the women stopped work and looked up, laughing. There was something she didn't know about that made them all laugh, something she couldn't ask. She shouldn't have told Ada about the boyman.

'You got your stack all wonky,' Ada said.

ten

'**A**re you going to the pictures?'
         He'd walked up beside her at the tram stop. His hands were in his pockets and he was looking out over the road as though he could be speaking to a car or a tram. She wasn't sure if he was talking to her or not. 'Are you going to the pictures?' he asked again. So she said, 'I go with Jean. Sometimes . . . But she's gone away.'

'On Fridays we go for a feed after the pub and go to the pictures, or we go up home and play cards.' She couldn't think of anything to say. He turned suddenly and walked out on to the road. She hadn't noticed the tram coming.

She moved with the crowd to board the number seven, wanting to follow him to the middle compartment, but she couldn't go in there where men go. It was for drunk people, singers and shouters, a bad place. She wasn't allowed to sit in the middle compartment of trams.

From where she stood she could see him sitting, leaning forward, smoke coming out of his nose.

So he had spoken to her. At first she hadn't been sure if he was talking to her or not, then she knew he was. He'd asked her something about pictures but she wasn't sure if she'd answered him, didn't know what she should've said and wondered what his question really meant.

Could've said you're ugly enough to like or love me. Could've said every day I see you jumping out in front of cars, running, running, through a crowd, through a doorway before the tram stops. I ride two extra stops, watch you hang from the tram, drop, run, dodge through the crowd of people, disappear through a doorway into The Boozer, The Central. Why did you talk to me? Is it because you have to like me because you are like me? My name is Mata Pairama. I have a name, Mata Pairama, Mata Pairama, a name of my own.

The tram neared his stop. He looked up from the doorway, lifted his eyebrows, smiled, hung from the handrail, leapt and ran. Do I like you because I have to like you? Will I love you, will you love me, and what was it you said standing by me at the tram stop with your hands in your pockets talking to trams and cars? Pictures. Are you going to the pictures, you said. Joe's, down Bridge Street, having a feed, and going to the pictures after. If you like?

But she wasn't allowed to go to the pictures, wasn't allowed to talk to boys or men.

Had to go home from work and help with the meals. After dinner she'd do the dishes and scrub the benches down, sweep the floors and set the tables for next morning. After that she could go to her room where there was a bed and a stool, three coat hooks, three coat hangers, one window, a photo of her mother that leaned up against a cup on top of the stool. One day she would ask Mrs Parkinson to let her have some money from her wages so that she could get a frame for it. She wanted new shoes and another cardigan, and different hair.

And she would like to go out in the evenings or on Saturdays, and to have time to look in the shop windows on the way home from work. Brown teeth when he smiled.

She stepped down on to the road hurrying back along the footpath hoping she wouldn't be late, hoping Mrs Baird wouldn't know she'd gone two stops past.

'Where've you been?' Mrs Baird asked. 'I was coming back from the shop and I saw you go past in the tram. You didn't get off at the right stop.'

'I wanted to walk back . . . to look in the shop windows.'

'There's work to do here. You know what Mrs Parkinson said.'

'Yes.' Then she said, 'I'd like to go to the pictures.'

'Huh. There are better things for a Christian girl to do,' Mrs Baird said.

Or she could just go, which is what Jean would have done. But Jean didn't have a guardian who told her where to stay and what job to have or how much money she could have from her wages. Jean had left the Home and gone to live with an aunt and one Saturday Jean and her aunty had come to take her out. Jean's aunt had told Matron that they were going to afternoon tea but they'd gone to the pictures instead, Jean wearing a new, green, tweed coat, her coppery hair just resting nicely on the shoulders of it. They'd loaned her a blue raincoat which had covered her Home clothes and made her feel good.

In the carpeted foyer of the picture theatre they'd looked at all the photographs of film stars before going up the carpeted stairs leading to a wide doorway where a man tore their tickets in half and nodded them in. Inside there was red carpet in the aisles and brown padded seats to sit on. There were pillars patterned in gold vines and flowers, and pale alcoves lit with green and pink light. The ceiling was domed, and babies, dressed in clouds and flowers, held hands in a circle there. What she'd liked best of all was the gold shimmering curtain, that, as the house lights changed colour, changed colour too and was drawn upwards in fine, glistening loops and folds. There was music. One day, one night she'd go again.

Not tonight. Tonight she would thicken the stew and turn the rice pudding down, set the table neatly and cut even slices of bread. In her room she had a photo of her mother whose name was Anihera Keita Pairama. She had her own name, Mata Pairama. Her name, her name, which couldn't be taken away from her, couldn't not be hers.

And you might like or love me, that's what I would like to know.

eleven

'So how's that bloke on the tram?'
            She didn't want to answer because Ada would tell
Jerry and Jerry would make a joke about it to the staple-machine
women who would grin onto their book covers or look at her
and smile. Also if she answered she'd lose her count. Her fingers
could walk down in fives now — four fives and a four to make
twenty-four. She could fan the bundles of twenty-four into
groups of twelve and put the twelve, straight-edged, onto the
stack on the skid.

'Still giving him the once over are ya?'
'On Friday nights he goes to the pictures.'
'Ask you to go with him, did he?'
'No yes.'
'Did you go?'
'No.' Getting better. She'd talked to Ada without missing her
count.

Ada slapped six lots of twelves onto the stack. 'Why not?'
'I have to help at the boarding house?'
'Don't you get a night off sometimes?'
'No.'

Ada lit a cigarette because the boss had gone out. The cigarette was in one corner of her mouth, smoke puffed out of the
other. It smelled good. 'And anyway they wouldn't let me, not
at night, not with a boy.' She hoped Ada wouldn't tell Jerry.

'Can't say I blame them, he might be a bastard. There's plenty
of bastards around, you know.'

'And I wouldn't have money.'

'Why, where's your money?'

'Mrs Parkinson looks after it for me, pays the board and just
gives me my tram fare and tea money.'

'She might be a bastard too. You got to keep your eye out
for bastards . . . Isn't that right, Jerry?'

63

'What's that, Ada my love?'

'You got to keep your eye out for bastards.'

'Sure thing . . . Hey look at that Ada, straight as a die. She's doing all right you know.'

'We better fold now,' Ada said, 'Getting ahead of ourselves.

'So they don't give you a night off, or a day off?' Ada shouted above the noise as the folder started up. The blade rose, Ada fed the paper in and the blade came down again, snapping the pages through the slot.

'Saturdays. Saturdays I get time.'

Too much time. After the breakfasts and the cleaning up she had time until four. Time to tidy her room but it was already tidy, time to rub the floor and the windowsills but they already shone, time to clean the little window but it was clean enough. If there was a ladder in her stocking she mended it, if there was a hole in her cardigan she darned it. The cardigan was thin, nearly worn out, but she could darn finely — slowly to pass the time. On cold days she shivered in her cold room.

On Saturday afternoons she went out for a walk, pulling her cardigan about her and hurrying as though she was going somewhere. She didn't look in the shop windows or watch the trams rattling by, but stepped out quickly as if there was someone to meet, somewhere to go. She'd think about the letter she was going to write to Jean and of the man whose name she didn't know, who talked to her each day at the tram stop. She'd think about being at work with the noise, the smells, the things that people said, about counting by fives and making a neat stack, of keeping up with Ada at the back of the folding machine and of Jerry shouting, 'That one there, she's murder. Tell her to go easy til you get the hang of it.' She'd think of Ada and the things she sometimes said.

'What do you do then?'

'I clean my room, wash my clothes, mend them, go for a walk around town.'

She could keep up with Ada now, even with the machine on high. Could pick up a bundle of six in each hand, turn the two bundles towards each other, knock them and stack them. Nicely.

'You should ask her for your money . . . for clothes, some new stockings, a coat for you.'

A coat was what she wanted, but she didn't want Ada to know about that. She had asked Mrs Baird if she could save something from her wages each week for a coat. It had taken her a long time to ask. Mrs Baird had reminded her that the money was for her board, and that what was left went to Mrs Parkinson, but had said she would speak to Mrs Parkinson.

People in the trams had coats — fawn with fur collars, tweed, astrakhan, gaberdine, green and brown check, black and white, blue, mixed-up browns. The workers had coats, shabby and warm, which they took off in the cloakroom and hung on hooks on the wall, belts to unbuckle, buttons to undo. Some of the women had headscarves, which they took off and put in the pockets of the coats before fixing their hair, pressing their lip-sticked lips hard together in front of the narrow mirror, one peering behind the other, lips sliding. She would like an off-white jeep coat, a grey skirt, new stockings and a pink chiffon scarf.

Two days after she'd asked about the coat Mrs Baird had said, 'Mrs Parkinson told me she knows somewhere she can get a coat for you.' That was a long time ago and she'd stopped thinking about what sort of coat it might be, stopped thinking about coats altogether until Ada mentioned it. 'And you're lucky,' Mrs Baird had said. 'You've got a tram stop right outside the door and shop verandahs to wait under.'

'Mrs Parkinson's getting a coat for me,' she said to Ada.

'It'll be too late soon, the winter'll be gone. I reckon what you should do . . .'

But Ada's words were lost as the lunch whistle sounded. She knocked the last few books into a pile while the machine slowed down and stopped. She straightened her back then followed the rush of people to the lunch room.

The seats were filling up as she went to one of the tables and sat down. People were bunched round the box of orders, looking for their names on the bags. Ada came with her pie, holding the greasy, steaming bag by the twist. In her other hand she had two cups of tea which she held high in front of her, making her way in and out of workers still coming in through the door. 'Here you are, mate, milk no sugar.'

'Thank you.'

In her room on Saturdays when there was no more mending to be done, she'd pull the damp paper from inside her shoes, stand them on more paper and scratch a pattern with her little nail scissors. Then she'd cut out the shape in six thicknesses and fit them inside the shoes. After that there was a nothing time, no more to be done, too early to go out and walk. She would think of the smelly lunch room, the swearing women, and of what Ada might say, like, 'Here you are, mate, milk no sugar.'

'Well what I was saying? You'll be getting a rise next week, so you want to take that extra few bob out and sock it some-where,' Ada said.

'What's this?'

'What for?'

'What's this all about?' The others were sliding into the seats with their eyes widening, wanting to know. She didn't want to look at anyone. 'It's these bastards who are supposed to look after her. They pinch her money and use her for a lackey.'

'Why?'

'How?'

'What do they . . . ?'

So Ada told them and they all talked about it. She was wedged into a corner and couldn't get away so she nibbled at her sandwiches wishing the lunchtime over, waiting for the whistle and the whirring and roaring of the machines as the switches were turned on.

Window, wardrobe and wallpaper. There was a tiny hole in the top part of the window, and when she had first gone into the room there'd been just one crack, going from the little hole to the top of the pane. When she'd tried to clean the window other cracks had sneaked across the glass in all directions, so now she didn't want to clean it any more in case the pane fell out. The little hole was six-legged and spread itself across the window like a giant spider. Her window spider. She kept the window spider as a secret for herself.

The bottom part of the window slid upwards when she

wanted it open. It wouldn't stay up on its own but she'd found a way of keeping it up by using a coat hanger as a prop. She used paper and water and a bit of her soap to wash the window with.

When she'd first been given the room she'd brushed all the little hills of wood dust out of the wardrobe that had fallen from the insect holes. She'd washed the inside, waxed the outside and made a little wad of paper to jam in the door to keep it shut. It was a narrow wardrobe but there was plenty of room in it for her dress, her skirt, her blouse and her cardigan. There was a space for her shoes, and beside the place for her shoes she'd put a box that she'd taken home from work where she kept her cleaning cloths and shoe polish.

'Yeah, yeah, that's what you do, pinch it out.'

'Hey, Dotty, she getting a rise next week?'

'How would I know?'

'You'll know when you do up the wages.'

'Hmm.'

'So don't stick her packet down, she's going to pinch some out.'

'Why? What for? What's all this about?' Dotty said as she came with her cup of tea, drawing her lips in, her eyes moving from side to side behind her old glasses. Now they were telling Dotty.

If she did take some money out and save it, she'd be able to get a photo frame. She'd seen one that looked about the right size in a second-hand shop just two streets away. It was a wooden frame with a gold-patterned edge around it. There was a dirty piece of glass in it and some layers of old cardboard. On the back there was a piece of dusty string tied to two flaky eyelets.

'Buggers, they should be bloody had up.'

'Should too, you should have them up.'

'What are you going to buy?'

'When you get your rise?' They were all looking at her. She had crumbs in her throat.

'A photo frame.'

'A photo frame?'

'What for?'

'My photo.'

'What photo?'
'You got a photo?'
'Who of?'
'My mother.'

She'd told them something that she hadn't wanted to tell. She was hot, had crumbs in her throat, and now they'd all be asking, wanting to know everything. They'd find out things to look at each other secretively about, and she wouldn't know what secret things she'd told them.

'She's dead isn't she? She died?'

'She gave it to me before she died.' She didn't know why she said it.

'What else?'

The whistle went and they all began shifting. The voices rose above the sound of it. 'Did your mother . . . ?'

'Did she leave you anything else?'

She walked away with crumbs in her throat, pretending not to hear over the push and bustle. The women were hurrying for the cloakroom to flick back the wisps of hair, fix up their lipsticks, pee, straighten their stockings and pat down the backs of their skirts.

On one of the walls the wallpaper had damp cloud shapes on it, and raindrops that sat, sometimes trickled, down under the shapes of clouds. The pattern of the paper had faded, but behind the wardrobe the green feathery leaves on a mottled-brown background could still be seen. When she'd first moved into the room there were places where the wallpaper had come away, so she'd stuck them back up with the sticky paper that she'd taken home from work. Cloud shapes, rain wallpaper and a glass window spider. These were her own things, her own secrets of her room.

Ada was stacking covers and waiting for the machine to come to the top of its warming-up noise. The bar lever came down and she started pushing the books through.

'So there you are, mate. Get a rise soon, in a week or two, and you can nip a half a crown out without them knowing. How's that?'

'I might . . .'

'Might? No might about it. Those buggers been robbing you left, right and centre.'

The frame only cost one and six. She'd give the wood and the glass a good clean, fit the photo in, back it with cardboard and stick it down with sticky paper. She thought her mother would like it.

'Anyway, how's that bloke?'

She bent low over the books so that Ada couldn't see her face and because she didn't want to talk about that over the noise of the machine. Also, she didn't know if she should tell Ada anything any more. It was only when she was alone in her room that she thought of the things she might say to Ada and of what Ada might say to her, or of what she'd write to Jean. Waiting for letters from Jean.

Ada didn't wait for her to answer the question but started singing the silver dollar song, keeping in time with the thrusting bar.

She knew his name now but it wasn't a proper name. Sonny. He'd talked again about the pictures — about them having a feed at Joe's on Fridays. Them? She didn't know who. Then she called to Ada over the noise of the machine and her singing. 'He wants me to go out with him on Friday to a place where you eat, but I haven't got the money and I wouldn't be allowed.'

Ada didn't stop what she was doing or look up, but she stopped singing and jutted her bottom lip out over the top one. After a while she said, 'Huh. I'll come and be your aunty. I'll come and get you and shout you a night out. We'll go to that place . . . wherever it is that bloke goes for a feed. I want to look him over in case he's a bastard. Tell that Mrs Thingamebob your aunty's coming to take you out. Tell that bloke you and your mate's coming to that place for a feed on Friday.'

Then she was scared. Better to just stay in her room looking at things, writing to Jean, waiting for Jean to write. Just the photo frame would do. She'd open the packet and get a half-crown out, buy the frame, get cardboard and sticky paper from Jerry.

'I can't . . .'

'Yes you bloody well can. Tell that thieving Whatsername at

your boarding house I'm calling for you Friday and we're going out for a feed.'

'She'll tell Mrs Parkinson.'

'Tell her to tell Mrs Parkinson your aunty's coming and you're going out.'

'Mrs Parkinson doesn't like my aunties.'

'What? What aunties?'

'I'm not allowed to go there.'

'Where?'

'Where my aunties live.'

'I thought you didn't have aunties. I thought you . . . Bloody bitch. You just tell her I'm coming, I'm taking you out and that's all about it. If you want to say aunty, say it. If you don't, don't.'

'I have to do the tea and the clearing up.'

'What time you finish all that?'

'Seven.'

'That's all right, I got shopping to do. Do my shopping then I'm coming round, could be two of us. Could be Daisy and me — my half-sister. Sometimes Daisy and me go out for a feed on Fridays, sometimes stay home and get into the whisky.'

But it was scary. Mrs Baird was too crabby to ask. She'd grumble and mumble then ring Mrs Parkinson. Mrs Parkinson would ask question after question then . . . maybe let her go. She didn't want to go because she wouldn't know what to do or say. Didn't have a coat.

Ada had two fingers in her mouth, whistling for Jerry. The bar on the folding machine idled up and down and Jerry was coming from the packing room bringing the trolley. She straightened up. The paper had pushed forward in her shoes.

twelve

'Done your shopping?' Ada asked.
             'I got some stockings and my photo frame.' She took
the frame out of her bag to show Ada.

'Needs a good clean up,' Ada shouted above the whirr of the
machine starting.

When Jerry came in she asked him for some scraps of card,
some sticky paper and string and showed him what she wanted
it for. He took the old cardboard out of the frame, trimmed some
new board to the right size on the guillotine and brought her
some gummed paper and string from the reels in the packing
room.

'What does she do with it anyway?' Ada asked as she paused,
waiting for Mata to catch up with the stacking.

'Who?'

'That one takes your money.'

'It's to pay back what I owe.'

'Like for what?'

'My stockings and underwear, pyjamas and things I needed
when I left the Home. And . . .'

'And?'

'My father owed her money for all the years.'

Ada resumed feeding the paper through the machine,
frowning. Then above the clatter she called, 'What years? She
didn't look after you. You didn't stay with her,' then left the
machine and stood by the stack with her man's hands on her hips
and her lined face fierce and said, 'What years? You were in the
Home. She didn't look after you at all.'

'She said he promised but he didn't send it.'

'So now she's making you pay?'

'It's written down in a notebook . . . what I owe.'

'She's a thieving bastard.' Ada returned to the machine and
thumped the paper through. 'You should get the police on to her

71

. . . except you don't know about the police either. Sometimes I think the bloody world's full of bloody bastards.'

Mata bent to stack the notebooks, hoping that Ada wouldn't ask any more questions. She didn't want to tell any more because she could see that Ada was angry — thought Ada might be angry with her. Also, Ada would tell the others who would tutter and frown, yet at the same time seem glad about it.

'So why did she have you?'

'Who?'

'That guardian, that bastard. Why be your guardian if she don't care, if she only want money and your father's not sending any?'

She knew the answer to that because Mrs Parkinson had told her many times. She knew she shouldn't tell Ada but then she couldn't help telling. 'So my grandparents couldn't have me, and to keep me away from evil and sin.'

Ada returned to her work without saying anything and didn't look angry any more. She just frowned hard at the gap under the lunging bar, judged the timing and began sending the notebooks through.

That night she took a saucer of water to her room and, with piece of rag and a little of her soap, cleaned the frame and the glass, working slowly so that it would take a long time. After that she placed the photo onto one of the new pieces of cardboard. The photograph was smaller than the card, which made a nice white edging for it. She put it into the frame, packed the rest of the board in behind it and gummed the back with the sticky paper, trimming it with her little nail scissors. She tied new string through the eyelets and it was done.

There was a nail that she'd been saving, which she poked into one of the insect holes on the side of her wardrobe. She hung the photo of her mother there and felt something aching and pleased inside her.

thirteen

She stopped in the doorway letting Ada and Daisy go ahead of
her, but the two older women paused too. Then they went
in and Daisy turned to her and said, 'Come on.' But she didn't
want to go in, didn't want Sonny to be there or for Ada and Daisy
to see. She was ugly with bad hair and had a mended cardigan and
ugly clothes.

'I don't want . . .'

Ada came and took her by the arm and she knew if she tried
to pull away, people would stare. So she went in but couldn't
look anywhere. Ada and Daisy were whispering.

'Over here?' Daisy asked.

'That'll do.'

They sat down at the table and she stared hard at the things
on it — salt and pepper, sugar, tomato sauce, Worcestershire
sauce and something else, which could be vinegar. Ada had a card
and she and Daisy were talking about what they would order.

'What'll you have, Mata?' Ada leaned towards her, reading
from the card. 'Steak and onions, sausages and eggs, fish and
chips, pea pie and pud, spaghetti on toast . . .'

Fish and chips was what she wanted. The School kids used
to have fish and chips for lunch, wrapped in newspaper. They'd
make a hole in the top of the packet and take the chips out one
by one. In the middle of the packet they'd come to a piece of fish
in bubbly batter, greasy and steaming, and she used to like sitting
where she could smell the hot, appetising smell, and where she
could listen to the kids talking about what they had — sixpence
worth of fish and chips, fritters and chips, chips only, with or
without salt, with or without vinegar.

Some would have a shilling's worth to share with brothers
and sisters, and the families would argue about it. She didn't
know if she should say she wanted fish and chips or if there was
something about fish and chips that would make Ada and Daisy

73

smile at each other in a secret way.

'I'll have the steak and onions,' Daisy said.

'Fish and chips for me,' Ada said.

'Yes, me too.'

'Fish and chips and a couple of eggs. Have a couple of eggs thrown on, Mata,' Ada said.

'Yes thank you.'

Ada gave the orders to a waitress, who shouted them through a hatch and returned with knives and forks and a plate of buttered bread. There was a hot-fat smell, a hum of talking, someone laughing over the other side of the room, but she didn't want to look, didn't want anyone to see her.

'Is he here? Whatsisname, the one on the tram?' Ada asked.

'Sonny.'

'Is he here? Or is he just giving you the runaround?'

'I don't know.'

'Have a look. There's four or five over the other side there a bit drunk. A couple my age, two blokes and a girl having a yarn and a laugh. Has he got a bullet head and big shoulders?'

'I don't know.'

'Course you do, have a look.'

But she wouldn't look. The waitress came with the food and she didn't know if she could eat it. 'Want sauce, want vinegar?' Ada said.

In front of her were two large pieces of fish and a heap of chips topped by soft-fried eggs. 'Yes, vinegar please.' She took the bottle from Ada and sprinkled the vinegar, and as she returned it she looked up and saw, through drifts of smoke and steam, the man Sonny sitting over the other side of the room leaning on one elbow talking. She put her head down and began to eat.

When they were partway through the meal he came and stood by the table and she had to look up, could feel the heat of the room and smell the heavy odours of it as he reached and shook hands with each of them.

'Sit down,' Ada said, nodding to an empty chair. So he did, sitting with his shoulders hunched and his fingers laced together at the edge of the table. 'You're the one she's been talking about, on the tram?'

'That's me.'

'Well, we thought we better come along and run our eyes over. Thought you might be a bastard.'

'Not all the time.' That made them all laugh but she didn't know why. 'Fridays I bring my aunty and uncle down, sometimes their kids. A few mates come in sometimes.'

'Bit long in the tooth aren't ya?'

'Twenty-nine last time I counted.'

'Haven't you got a girlfriend or a wife?'

'Nah.'

'No girlfriend, no wife?'

'Nah.'

'Why you been asking her?'

'Seen her on the tram giving me the eye.'

They all laughed again. At her. She was hot and uncomfortable, wanted to be home in her room where her mother looked down from a photo in a frame, where there was rain paper, a glass window spider reaching its long arms. Tried to think about that, about having a name of her own, about how she'd taken money from her packet to buy a frame for her photo, bought stockings and underwear as well.

Ada and Daisy stood to meet the old man and woman and two younger ones who had come over, shaking hands, kissing — as though they knew them. Ada got her up to greet them and they kissed her too, but she wasn't used to it. Then Sonny said, 'What about me?' and kissed her on the cheek and laughed. They all laughed and she felt her face getting hot, couldn't look at any of them.

Sonny's aunty and uncle sat down at their table and began talking to Ada and Daisy in low voices in the language she couldn't understand. And she noticed that as Ada spoke she began to move her head and eyes and hands in a way that she hadn't seen her do before. Her stern face changed as though it had melted and all the hard lines had been modelled away.

Then the aunty turned and spoke to them all. 'We all going up my sister's place to play cards so come on up.'

'One day,' Ada said. 'But we got to take Mata back in a few minutes.'

'Stay there then, drink your tea.'

'And you all go. Another day we come and meet your sister.'

The air outside was cold after the heat of the grill room, and she held her cardigan close about her. The stores were shutting and people were gathering at the tram stops with their shopping, stepping out onto the road as the trams lumbered forward. Faces were pale under the white-blue light of the street lamps, and the parcels and bags that people held gave them strange shapes as they stood out on the black road. She walked with Ada and Daisy, with his kiss on her cheek.

'So that's him,' Ada said. 'Well.'

She'd write and tell Jean about it because Jean knew about kissing and going out with boys. When Jean had gone to live with her aunty she'd been allowed to have make-up and nail polish, and could buy anything she liked with her money. She used to dress up and go to the milkbar with other boys and girls. A lot of boys had liked her, taken her for rides on their motorbikes. At church on Sundays Jean would tell her what they did.

Then Jean had started going out with just one boy called Rick. She was in love with him and he was in love with her, and now she had someone of her own, a baby of her own too. But she didn't write any more.

'Well, I don't know about him,' Ada said. 'I think you got to be careful about him.' As though Ada knew him. People always seemed to know things that she didn't know, seemed to know each other even when they'd only just met.

'Might not be the one for a girl like you,' Daisy said.

But who will there be? Who will there be, ugly enough to like or love me, so that I can have someone of my own?

She opened the door and went up to her room. It was cold. It was Friday night and the weekend stretched out rawly before her. Tomorrow she'd get her work done then sit in the room and wait. Then she'd walk, pretending to go somewhere, returning in time to help with the meals, wash the dishes, scrub and clean. Then she'd come back to her room and think of having someone of her own, with a house just for the two of them — a house painted cream with red window frames and a glass front door. They'd open their gate, walk along their path, unlock their door and go into the kitchen with its floral curtains, green cupboards and drawers, Neeco stove, pots and pans, dishes, cutlery, tablecloths and teatowels.

In the evenings they'd sit in armchairs with the wireless going. There'd be tasselled blinds to pull down over the windows, feltex on the floor and pale wallpaper with silvery stripes running down it. On one wall would be photographs, one of her mother. She couldn't think who the other photographs would be of. Anyway there'd be lace curtains at the windows, gathered to the sides and held into place by frilled ties. There'd be glass swans and wooden elephants on the varnished windowsills, a clock and a vase of flowers on the mantelpiece.

Jean and Rick had a house with a lawn in the front and a yard at the back where there was a garden and a revolving clothesline. They had furniture, some of it new, and they were saving for a washing machine. They would have the washing machine by now, she thought. Sometimes in the letters Jean told her what she and Rick did, what men and women do, but Jean hadn't written for a long time.

She knew she didn't want to do what men and women do.

On Sunday she would go to church and walk back to Mrs Parkinson's to spend the afternoon there, and Mrs Parkinson would give her church papers to read. Perhaps there'd be a coat for her. In the afternoon she'd walk home in time to help, then after the cleaning up had been done she'd go to bed and wait for Monday.

But there were more things now that she could think about while she waited for Monday to come. There was a warm steamy grill room, fish and chips with runny eggs on top, and a kiss on her cheek that no one could take away.

fourteen

Sonny leaned across the table and said, 'It's my aunty, always on about it, always nagging.' Then he continued eating his sausages and eggs, looking about at the ceilings and walls as though he'd lost something there. His eyelids were drooping and he had a beery smell.

He'd come in late to the restaurant, just as the rest of them had finished eating. Ada and Daisy had gone with his aunty and uncle to play cards, and had told him to walk her home and get her there by quarter past nine. She was uneasy because she knew that if Mrs Baird saw them walking together she'd tell Mrs Parkinson.

Then she thought of how, for nearly two months now, she'd saved her half-crowns and bought a photo frame, stockings, underwear and a pair of shoes, as well as pies and doughnuts at work and meals at Joe's. No one had found out. Also she had a brown cardigan, which at first she'd hidden, but had then begun wearing right in front of Mrs Baird, who hadn't even noticed.

The Monday after their first meeting in the restaurant Sonny had arrived at the tram stop carrying a parcel. He'd taken her elbow and guided her through the crowd to the middle part of the tram, the place where men and bad women went. But she'd sat down beside him, nearer to him than she'd ever been, liking the smell of smoke and hair oil, liking having someone to sit close to.

'What's your name again?' he'd asked.

'Mata.'

'Mata, I got you this,' he'd said, showing her the parcel.

'What . . . What for?' Then he had placed the parcel on her lap.

'Because I heard what that aunty of yours said to my aunty.'

'It's not my aunty. It's Ada. She works with me.'

'Gabbing away in their lingo . . . Open it.'

'I can't.'

'Why not?'

'I don't know.'

Then he'd popped a hole in the parcel with his finger, pulled a bit of the paper away, and she'd seen that there was a brown knitted garment inside. 'They don't want you to have a jersey, I give you a jersey,' he'd said. 'Go on.' So she'd begun unknotting the string while he leaned back blowing smoke, one arm stretched along the seat behind her as if he had his arm round her.

Inside the parcel was a large cardigan, a man's cardigan, with four big buttons down the front.

'I can't have it, they'll see,' she'd said.

'Hide it in your bag. Tell them that mate of yours give it to you.' He'd picked up her bag and pushed the cardigan down inside it. 'And don't forget. They don't let you have clothes, I get you clothes. They don't let you have money, I give you money . . . Gone past our stops you know.'

That night in her room she'd tried the cardigan on. It was too big at the shoulders but looked all right if she left it undone. The sleeves were too long but she'd tucked the cuffs under and stitched them down. It was nice and warm.

'Yes, my aunty . . . she likes you,' he said sawing the sausage. 'Said you're a quiet one, said she likes the quiet ones.'

What if she told him things, talked to him, tried telling him something?

'When I say things people laugh,' she said, 'and I don't know what's funny . . . I don't know why they laugh.'

He looked at her with his head on one side, put his knife and fork down and leaned forward with his hands on his knees and his elbows poking out. His eyebrows went up and his pink eyeballs popped as though leaning had made them roll forward, then he leaned back, dropping his head backwards, and laughed. She was looking up into the back of his brown teeth and could see the bulge in his short neck riding up and down. It reminded her of the bar on the folding machine. People stared. She didn't know what was funny.

He picked up his knife and fork again, grinning down onto

the food, looked up and caught the eye of the waitress and asked for tea and bread. He put his head back and laughed again. The room was filling with people as it neared shop closing time.

'I have to go. In a minute I have to . . .' she said.

He stopped laughing and began eating again. 'Time I got married, she reckons. Reckons I got to get married, too much on the loose.'

There was tea and bread there for both of them and he poured tea, slid the plate of bread towards her. 'That's what the old lady said. Hmm. So what do you reckon?' But she couldn't think of anything to say, thought she was being asked a question but wasn't sure what, so she just ate some of the bread and drank her tea, quickly because it was getting late. He was swishing bread round the plate mopping up tomato sauce and gravy and she stood to go. 'Hang on,' he said. 'Put you on a tram and you'll get back in time, easy.'

As they walked along the footpath he said again, 'What do you reckon?'

'Sometimes people say things to me and I don't know what they say.'

'About you and me getting hitched.' She knew it meant married. He went out on to the road looking to see the number of the tram that was coming then returned to the footpath. 'So what do you reckon?'

It wasn't her tram and she was going to be late, but what did it matter because she was going to get married and have someone of her own — if she could, if Mrs Parkinson would let her.

'Yes, but I won't be allowed,' she said. She walked out on to the road as the next tram came to a stop. He went with her to the step.

'Says who?' he said stepping back, and then he called, 'I'll get a ring. Aunty said I got to get a ring.' He was laughing but she didn't know what was funny. It made people stare.

fifteen

Ada went with her to tell Mrs Parkinson that she wanted to get married. 'That'll have to wait,' Mrs Parkinson said, 'until she's free to do as she pleases.'

'Early next year,' Ada said, 'would be a good time.'

'It won't be possible unless she is to marry someone of means,' Mrs Parkinson said. 'She has debts, you know.'

'How much?' Ada asked.

'All these years I've been trying to make good from bad, and this is the thanks I get. Her mother was bad and her father told lies, but I did my best no matter how bad the blood.'

'How much?'

'I'm her guardian until she's twenty-one. By then it'll all be paid.'

'How much?'

'A hundred and five pounds.'

'She's coming to live with me . . .'

'I am her legal guardian, I'll have you know, and I won't have the likes of you . . .'

'She's coming to live with me. In three months the money'll be paid.'

Mrs Parkinson hesitated, shifted her eyes. 'I doubt that. It's easier said than done.'

'We'll give you thirty-five pounds now and twenty-five a month.' Ada opened her handbag and took a purse from it.

'Hmm. Well, we'll see . . . All right, I'll give you three months then we'll see. If it's all paid up I wash my hands of everything. After that don't expect a thing after all I've done. After that don't come running to me about any wedding.'

The two of them walked solemnly along the path, clicked the gate behind them and then Ada leaned on a lamp post and laughed. She laughed so hard that her eyes watered and she took her hanky out of her sleeve, wiped her eyes and blew her nose saying, 'She only has to get paid. It was only easy, she only has to get paid.' It seemed to be the funniest thing in the world.

After that they went back to the boarding house to get her belongings. 'I've asked my niece to come and stay with me now,' Ada said to Mrs Baird. 'We've come for her things.'

'I'm sorry but you can't come in here like this taking my boarder away,' Mrs Baird said. 'She's got a guardian, I'll have you know. Nothing to do with you. It's her guardian who arranged for her to stay here.'

'We've been to see Mrs Parkinson,' Ada said.

'How am I to believe that? Mrs Parkinson said nothing to me. There's work to do here and you can't just come here taking my worker away. You can leave her things here until I say so, until Mrs Parkinson gets in touch and tells me herself.'

'You could phone her,' Ada said.

There was something about Ada that made Mrs Baird nervous. She dropped a fork in the sink and went to the telephone.

When she returned she said, 'Mrs Parkinson said she's got someone else for me if you can leave May here until Friday.'

'We'll go now,' Ada said.

From Ada's they could walk to work and home again. For the first few days they went together to the tram stop after work to see Sonny, to tell him why she wouldn't be travelling on the tram any more, but he wasn't there. On the Friday they went to Joe's and he wasn't there either, neither was his family.

'Someone must've died,' Ada said.

For a moment Mata thought Ada was saying Sonny had died. She didn't ask Ada what she meant, but thought she mightn't ever see Sonny again.

At first it was strange to have money of her own. Ada told her to save it all and at the end of each month she'd have enough to pay Mrs Parkinson. 'You don't need to pay any board,' Ada said, 'and you don't need any tram fare. When you're all squared up, then we'll see.'

It was a month before she saw Sonny. He'd been away to a funeral and had decided to stay on a while. On his return he found that he'd lost his job at the meat works, but he'd gone down to the wharf and got work there without any trouble.

The story that Ada told about the two of them going to Mrs Parkinson made them all laugh, and their laughter had made her laugh too. She wasn't used to laughing, felt uncomfortable when the other people in the restaurant turned to look at them.

'I got you this,' Sonny said, putting his hand up his sleeve and producing a watch as though he was a magician. It was a man's watch with an expanding strap.

'Looks like a hot potato,' Daisy said. 'You been perking?'

'Got it from a mate, just helping a mate out.'

'Pull the other leg.'

'Nah, true. My mate had a bad accident. Fell down the hold this morning and busted his legs and arms and cracked his head open. Laying there nearly dead and he says, "Get these watches off me before the Zambucks come." We looked on his arms and he's got five up one arm, five up the other, all the same, like that one. So we got them off him . . . just helping.'

At the end of each month she took the money to Mrs Parkinson, and on the day of the last payment, even though Ada wasn't there with her to help her feel brave, she asked Mrs Parkinson for the papers.

'What papers?' Mrs Parkinson asked.

'That could be about my mother and me.'

'There's no such thing,' she'd said. Then she'd gone to a drawer, taken out an envelope and handed it to her. 'Here, take this. It's the paper and the birth certificate, and then I can wash my hands of everything.'

In the envelope was a document of guardianship and a birth certificate. Also there was an old letter from her grandmother: 'I am answering your question about the land. It is our family land and the children inherit it when it is their turn for it. There is land here for my daughter who is deceased, the one who is the mother of Mata. Our granddaughter can come here at any time you allow. But the land can only come to her when she is freely our own, when she is freely our daughter and not her father's daughter or someone else's daughter. That is because the land

must not be taken away. Yours sincerely, Keita Pairama, grandmother of Mata Pairama.'

She undid the back of the photograph, put the birth certificate
and the letter in between two pieces of the backing cardboard and
did it up again. She threw the document away.

sixteen

When she and Sonny first married she thought it meant that
she had someone of her own. For a short while it seemed
so. While they were staying with his family it seemed that way.
It was like having someone of her own and her own family as
well.

Sometimes even then Sonny didn't come home at night, but
the old people were there and they were good to her. Their
granddaughter, her husband and baby lived there too, making it
seem like a real family. 'Have to change his ways now he's married,' his aunty would say when Sonny didn't come home. 'That's
him, always on the loose. I want to see that boy settled before we
head up north.'

When he did come home it would usually be in the early
hours of the morning. She'd hear him stumbling in, moving
round in the kitchen and heating up food. Later she'd hear Aunty
get up to see if the stove had been left on. Sonny would be asleep
at the table and she'd hear Aunty trying to wake him. If he didn't
wake, Aunty would ease him on to the floor and put a blanket
over him.

In the mornings he'd be up early no matter how late he'd
come in. She'd hear him moving about in their room putting his
clothes on and would pretend she was still asleep because she
didn't know what to say to him. Someone of her own but she
didn't know how to own him, often glad when he didn't come
because she didn't like to do what men and women do.

By the time they were all up he would have breakfast

cooking and Aunty would start telling him off. He'd listen for a while then he'd sometimes say, '*She's* not moaning about it. I can't hear *her* moaning about it.'

'Don't mean she like it,' his aunty would reply.

She felt she should say something too but didn't know what. After that breakfast would go on in silence, and when it was time for Sonny to go he'd walk out as though he'd forgotten them all, whistling down the path to the tramstop.

'Only good thing I can say about him,' Aunty would say when he'd gone, 'he goes to work every day. But what's the use if he don't bring home money, just drinks it, buys silly things, bets on the horses, gives it away. You want to give him a good telling off.'

But she didn't know how to tell him off. As well as that, she quite liked it when she heard him say, '*She* doesn't moan about it, can't hear *her* moaning about it.' They had their names down for a state house and once they were on their own Sonny would be different, she thought. He'd change his ways because there would be just the two of them. When they had their own place she'd know what to say, they'd know how to talk to each other and she'd try her best to like what men and women do. They'd have children and be a family all belonging to one another.

They'd been married a year before they were allotted a house. It was painted turquoise and had a roof of brick tiles. It had hard brown lawn front and back and a thin hedge. There was a low wall at the front with a letterbox by a wooden gate. Even though she hadn't heard from Jean for a long time, she decided she would write and describe the house to her. There would be an answer this time, perhaps, which the postman would put into the letterbox so that it would be there waiting for her when she arrived home from work.

Inside the house there was a floor of varnished wood and she was going to save up for linoleum and a bisonia square. Sonny's aunty and uncle had given them all the furniture they needed for the time being, bedding and towels as well. Ada had given them some green curtains and a table.

On most nights Sonny would be home late and she'd wake to hear him stumbling about in the kitchen. Sometimes she'd go out and heat food for him, help him into bed.

Now and again he would come home early from work and then she'd be glad to have someone to eat with, someone to talk to even though it was hard to know what to say. He'd sit and eat, staring in front of him and she'd sit opposite him wondering if he had forgotten she was there.

And on the nights when he wasn't home she'd sit and look at wallpaper, at windows and old curtains, at nailholes and cracks in the floorboards, insect holes, door handles, watermarks on ceilings, trying to find something to hold as her secret, something to be her own. Once in a while she'd write to Jean, but mostly she sat thinking of work the next day when there would be the noise of people shouting above machines, the crush and hurry when the whistle went, the smoke-and-pie smell of the canteen, the gossip, the swearing, Jerry having them all on. She'd think of what she was going to tell Ada.

Then one day Ada sat down on a box by the folding machine and when the lunch whistle went she stood up and went home. That night she died.

When Ada didn't arrive at work the next morning she had to work the folder on her own, putting the books through then going round the back to stack. It was nearly knock-off time when they heard that Ada had died.

She didn't feel anything inside when she heard, not sorrow, not anger, not anything. Some of the women cried but there was nothing inside her that could make her cry. She sat on Ada's box by the machine and there was nothing in her legs and arms to make them move. 'Come on, lovey,' Jerry said. 'Time to go home. Go home and have a good cry. It's a good way for our mate to go you know. No suffering.'

When she arrived home she took the photo of her mother off the wall, sat on the edge of the bed and held it against her. There was nothing inside her that could make her cry but she thought about the time she'd gone running along the track shouting for Aunty Gloria, nearly crying, and the day after that when they'd sat on the hill where her mother was buried, pulling out weeds and putting flowers in a jar.

People went away, or they died.

She sat there for many hours hoping that Sonny would come so that there would be someone to tell, someone to talk to. He rarely came, but occasionally called to bring her something. Nothing to make her move, and eventually she lay down on the bed and went to sleep.

The next day she woke late, feeling swollen, as though something angry had found its way into her. She stayed in bed all morning then got up, dressed and sat at the kitchen table and waited. She didn't really know what she was waiting for — unless it was her children. Where were her children? There was nothing inside her that would make her move.

That night Sonny came with a leg of mutton wrapped in sticky brown paper. 'Thought you wasn't here,' he said. 'Why you sitting in the dark?' He put the meat on the table in front of her. 'I come to drop this off . . . Why you sitting in the dark?'

'Ada,' she said. It was not knowing what to say next that almost brought tears to her eyes.

'What's the matter?'

'She died.'

She heard him groan as he sat down beside her and then he banged a fist against his chest and cried. Not like the women at work dabbing at their wet eyes, not like herself a moment before with two sudden tears popping into her eyes but not running. But crying with noise and wetting tears. He reached out for her and she held him until his crying stopped. For a moment it was as though he belonged to her.

'When?' he asked.

'The night before last.'

Then he looked at her in a puzzled way and started to ask some questions that she didn't understand.

'Where is she then? You been over?'

'Where?'

'Where they got her.'

'Who?'

'Ada?'

She didn't know what he was asking her so she told him about Ada feeling sick at work and going home when the lunch whistle went. The next day at work Ada hadn't turned up and in the afternoon they'd found out she died.

'So you been over?'

'Where?'

'Ada's.'

'I've been home here.'

'Have they gone?'

'Who?'

'Ada and them.'

'Where?'

'I dunno. Back. Where Ada comes from.' But she didn't know how to answer, didn't know what he was asking her.

He put his hand in his pocket and took out a pound note and some change. 'We'll get a taxi,' he said.

'Where to?'

'Over Ada's, and see . . .' There were things that she didn't know that everyone else knew. She put her coat on and followed him. He had the parcel of meat and was rattling change in his hand.

Sonny directed the driver to his aunty and uncle's place and asked him to flag another car. When they arrived he went inside, and it seemed a long time later that he came out with Aunty and Uncle and the rest of the family.

A woman answered the door and when she saw them all standing on the path she began to cry out. She called them to come in, embracing them one by one. They went into Ada's sitting room and sat down and the woman went into another room where they could hear her waking others. Then she returned and sat with her head bowed, holding her hanky to her eyes. Sonny's uncle stood up and began speaking in the language she didn't know. As he spoke the woman nodded, smiled down at her hands, folding and turning the handkerchief.

When he finished speaking there was a long silence, then the woman said, 'I'm happy to see all of you, thank you for coming, you're all welcome. I'm the sister-in-law of Ada's sister's husband. They left here yesterday early but someone had to stay back and keep the house warm. Just me and my two kids stayed back. You're all welcome here.' They could hear the two kids out in the kitchen preparing food and after a while they came in. 'Here's Jacky and Ann,' the woman said. 'They've made a cup of tea for us.'

In the kitchen the table had been set up with bowls of meat and vegetables and plates of bread as though they had all been expected. The old ones started joking and laughing as though they hadn't just now been crying, going on as though Ada had played a trick on them all and as though they were all about to play a better one on her.

'Mum and me's going back home in a couple of months,' Uncle said.

'Mm, cheaper to go on two legs than let them take you in a box,' Aunty said.

'She thinks I won't pay for her to go back, that's why she wants to go now.'

'Where will you be? Under by then, huh.'

'She thinks I'll bury her where she drops.'

'The way you cough you could drop tomorrow . . . And now, dear,' Aunty said to the woman, 'you come from the same place Ada come from?'

'Further north, right at the top. I been here twenty years now and been back only twice.'

'There's an old lady, Paritainoema . . .'

'A half-sister to my great-grandfather. Same fathers but she's from the second family.'

'Yes, well it's that first family. One of the daughters was brought down and married to an uncle on our mother's side.'

'I heard about it, and there's some of that family down here too. It's . . .'

She listened to the talk that became more and more difficult to follow, sprawling everwhere, sentences begun by one person being finished by another. It seemed that they all knew people, the same people, even people who had died a long time ago, seemed they'd all known each other for a long time and in another life, even though they had only just met. The woman was called Johnny but her real name was something else. Other people knew things that she didn't, there was a secret to it. The talk went on until daylight.

'We go home for our things, girl,' the old man said to Johnny as they stood to leave. 'Tonight we come back and stop here with you.'

'Ae, we stop here until the family come back. No good just you and your two kids,' Aunty said.

'Thank you, Mother and Father. My kids and me'll get your beds ready for you.'

They went out onto the footpath into the half-light of early morning, into the pallor of street lights as the first tram went by with its trolley clacking, bearing on the front of it its name, its number and its three blue lights. It traipsed fully lit, pulling its clangour along the grey dawn street.

Ada was gone. Dead, and gone . . . back, she didn't know where. Everybody knew each other, knew how to finish each other's sentences, knew what to do and say, belonged to each other. There was a secret to it that she knew nothing of.

seventeen

Where were her children? For years she had waited for her children. Long after Sonny had stopped coming home she'd waited for the children who would belong to her and to whom she would forever belong.

She was often asked at work about her family, about her children. One by one young women left work to have babies. Often they'd bring their new, dressed-up babies for everyone to see and the women would all gather round talking, smiling and clicking their tongues. Sometimes they'd give her the babies to hold and they'd say things to her that made her sorrowful.

Once, a long time ago, Jean had come, stepping out of a taxi with two grown girls and a little boy. At first she hadn't recognised the woman getting out of the taxi, but the two girls, who looked to be about seventeen and eighteen, were so much like the Jean that she hadn't seen for nearly twenty years that she knew the woman must be Jean with her daughters Kirsty and Jennifer. Jean was carrying the little boy up the path while the two girls waited by the taxi.

'Jean,' she'd called from the window. 'It's the right place. Send the taxi away.' She'd gone out and helped them in with two big bags.

'I thought you mightn't be here any more. I never got round to answering your letters,' Jean said.

'Never mind . . .'

'I kept the address but then I wasn't sure . . . I thought I might stay a while, if there's room.'

'There's plenty of room, you can stay as long as you like,' she'd said, taking the bags and putting them into one of the bedrooms. 'There's only me here.'

'What about your husband? Kids?'

'No kids. And Sonny's not here any more.'

'Like Rick. Rick buzzed off years ago,' Jean said. 'Good riddance too. I've been married again since then. Lasted two years. It was me that buzzed off that time, and since then I've been round having a good time . . .'

'There are two spare rooms and I've got beds and blankets here that Sonny's aunty and uncle left when they went away.'

'Did he go with them? Sonny?'

'No.'

'Got another woman?'

'One and then another.'

'He must be a bit of all right, is he? Is he a bit of all right?'

She didn't know how to answer Jean. Sometimes she forgot what Sonny looked like. He had a wide body, she remembered, and his head sat between his shoulders as though he had no neck. His face was oval-shaped and his eyes were small and dark brown. His legs were short and he swayed from side to side as he walked.

'He's ugly.' She didn't know why she said it but it was true. He was ugly enough to like or love her, to be someone of her own, but there were secrets to it that were difficult to know.

'Go on. He can't be that bad,' Jean said, 'otherwise why would he have all the women after him?'

The little boy Terry had gone to sleep on his mother's lap. He had a round, moon face and white curls, and it seemed as though his head was too big for the rest of him. It lolled on a wisp of a neck and his skinny arms and legs dangled like pink ribbons.

Three weeks later when she arrived home from work, Jean's bags were packed. Mata was sorry to see the bags by the door and to realise that Jean was leaving, because she looked forward to coming home after work knowing there would be someone there.

Terry was asleep in the bedroom and the girls had gone. 'I've sent them to their father,' Jean said. 'He's going to get them jobs. Besides, he's got his own house and he can afford to have them.' And then she'd said, 'I've decided to go back to Terry's father and I was hoping you might have Terry for a little while. Doug's not very good to Terry because he reckons he's not his . . . What do you think, May?'

'I'd like to have him,' she'd said.

'Just for a while until I can talk Doug round. He's got this nice place with everything in it, every gadget you can think of, really modern, but it's no place for kids. Terry wouldn't like it there. I rang Doug this morning and I can tell he wants me back, so I told him I might have someone to look after Terry for a while.'

'I'll have him.'

'Until I work things out. I know Terry likes you.'

'It's all right, I'll have him.'

'And I'll ring you. I'll ring in a week or two and let you know how it's going . . . I thought I'd go now while he's asleep. He won't mind, he's used to being looked after by other people.'

After Jean had gone, Mata looked at the clothing that had been left for Terry and realised there wasn't much. She didn't mind because she liked the idea of going out and buying what was needed. She'd get clothes, some nice shoes and some little gumboots so they could go out walking when the footpaths were wet. He had a few nappies and she'd get a few more, not too many because Terry could ask to go to the lav now and only needed nappies when he went to bed. He could say several words. He called Jean Mumum, and sometimes he called her Mumum as well. If he wanted to call her Mumum she'd let him. As well as the clothes she'd get a pushchair, a cot and a highchair. She could get them from the second-hand shop and paint them up. The idea filled her with pleasure.

Then she wondered how she was going to afford all the things for Terry if she wasn't able to go to work. In her excitement she had forgotten about work. But she had some savings so she'd use them. By that time Jean could be back and she'd return to her job again.

She'd had Terry for six months before her savings ran out, then she wrote to Jean and told her she needed money. Jean replied saying that she'd send money every fortnight. It was a relief because she'd thought Jean might come and take Terry away.

Terry was six years old before his mother came for him. Jean had left Doug and met someone else, a man who wanted a family.

'I'm not sprouting any more kids at my age,' Jean said. 'And anyway, if I did have another baby who's to know this one won't turn round and say the kid's not his too?'

She'd said that they were lucky there was Terry, and anyway it was a nuisance sending the money every fortnight. She'd promised to let Terry come back for a holiday every now and again if they didn't go to Australia to live.

Terry turned and waved to her as he got into the taxi ahead of his mother and she never saw him again. It was as though he had died.

She thought of him every day and whenever she went out she'd look for him. When she saw children playing, or walking to or from school, she'd look for the one that was most like Terry, or the one that would be nearest to his age. At first she'd sent cards and presents on his birthday to the address Jean had given her, but these were always returned to her with 'Address Unknown' stamped on them.

She returned to work and when she was asked about her family she'd sometimes say, 'I did have a little boy once, but he died.' It seemed the right thing to say.

After that she waited, but it was difficult to know who or what she waited for. Once again she was looking at wallpaper, at windows, cracks in walls, watermarks on ceilings, cracks in floorboards, nailholes, insect holes, handles of doors, trying to find something in a room or a house to hold to herself, something to be her own. But always, in the end there was only herself. All the other things that she had never had, had gone.

For a short time, a time she could barely remember, she'd had a mother who had left her and who had then died. At first she'd remembered only her mother's clothes and her hands, but not her face.

She'd been taken to live in a children's home where there was night crying and bedwetting, and where she was always bad and strange — where she'd had a dirty skin and the kids had called her dirty. Her bad hair had been chopped with large scissors by Matron every time the curls grew and she'd had two long clips to keep the hair close to her head, but always her bad hair had loosened the clips and sprung into wrong twists and waves and curls. How could they keep the Home free from nits and lice when there was hair like that?

She had never wanted to be bad so she'd scrubbed her skin, watered her hair down and prayed to be good, tried to be obedient and to work hard, yet all the time there was evidence that she was bad — other children would not walk with her to school and they didn't let her join in their games. At school she was called names that made her feel ashamed. Once she'd made a mother angry.

Sometimes on the way home from school, kids had hidden in wait for her, running out and attacking her with their school rulers. She would swing her bag at them and try to run but there were always too many of them and they'd hold her and hit her. As soon as they saw blood they'd run away, turning every now and again to shout.

If she knew they were waiting for her she'd go the long way home, which meant going through the pine plantations where there were bad men who could tell that she was bad too. They'd open their coats and trousers and hold out their bad things to her, and she'd run away feeling sick with the knowledge of her own sinfulness.

She'd had a friend once, who hadn't been a friend for always. Jean told lies and swore, giggled in the dark and told her secrets that were rude and awful. Sometimes Jean would take all of her clothes off and jump and dance around naked in their room, just to be bad. Her skin was as white as cups and saucers and her hair was terrible and red.

Once she'd gone for a holiday to a place where there were people like her, but she wasn't like them. They hadn't sent for her again but she'd been given a photograph that showed her mother's face.

She'd had a diamond ring once that Sonny had given her. It was a band of thin gold with a single large diamond held by a platinum claw. The women at work had come to her, red-faced and greedy, to look at the ring and to ask her one thing after another. Her answers had made them look at each other, winking and blinking their eyes. And after that there was the wedding ring. She'd thought that it meant she had someone of her own.

So she'd waited. She'd examined the faded patterns, the cracks, the marks. She'd listened to the dripping tap and watched the clock hand moving, wanting to make something her own. Felt the ache of it spread through her in wide beams.

Sometimes at night she would hold the photograph of her mother against her as though it would pull the ache out. She thought of the hard waiting thing inside her being softened and loosened and drawn out of her through her mother's eyes.

Then one day she had put on her coat and her shoes, put the photo in her pocket, opened all the doors and windows of the house and gone out following her feet, wanting nothing and going nowhere.

MAKARETA

eighteen

I waited until Keita and I were alone before I told her I wanted to leave. I said nothing, at first, about taking Makareta with me. 'I've heard from my sister,' I said. 'She's sick and wants me to come and stay.'

Keita dabbed the brush into the blacking and began spreading it over the top of the stove. 'For how long, Polly?' she asked.

'To stay, Keita, to live.'

She didn't look up or stop what she was doing. I feared her eyes.

'What's wrong with here?'

'Nothing. Nothing wrong.' I took the kettles and teapot from the stove, anxious to have something to do, and began wiping them down at the bench.

'Then this is where you stay.'

'My sister . . .'

'You're talking about Cissie,' she said, working down the stove's front, sweeping the brush over and around the hatches, 'who lives in two rooms on top of a shop with a no-good husband and three children.'

'She's sick.' The words came out louder than I intended.

'So then you must go and look after your sister a while. There's nothing wrong with that.'

'On Saturday,' I said. 'I want to go this Saturday to my sister's, to live.'

She stopped then and put her hard eyes on me. 'I won't agree with it,' she said, returning to her task as though there was no more to be said.

I had to pull words up from inside myself. 'I promised my sister.' It wasn't easy when I'd always been treated as a daughter.

'Promised your sister? No, Polly, it's not your sister begging you to come. It's you wanting to go. That's why I'm asking you, what's wrong with here?'

'Nothing wrong.'

'Too quiet here for you? No men here. That's the truth, that's the reason. Your sister lives in a big town so there must be plenty of men there to want you. Plenty of soldiers coming back from Italy, so you want to go to Wellington.'

'No, Keita . . .'

'That's the truth of it.'

'I haven't forgotten Rere,' I said.

'We had other plans for our son but he wanted you and we allowed it. We didn't turn you away. Now our son's dead, two years dead . . .'

'And four, nearly five, since he went to war.'

'So there,' Keita rattled the gratings and banged the flaps. 'It's what you're saying. Four years or five, now you want another husband.'

'No, no . . . But I just think there could be more, there could be work. Women go to work now. And Makareta . . .'

'Makareta? Don't talk about Makareta. Our son's child stays here.'

'She's my child too. Soon she'll be five.'

'We've got our little school here and this is where she stays, right here with her family.'

'I'm her family too.' But Keita wouldn't hear me. 'Our granddaughter was born right here, she's lived here until now and this is where she stays, with her father.'

'But he's not here,' I said, 'Rere's not . . .'

'The father's the family, the family's the father.'

'And I'm her family too.'

Keita turned away from me, putting the brushes on the rack and wringing out a cloth, 'You want to go, want to forget, then you go,' she said. 'If you stay then you are our daughter and we will look after you always. As for Makareta, you can cry all you want but you're not taking her. You can't take her from Kui Hinemate, the one that baths her, washes her clothes, cooks special food. The one who, when our granddaughter was a baby, massaged her, treated her colds, got up in the night to stoke the fire and keep the kitchen warm.'

'I looked after my baby, I cared for her.'

'Nobody's saying different, but Makareta is Kui's whole life. You can't take a whole life away.'

'I'd bring her back . . .'

'Do you remember, Polly, that Makareta's whenua is buried up there with her father?'

'He's not there, Keita, not buried there, there's only the place . . . ready for the stone.' I had the courage to say the words even though they were not words that Keita would listen to.

'This is her home always.'

'It'll be here still. I'll bring her back.'

'That's what you think now, but the town has it's way of eating people. If you want the town to swallow you, you go, Makareta will be cared for here. Cry all you want, you can't take our granddaughter away.'

Keita went out, taking the ashes, and because it was what I always did I laid the paper in the grate and set the kindling. I wondered what I would do now, knowing that Keita would never agree to my going and taking my daughter with me.

I was surprised when she came back in, and, taking off her headcloth and overall, came to sit down by the stove to talk to me. 'I would wait to tell you this,' she said quietly. 'I would wait until next year or the year after that. But now, with you talking like this — about going to live with your sister — I want you to know that we have thought of you. I want you to know we have a plan for you.

'When our son Rere brought you home we didn't refuse you. We know your family and we were happy to have someone from that good family to be part of us. You're a good-looking woman, you know the ways of the people, you know how to work and you've had an education. What more could we want for our son? Then Rere went to war and we lost him. We lost our son, you lost your husband, but you are our daughter still. We don't expect our daughter to lead a life of loneliness, of course not. We don't want our granddaughter not to have brothers and sisters. So this is it. We have planned for you to marry our son Aperehama. I wanted to wait a year or two before telling you because Aperehama is still young and it is only two years since Rere died. But now, because of what you've been telling me, it's the right time to speak.

'You and Aperehama will marry, that's our plan, and this will be your home always. You'll have other children with Aperehama, to be brothers and sisters for little Makareta. That way the whakapapa is not upset, the ancestry of the children remains the same. And Polly,' Keita lowered her voice to a whisper, 'you and your children will have land, plenty of land. You will have land through our eldest son and land through our youngest. We know your family. It's a very good family, from a strong line, a family strong in the customs, but, Polly, they've got no land. Through no fault of theirs they've got no land. Never mind that, their daughter is our daughter.' Keita stood. 'That's all, that's our plan. We want you to know that you are our daughter and this is your home. We want you to know that although our son has died we don't forget you.'

It was difficult at first to take in what Keita was telling me. Marriage to Aperehama? I could understand how it made sense to her in that the lines of genealogies and inheritances would be kept. Also, if I married Aperehama it would mean that Makareta could not be taken away from them. It was true that Makareta was Hinemate's life, the life indeed of the whole household. Taking Makareta away from Kui was the most difficult part of the decision that I had made. But my own life was a lonely one, an empty one in many ways now that Rere would never return. For me it was time to do something new.

Aperehama was like a brother to me. I couldn't stay there now that Keita's intentions were known.

I also knew that if I wanted to take Makareta with me, she and I would have to leave secretly.

nineteen

During my pregnancy, the women of the household had taken over my whole life. Every morning Gloria was sent to the washhouse to heat water in the copper and prepare a bath for me. Kui Hinemate would come and wash me and massage my stomach and breasts, all the time talking about the feelings and thoughts of a baby in the womb — about its listening and its knowing, its love of good, its rejection of evil. 'A baby curls itself to hide from bad things,' she would say. 'Hides its face with its hands. A baby is old. A baby knows.'

I had to accept the bathing and to allow the towelling and the massaging, but I had my own ideas about the baby growing inside me. Kui's voice was just a drone, an interruption across my own thoughts. I remember the looks of resignation that Gloria and I sometimes exchanged.

At mealtimes I was given the tenderest pieces of meat, the first slice from the loaf, and sometimes special dishes were cooked just for me.

Once, at the beginning of my pregnancy, Rere and Wi went into the bush to get two kereru, which Keita baked in the camp oven, frequently basting the juices over the fat breasts of the birds to keep them moist.

At the evening meal they were brought to me on a large dish and I ate while the family watched. As I pulled the breast flesh away and parted the front bones, they commented on the size and fatness of the birds and exclaimed over the berries that filled them. Wi and Rere told stories about where they had gone to find them and in which trees they had searched. They talked about the size and ripeness of the miro that the kereru had been feeding on, described the noisy flight as the pigeons went from branch to branch, told of the heavy falling as they were brought down. I ate as much as I could, eating to please, before passing the dish to share what remained.

I thought of those days as the best days of Keita. Keita, as sharp and as watchful as always, but gentle sometimes, excitedly awaiting the firstborn of the grandchildren. But in spite of all the attention that was given me, I was often lonely for my own family. My own parents were dead by then and my brothers and sisters lived in distant places.

In the late stages of my pregnancy I was lonely for Rere too. In spite of Keita's disapproval, he had volunteered for army service and gone into training camp. Not long after Makareta's birth he went to war.

One day when my baby was almost due to be born I went to the creek with Kui Hinemate, Keita and Gloria. They would not allow me to help with the washing so I made my way downstream, undressed, and sat in the water, cupping it in my hands and letting it run over my shoulders and down over my big, stretched body.

Rere and I had come to that place often, just to be alone. I remembered that our baby, soon to be born, could have been made there, under the big manuka tree, which now dropped its white flowers in the water about me. In its branches a pipiwharauroa chick screeched for food while its small foster-parent hurried back and forth to provide. The grass was long and green there still, in spite of the dryness of the summer.

But I knew those days were over for Rere and me. There was a war and Rere was going away. At times it seemed that he'd gone already, because now when he came home on leave he was different in his manner — quiet, as though waiting — as though to speak or to laugh would reveal the excitement he felt inside him. It was as though the Rere I knew had already left us.

I dressed and went to where the others were, stooping to spread a towel on the ground in the shade. It was as I straightened that I felt my breath scoop and fill me, then release itself, groaning, from somewhere deep inside. I went down spreading my knees apart and my baby slid from between them on a surge of water, as though she had come to me, swimming, from somewhere upstream. I put my hands beneath her, turning her. Her eyelids moved, her mouth opened, she sneezed, and as I lifted her, she arched, like a swimmer, her little arms stroking. That's how our Makareta was born to me and to her family, without pain, in wartime.

Kui Hinemate came towards me, calling to Gloria to bring towels and asking Keita to cut flax for the muka ties. I lay back against a tree while she attended to me, thinking of Rere, praying that he would be home to see his daughter before the battalion left for overseas. 'An aunty, just like that,' I heard Gloria saying. 'An aunty to a girl baby with a woman face, a kuia face.' I could tell she was excited and tried to lift myself from the sorrow that I had suddenly felt. 'Did it hurt, Polly?'

'I felt nothing,' I said, then started to cry.

'Too quick,' Kui Hinemate said. 'And no pain, that's why you're crying now . . . And there's a war.' She wrapped our baby in a pillowslip and bound me with towels. 'Lie down and sleep before we take you home,' she said. 'Sleep your sad heart away.'

I did sleep, my baby beside me, and when I woke Gloria had made tea for me. The washing had been bundled, the water tins were full and Keita was scooping the placenta into a basket she had made. Pipiwharauroa squealed on and on in the manuka.

Kui took our baby and the basket and went ahead of me on the track up through the scrub, talking, talking. 'Maybe you'll be my last one, maybe not,' I heard her say. 'But I'm glad of you. I don't get wood or carry water any more, don't milk a cow or get kai from the creek. The garden is only small now because the men have gone. There's work on the land, but I'm told that's for younger ones to do. But now there's a baby to look after, a baby and a mother. I'm glad of it.

'A long time ago your grandmother was given to me when her own mother died because I had a new baby of my own and milk enough for two. She was a round-faced baby like you, and I had the job of my young life. It was like twins for me, Anaru and Keita, a sister and a brother for each other. One grew into a little black, talking girl, the other into a long-legged, quiet boy, tall and white like me. He went to war and didn't come back.

'But the war let us have Wi back and I was here to be the mother while Wi and Keita worked the land. Now I have you. I'm glad to have my work back again.'

We made our way through the stalky grass, and at the top of

105

the rise took the track that led down into the bush where, in and out amongst the ponga, the karaka, the nikau and the manuka, the fantails jibbed, angling their fans, snapping their quick beaks, turning and tailing.

We rested there a while, sheltered from the afternoon sun, and Kui adjusted baby's wrapping so that sun would not touch the new skin. 'Are you better Polly?' Gloria asked, putting her arm round me.

'There's a war,' I said. 'I didn't want Rere to go but he's going. We don't know if there'll be a final leave or if we'll be allowed to know when they sail. I just want him to see our baby before he goes.'

'They'll come. They'll come on last leave, so we've heard, so we believe,' Keita said. 'And when it's time for them to go? Well, the horses are in the home paddock ready to take us to the train.'

'Wellington,' Gloria said. 'We'll see the soldiers go and we'll see Anihera.'

'There is no Anihera.'

'My sister . . .'

'There is no sister called Anihera,' Keita said.

twenty

Gloria sat sideways on the seat, shielding me from the eyes of other passengers who had begun to move up and down the train. I opened my coat and blouse, put Makareta to me and she took the milk in long, strong pulls. It was a relief to have her sucking on my full, sore breasts. I wished that other, deeper hurts could be drawn away as easily. In another half-hour we'd be in Wellington.

The days since Makareta's birth had been days of anxiety for me, not knowing whether Rere would come home before leaving for overseas, or whether the battalion would just sail one day, secretly. 'There's special leave,' Keita said, 'for fathers with new babies or for death in the family.' But she was anxious too.

After we'd sent the telegram telling Rere that our daughter had been born, Aperehama went each day to the railway station with the horses to meet the train. Each day he returned alone, but with broken pieces of news from the guards and train drivers. It was news that was not allowed to be known, so it had been gleaned from a feeling, a word, a hint of change observed by those close to the camp town, and passed on. It was news not allowed to be told, so it came under the hand, under the breath, and always only in part — there'd been a special visit, a parade, a word, there was something going on.

One day Aperehama came home and said, 'Any day,' and we knew then that Rere would not be home on 'compassionate leave' at all but would come instead on 'final leave' before he left for war. The day after that he arrived, along with his cousins Hori, Nonny and someone else we didn't know.

Watching from the window, Kui and I saw the men and the horses as they came up the hill and round the last bend. At the fence to the home paddocks Rere, Hori and Nonny left the horses, their kitbags and their companion and came running.

'Coming,' I called as I went out into the yard. Keita and Gloria were shifting embers around the camp oven, and Wi was blocking his knives. Their heads turned towards the track where they had heard the men running.

They came into the yard kicking up dust with their soldier boots and my Rere and I were holding each other as though everything was as it had always been between us. The cloth of his uniform was rough against the tenderness of my breasts, which were aching and hardening, and from which milk began to pour, wetting my clothes, wetting us both. 'Where?' he asked.

Kui came out bringing Makareta, who blinked in the outside light and moved her head from side to side. Rere took her, unwrapping the blanket and letting her lie on his hands. Hori and Nonny came leaning in to look.

'What do we call her?' he asked.

'Makareta after my mother,' I said, 'And Hinemate after Kui.'

'The only one with my name,' Kui said.

'Beautiful then, just like you, our Kui.'

Someone else arrived just then — a small, surprised-looking soldier with his swag on his shoulder and a ukelele in his hand. 'Our mate Bobby,' Nonny said. 'Their river bust its banks and he can't get home for a couple of days.'

The soldier called Bobby put his things down and came to greet us all. Not long afterwards we heard other relatives coming over the hills on horses. We could hear them calling, 'Hori Hori, Nonny Nonny, Re Re Re Re.'

It was not only anxiety that I felt in those days of waiting for Rere to come. Mixed with anxiety were the usual fears and sorrows that are to do with war and parting. I felt those things too even though war was something far away, not really comprehended, and parting was not yet a reality. What was real to me, what I held inside me, was the knowledge that Rere was going to war because there was a war to go to. In the excitement that he felt, in the happiness that I could see in him but could not share, I felt him becoming a stranger to me. We had shared so much, loved so much. We had dreams and plans, but even though I'd pleaded with him he hadn't waited six months, six weeks or even six days before volunteering. He was starting out on the biggest adventure of his life, that was what I felt and what I knew, and there was hardly a thought in his head that was for me.

That night as we held each other I tried to bring him back to me, tried to make him remember the creek, the tree, the dark, laughing paddocks where we'd grown in to each other, where we'd guessed our futures, planned our lives. 'The manuka tree was covered in flowers the day baby was born,' I said. 'The grass was long and green.' But I don't know that he heard. He spilled and lay over me, motionless, as though asleep, and loneliness was the seed that I held. Close-to-anger sadness is what I felt. 'One day . . .' he said in his half-sleep, but the memories were eluding him. They belonged to another time.

It was Kui who tried to help me through those days. She would take Makareta from me saying, 'Don't cry, Daughter, or your milk will fill with tears. Our baby will be drinking tears.' Or, 'We don't let tears fall on a baby's head. A baby is old, a baby knows. Remember we're the ones who wait, the mothers. That's what this old woman has learned to do — to wait and wait, hope and wait, on and on. Otherwise how can the world turn?' Her words didn't comfort me. She was old. I didn't want her life of waiting to be my life. I didn't want a life of waiting and hoping to be my daughter's life.

Rere and I had little time together during that fortnight of final leave. They were days claimed by his family — days of visiting elders, attending farewell functions, listening to speeches, drinking, singing and not being allowed to sleep. At the end of it we put him and his cousins on the train with their kitbags and parcels. They were exhausted. As we waved them off, their eyes were closing. I knew they were glad to be going.

A month later the news came that 'the boys were packing up' and we dressed, picked up the boxes, bags and blankets that we had ready and set out for the railway station. It was a busy road that day as people made their way on foot or on horseback to the midnight train, all anxious to know details — but there was no one who knew. We were not sure if the overnight train that reached our station at midnight would get us to Wellington in time. I needed to kiss Rere goodbye, to say something that would make things be as they had been between us, or close to it, or to pretend. People pretend in wartime.

Also there was something else that Kui had said that was biting into me. 'Kaua e harawene mona,' she'd said one day. I didn't want the words but there they were, spoken. They bit and began to eat. Don't be jealous of him? I knew that Kui was looking into me to somewhere that I hadn't wanted to look, at something in me that was more than sorrow and harder than anger. Rere was going to war. My brother had joined the Navy and my two older sisters were in the Red Cross learning to drive trucks. Sooner or later they would go to war too — all the ones I loved — while I was staying home to write letters and wait, to listen to the wireless, feed baby, carry wood and water, wait for a telegram, hope for it not to come.

But if I could I'd have been off to see the war and the world too. That's what Kui knew. Before she'd spoken I hadn't dared to look at my sorrow, my anger, and to ask myself what it was really about. If it had been me, I'd have gone. That's what I needed to tell Rere.

Also I wanted him to see Makareta. She knew us all now, smiled, talked to us, and that was a memory I wanted him to take with him.

The train entered a tunnel and the sooty engine smoke layered back through it, seeping into the carriages, stinking. Hills slanted away and up on either side as we came out, then we cut through them into a second tunnel. Coming out of it, we saw the buildings, the houses, the hills and the harbour of Wellington. At another time it could have been exciting. In the harbour were the ships that would be taking the men across the sea to no one knew where. I passed Makareta to Gloria and buttoned my clothes. 'I've got a photo of me, for Bobby,' Gloria said.

We stood, collecting our bags and bundles, and waited in the aisle. People, crowding the platforms, pushed forward as we pulled in, then, discovering that this was not the train they were waiting for, moved back again. They were asking if we'd seen the troop train or if anyone knew when the boys would be in. They spoke in whispers. Out on the walls and pillars were notices and posters warning us to keep silent. Our careless words could cause ships to sink and bombs to fall, the notifications said.

The main building of the station was crowded with people, some sitting on seats or bags, or on coats or blankets they had spread on the floor. Others stood, or wandered. All waited — for a train they knew was coming, or for the end of the war or the world, or for whatever might be. We went through to a space by a far wall, put our belongings down and settled ourselves.

Coming. Coming. It wasn't a shout or a whisper, but a movement that ruffled the crowd. It was like a knowing that came from the air — air that had become cold enough to show breath as we began to stir, to stand, turning first one way and then another, not knowing which way to go. There was a train coming, a sound far back, but no one knew which platform it would come into.

Then the station began to empty. The train was coming, but not into the station.

We followed the people out on to the street and there we saw it making its way slowly along the wharf tracks. There was no sign that this was a train filled with soldiers on their way to war. It looked instead like a line of empty carriages with their shutters down being taken to a wharf shed or a side track, finished for the day.

Then the wharf gates opened, the train went through, the gates closed. 'It was them,' someone said. 'Blackouts down and guards by the doors.' And we all hurried across the road to the gates, calling to the officials to let us through. We had gifts to give, letters, messages, photographs, keepsakes and food. We had husbands, sons, fathers to see on their way to war. But our pleas were not listened to.

After a long while of waiting we knew that the gates were not going to be opened for us. I needed to get Makareta out of the cold.

Kui, Gloria and I returned to the station while the others remained at the gates. We tended to Makareta then sat in our blankets to wait. 'In the morning,' Kui said, 'they'll open up in the morning.' But I knew the men would all be on board by morning. The ships could have gone by then.

It was early morning and still dark when we picked up our baby and our parcels and made our way back to the wharf, where the crowd still waited. As we were about to cross the road a bus arrived and turned in. We saw the gates opening and began to hurry. But the guards, keeping the crowd back, let the bus through and closed the gates again.

People began banging on the fences then, angry that some had been let through, demanding to know who. After a while I knew who it was because through the dark I heard singing. The Ngati Poneke Concert Party had been taken on to the wharf to farewell the soldiers. Yet we had our songs too, our gifts and kisses to give.

It was daylight when the gates were opened at last. We pressed through onto the wharf only to find that the *Aquitania* was already out in the stream and the soldiers were just blurred lines of khaki down the sides of it. At first we cried with sorrow and anger. Then, after a while, as the ship waited out in the harbour for another two to join it, we realised that the only way we could reach out to the men on their way to war was with our voices. We made our way through and stood with the Ngati Poneke group joining in their songs — 'He Putiputi', 'He Aha Kei Taku Uma', 'Me He Manu Rere', 'Tahine Taru Kino'.

Later, from across the water, we heard the men's voices singing 'Po Atarau' and we joined them in the singing of it. There could be no more songs after that. It was our last touching. We cheered and called as the sirens sounded and the ships drew away.

'I'll send it,' Gloria said as we went back towards the gates, 'the photo for Bobby.' She was fifteen and in love. Her face was smeared and her eyes were red and the lids swollen, just as I knew mine would be.

We were almost to the gates when we heard someone call, and as we turned Anihera came out from behind one of the wharf sheds carrying her newly born baby wrapped in a coat. She wore only a thin smock and open shoes. 'I heard about the boats,' she said. 'I wanted to see Rere, wanted to see you all.'

'Come home with us, Ani,' Gloria said. 'Bring Baby home.'

'I can't.'

'Come to Keita, come and see Wi, over at the station . . . Ani?'

'I saw Keita, saw Wi, saw them all . . . Just to show you my Mata, and to see you all.' And she left us, hurrying along the quayside in the crowd. Gloria ran after her, giving her the parcels she was carrying — a packet of smoked eel and a tin of bread. 'Don't tell them, Glory,' we heard Anihera call.

We took our Makareta home. She was two months old and had a dark brown skin that pulled over tight fat and went deep into dents and creases. She had thick, black hair that covered her ears, and dark eyes that seemed small when she was that age because her eyelids were so plumped out that they wouldn't open properly. She knew us through slits, watched us, always ready to play. We hardly ever heard her cry, but there was no need for her to cry in a household of so many adults who looked to every need.

Two and a half years later, in a telegram that was sent to Keita and Wi, we received news of Rere's death at Alamein. I was deeply lonely after that and unable to see an end to loneliness. Makareta was nearly three years old, a little grandmother of a girl who accompanied the old people wherever they went. She spoke Maori in the old way, like the grandmothers, and had the unhurried manner herself that the old people have. She spoke English too, but only to me. I thought it was right to speak to her in English.

She was nearly five by the time I decided I should leave. I thought that there could be more for her than a life with old people, and thought there could be more for me to do in the city. At first it was the letter from Cissie that gave me the excuse I needed, but after Keita had spoken to me of her plan, and later when I had spoken to Aperehama, I knew I had to leave. There was no longer a choice.

twenty-one

Aperehama leaned forward with his forehead resting in the cow's flank. Two streams of milk criss-crossed into the bucket. He was eighteen, just as Rere had been when we first met, like Rere to look at, broad-featured and dark with wavy, black hair. But he was taller than Rere, and quieter. Sad, I thought.

He shifted the bucket, undid the legrope and stood. The cow walked off and he tipped the milk from bucket to billy. As I watched I wondered if he had any idea of Keita's plans for him and me. If he had guessed, I wondered how he felt. It was loneliness that suddenly made me want to know. 'It used to be Rere's job, milking, when I first came here to live,' I said. 'You were thirteen.' I noticed his hesitation as he wondered where my words were leading. He was wearing old army trousers tucked into gumboots, and a grey jersey that was too small for him. Looking at him, I could see a loneliness that matched my own, and at that moment I wanted to put my arms round him and love him and be with him always. One step forward and it could have happened, whether it was Aperehama who took the step or whether it was me.

It was the thin wrists and the long child hands extending from the too-small sleeves that shocked me, that prevented me from taking the step and kept my feet on the spot where I stood. He hadn't finished growing yet, and looking at him I could see his thirteen-year-oldness looking back at me from puzzled, lonely eyes.

We turned away from each other and began walking back across the paddock. 'I miss him,' I said, as though there was something that needed explaining. 'I miss him, but those days are gone.'

'And now you're a prisoner of war, like me,' Aperehama said. He understood more than I thought.

When we reached the track that led to Gloria's I told him I was leaving. I saw that he was relieved and realised that he did know something of Keita's plan. 'One day soon,' I said. 'Makareta and me.'

'Makareta?' He was thinking of Kui Hinemate.

'I'll get Gloria's milk and take it to her each day. Sometimes I'll take Makareta with me. One day Makareta and I will leave Gloria's, head for the railway station and take the train to Wellington. I have to do it that way. Keita won't let me go and take Makareta with me.'

'It's my mother . . . why I stay,' Aperehama said. 'But if the war keeps on I'll be going.'

'You don't blame me?'

'You're my big sister, like Anihera.' It was an answer to something else rather than to the question I'd asked, an explanation, perhaps, why a step that could have been taken was not taken. Big sister? Even if I had wanted to stay I couldn't, now that it had been said.

twenty-two

Makareta wrote her name on the window and underneath it wrote her school words — *mother, bird, bed, hop, little.* Today at school they'd read a story about a germ who lived in a rubbish tin. You had to fight against germs. She thought it might be something to do with the war. There were more words that she could've written but the pane was full.

There was another window in the bedroom but it was already dark in there and she thought it could be past four o'clock by now. Her mother was supposed to be home at four. From where she was sitting she could see the dark doorway and the dark space behind it, but couldn't go in and turn the light on because the blackout curtains weren't drawn. There could be parrots in there too, she thought, watching from the dark ceiling — red, green, blue, white, orange, pink — with glassy, glinting eyes, ready to drop down. The ones in her dreams filled rooms, walked the footpaths and roads, picking and pecking.

She left the window and sat in a chair with her feet drawn up under her. Now that she'd remembered the parrots, she thought there could be one under the chair, its long leg and heavy claw reaching out to snatch her.

On the table was the piece of bread that she'd taken from the cupboard when she came home from school. She'd had two bites from it then noticed the steamy window, so she'd left the bread and gone to write her name. Now she wanted the bread but she was afraid to put her feet on the floor, because of the parrot under the chair that was pretending to be dead. Any movement would wake it and out it would come, clawing, waddling, cracking its beak, hunting her with its bead eye. She made herself as small as she could in the dark and sat without moving.

After a long time she heard movement on the step and the door handle turned. 'Mum,' she called.

'Not Mum.'

'Mum.'

'It's Keita, Little Daughter, and your uncle too.'

'Keita, Keita.' She jumped down from the chair and ran to her grandmother, telling her something in such a jumble of words that her grandmother couldn't understand what she was saying.

'Now, now, never mind,' Keita said. 'Show Keita the curtains and the light. Tell Keita where your mummy is. Show me where your clothes are so we can pack them in a bag.'

twenty-three

I was worried about Makareta, who would be at home waiting for me. Cissie had been taken into hospital the night before and I'd come to look after the children until Ben came home from work. He'd said that he'd be home by four, but it was after five now and I realised I wouldn't see him until after the pubs closed at six.

Makareta and I had stayed with Cissie and Ben for two months after arriving in Wellington. They were not happy days for Makareta, who kept talking about Kui Hinemate and asking to go home. She was unhappy at school too, didn't like children she said, and didn't want to be called Marguerita. I didn't want her to be called Marguerita either, remembering that I had lost my own name when I first went to school, but I tried to comfort her. 'It's just a school name because Makareta is too difficult for the teachers to say,' I said, 'but you're still Makareta.' I had wanted her to go to a big school, where I thought there would be more for her — more children who were clever, children who spoke good English. Now she was so unhappy I wondered if I'd made a terrible mistake in coming to the city to live.

But then there were Cissie and her children. They needed me. My sister's condition was worse than I'd thought and the children were pale and always crying. I did the best I could, stretching my widow's pension to pay for rent and food that Cissie never seemed to have money for. I used our ration coupons in the best way I could to get what was needed for ourselves and the children.

At the end of two months Cissie seemed much better and I decided I would try to find somewhere nearby to live, believing that once we had a place of our own Makareta would settle down.

But it wasn't easy to find a place. Makareta and I went together in answer to 'To Let' advertisements only to find ourselves turned away. Sometimes doors would be slammed on us before I'd had time to speak. At other times we were shown sheds, cold basements, or leaking rooms without heat or water. Then we met the parrot lady.

One Saturday morning we called at a house three blocks away in answer to a notice we'd seen in the paper. I was about to knock on the door when a window opened and a man called, 'It's been let already,' and banged the window down again.

I was hurrying away, pulling Makareta by the hand, when from across the road I heard a woman's voice call, 'Hoy, hoy,' as though she could be calling me, but I put my head down and kept on walking. Then I heard the voice again, 'Hoy, hoy, Maori lady with the little girl.' So I looked up and saw a small face looking over a gate, and a pale hand above the gate, waving, 'Hoy, hoy. Cross over. Come, cross over.'

So I crossed and looked into a little, grey, old face, and into two eyes as blue as flags. 'Now come in, come in the gate, I've got a place for you,' the woman said. 'They don't like a Maori woman to rent their house, but I've got a place for you and your little girl . . . And your husband. Now where's your husband, dear?'

'Killed overseas,' I said.

'They don't like a woman with no husband, but don't you worry. Inside, dears. Follow me.'

She led us along the path to her house, turning her head from side to side, talking back over one shoulder then the other. 'You can have a little sit down and a rest first, and a cup of tea and shortbread. Then I'll take you and show you the house I've got for you. Don't you worry at all.'

We followed her through shrubbery and up some steps on to

a verandah where there was a row of empty cages hanging from wire hooks.

'I was just cleaning them when I saw you at the house over the road and heard what was going on,' she said. 'Come in now and don't you worry. You'll see, little girl, there's a surprise.'

We went along a dark passage until the woman stopped by a door. She turned the handle slowly, opening the door just a little. 'In,' she said, and went through the gap in the partly opened door, leading us through.

As we entered there was a loud screeching. Wide shadows came beating down from the ceiling and Makareta leapt up into my arms as the woman closed the door behind us. 'Naughty girls, naughty fellows,' she called, waving her arms.

'Hello, hello, hoy, hoy,' the parrots replied as they returned to perch in different parts of the room.

'That's better, that's better now,' the woman said. 'There, little girl, you see. It's all my naughty friends.'

Makareta lifted her head from my shoulder and looked about at the sidling parrots that eyed us from their perches, then buried her head again. 'Come on then, mother; come on, little girl, we'll go and have that cup of tea and the shortbread. Then I'll show you the place.'

She opened the door, flapping her arms at the birds as they launched themselves at the gap again. We were led through to a bright kitchen, of parrot colours, where we were sat down on red chairs at a yellow, oval table.

'Visitors,' she said, as she made tea for us in a silver teapot. 'This is my teapot for visitors — but I never have any visitors because people think I'm mad in the head.' She spread an embroidered cloth on which bonneted, crinolined girls with watering cans walked along garden paths sprinkling tall flowers. 'It's my sister's cloth,' she said. 'She was the one who did work like this. She was the embroidery one. I'm the patchwork one.' Then she went out of the room and came back with fine china cups, saucers and plates, which she said were visitors' things too, and she stood on a chair to take a red tin from a high, blue shelf. 'I still make shortbread since my sister died,' she said. 'I have to save my butter and sugar rations until I have enough to make just a few pieces. My name's Alma. Tell me if you have milk. Tell me your names.'

'I'm Polly. This is Makareta. Yes, milk please.'

'Tell me the little girl's name again.'

'Makareta.'

'There you are, Polly; there you are, Makareta. Have sugar now and some shortbread. Naughty birds frightening a little girl like that, but they won't hurt you, no.

'Dears, my sister and I came to live in this house after the first war. We lived here for ten years together but we always quarrelled. Do you know why? Because she liked cats and I liked birds. But we solved it. We bought another house, six doors down, for my sister and her cats to live in and I stayed here with my birds.

'Every Wednesday we had turns at visiting each other like real visitors, with silver teapots and pretty cups, and shortbread on a special plate. I'm the shortbread one. Her speciality was caraway cake. On Sundays we would have roast dinners together and we never quarrelled again. But my sister died a year ago, and now, Polly, Makareta, I have two houses. I wouldn't let anyone else have my sister's house. Why should I when they won't even say good morning and they teach their children to run away from me? Why should I when they killed my sister's cats? They don't like a woman without a husband. They don't like old sisters who keep cats and birds.

'But you can have the house, you and your little girl. All the cats have gone. I went one morning to feed them and they weren't there. I called them but they didn't come. After a while I found them, all dead, in my sister's slit-trench in the back yard. I don't know who did it, but never mind that now. Have some more shortbread Makareta, I can see what a dear little girl you are.'

When we'd finished tea Alma took us along the street to a small house and showed us inside. 'It's rickety,' she said, 'but it's got a fireplace so you can be warm, and there's furniture, just ordinary and plain. I've taken my sister's cutlery, crockery and linen from the cupboards but I'll put it back again. I won't charge you too much, dear, because I've got so much money. Oodles.

Money and cheeky parrots, that's what I've got. I had canaries and budgies too, but now it's just the parrots, naughty parrots.' I could see that the house would be just right for Makareta and me.

I knew that I should've arranged for Makareta to go to Alma's place after school instead of trusting Ben to be home in time, but Makareta didn't like going to Alma's. The parrots had got into her dreams. In her dreams they waited under beds and chairs or waddled about the house following her. Outside they walked the roads and footpaths along with the children who, on their way to school, spun themselves, twirling their bags, or ran one behind the other making noises like trains. I felt unhappy when Makareta told me her dreams. I didn't know what to do except hope that things would get better soon.

She would be waiting for me, frightened, and I knew I couldn't wait any longer for Ben. I put jerseys on the children, tied some clothes and blankets into a bundle and went downstairs to ring a taxi.

It was when the taxi turned into our street that I saw Wi's truck parked on the road outside my house and knew that they had come for Makareta. I ran into the house calling to Keita not to take her. 'Mummy, Mummy, they've come,' Makareta said as I went in. Her clothes were ready in a bag.

'We came and found her alone,' Keita said.

'Cissie's in hospital,' I said. 'I had to look after the children. But it's all right now, it'll be all right. I've brought the children with me.'

'Well, Polly, you're quite right,' Keita said. 'Your sister's sick so you have to help her.'

'Don't take her, Keita.'

'Of course we won't take our granddaughter if she doesn't want to come.'

'Aperehama's come in the truck,' Makareta said. 'Keita's taking me home.'

twenty-four

So I had to say goodbye to my Makareta, and when it was found that Cissie would be in hospital for a long time, I had to organise my life around caring for her children. They were fretful babies, all eyes and bones. Heni was three, Benny was two and Bonnie was nine months. I wanted to do my best for them, always having in mind our cherishing of Makareta, her happy growing, missing her, searching for her face everywhere I went.

Not long after Makareta left, Gloria wrote to me and told me that Anihera was at home dying of tuberculosis and didn't know where her daughter was. Keita had been to Wellington looking for Mata but hadn't found her at the school or at the home for children where Anihera thought she might be. In the letter, Gloria asked me if I would try and find her, because Anihera would be happy to die, she said, if only Mata could be found. I knew my life was all right when I compared it to what had happened to Anihera. I had my sister and her children to care for, I was strong enough to do it and my daughter was safe at home.

On most afternoons I would go out looking, taking the children with me. I went first of all to the schools that were within walking distance, then later went by tram or bus to different schools I'd found out about. But my face wasn't welcome in the corridors or grounds of schools. Little children were not welcome either. I was told that I wasn't allowed on school property, or that I wasn't supposed to come into schools making enquiries. Sometimes I would wait by the school gates so that I could watch the children as they came out, but often a teacher would come with a message that I was to go away.

There was a woman I'd met called Awhina who was a trammy, and I asked her to look out for Mata for me. 'If there's any Maori face round town I see it,' Awhina said. 'Count us on a hand and a foot.' I loved to watch Awhina clicking her clippers through the tram, swinging out on the steps and in again at the stops, getting out on the road with the crank to switch tracks, or hanging on the ropes when the trolley slipped off the overheads. I was amazed that a Maori woman could have a job like that.

If I could have, I would've spent every hour looking for Mata. It was Makareta's face in my mind as I searched, but it was Anihera I felt for. My life was good compared to hers.

Three months later the war ended. When the sirens went and the bells began to ring I went out to the front gate and watched the people coming out of their houses. 'The war's over,' they were calling. 'We won the war.' They were heading for the city, with flags and streamers, to celebrate. Later in the morning Alma came to my door. 'We'll go to town and dance in the streets,' she said.

So we put Bonnie in her pram, sat Heni and Benny on the front of it and joined those already out on the footpaths. Trams went by packed with people who called from the windows and steps that the war was won, the boys would be home, there'd be no more rationing, the lights would be on again.

It was true that there was dancing in the streets. In the city people flooded on to the roads, some drivers abandoning their vehicles to join them. They danced and sang and embraced each other as we made our way along. From the verandah roofs we were showered with confetti, and people came out of the shops with cakes and lollies for the children. 'Everything's free,' a man said, lifting Heni onto his shoulders and walking with us for a while.

Every pub was full to its windows with noisy, singing people. Barrels had been rolled out to the kerbsides and the beer was flowing. As we made our way back, there were broken bottles and patches of vomit to step round, but nothing mattered. In the doorways people kissed and laughed or cried.

The end of the war and Rere was not returning. Children to look after but no Makareta, yet it was a happy day. It was good not to be alone on such a day, to be out in the streets with the crowds and to have a friend with me.

Early the following year the *Dominion Monarch* came in bringing the 28th Battalion home and we went down to Aotea Wharf, where the ceremonies would be held. It was summer but there was a dark sky and a wind that chopped across the breadth of the harbour, flipping up the white edges of the waves. As the ship came round the point we heard the men's voices coming to us across the water, and as it came nearer we could see the men on the upper decks and on the high points, clinging to the masts and about the funnels. They were singing their Maori Battalion song.

Alma decided to take the children home after the ship berthed. There would be a long wait while the men disembarked and reassembled for the march down the street. I knew by the size of the waiting crowd that the ceremonies would be prolonged. 'You stay,' she said. 'Seeing the boat come in and hearing the soldiers singing was extraordinary. That was enough for me. But for you? You should stay.'

So I stayed, feeling very much alone after she'd gone. When Rere died, the grief and sorrow that I'd felt had belonged to all of us. I'd had a place, belonged in that grief and was part of something. The loss I'd felt when Keita took Makareta was because of a decision I'd had to make for myself that wasn't right for my daughter. I'd known my part in it and had known who I was. I was, and always would be, her mother.

But at that time on the crowded wharf I had no belonging, no part in any ceremony, no place in the customs to do with receiving the dead home. I was not a wife, a widow or a bereaved daughter-in-law, but an onlooker, and I realised then that I should've returned to be with Keita and the families to receive the deaths of Rere and Hori according to the custom.

As the soldiers came towards the gateway the crying and calling began, the challenger sprang forward to place the baton and the haka groups came stepping and stamping forward while the soldiers came on to the gathering place. *Haul home the canoe*, the words of the haka said, *Haul home the canoe to its beaching place and let it remain here.* What a large canoe it was. The hundreds of soldiers came through the gateway and settled themselves for the rituals that would free them from the spirit of war — to be followed by the ceremonies that would welcome them home. I climbed up on to the roof of a small shed where several others were already gathered and from there was able to see all that took place.

There were iwi there from all over the country, all with their speakers, their chants, their dances and songs. There were trucks coming and going and workers carrying goods into the big wharf sheds where the welcome home feast was being prepared. Trains, which would later take the soldiers to their different destinations, were already lined up on the rails by the wharf side.

I could see Nonny's family there waiting for him. In the morning they would take him back, bearing the deaths of Rere and Hori home, but I would not be there.

I turned my thoughts back to Cissie in hospital and to the children who would be waiting for me, and began making my way out through the crowd. I thought, as always, of Makareta. She would be down at the wharenui with the grandmothers while the preparations were going on for the homecoming, chatting with the elders in her own serious way, or watching other children play. She would have new clothes for the ceremonies.

twenty-five

Makareta watched the men light the fire in the pig paddock. Two of the pigs had been shot and Bobby and Aperehama had stuck them between the front legs, letting the blood squirt out into the buckets.

After the pigs had been bled they were put on the fire and turned and rolled from side to side so that the hair burned off, and every so often the men dragged them out of the flames and scraped them with their knives until they were whitish, smoky-looking and clean. Big kids were waiting for the footballs.

She watched the men lift the pigs onto the sheets of corrugated iron where they slit and trimmed them right down, pulling the insides out and cutting away the parts that they wanted and tossing them into a bucket. Wi and Bobby squeezed

the mimi out of the bladders and threw them to the kids, who
blew them up with straws, tied them with flax strings and ran
away to play, the dogs chasing after them. After that the pigs
were taken to hang in the shed. It was getting dark.

The next morning, when she went to the marae with Kui and
Keita, the marquee was already up, the fire was being lit for the
hangi stones, the meat was being cut up and vegetables prepared.
It had been raining. People kept looking at the sky and not saying
anything at all about it.

In the big tent the tables had been put in rows, covered with
cloths ready for setting, and some of the women were covering
planks with white paper to make another tier. The older girls had
lined the tent walls with ferns and were threading flowers into
them. Others were tying little flags to the tent poles. Makareta
helped them until it was time to go home and get changed.

She had new clothes for the homecoming. Keita had made her
a navy skirt and a white blouse and she had new black shoes that
her mother had sent. She was going to wear Kui's tipare, which
had been fixed for her to keep her hair from blowing.

When she returned the grandmothers and aunties were all
sitting on the verandah in their black clothes, talking and smoking
and twisting leaves for their heads. Back by the trees her uncles
stood in a circle playing two-up. She watched the circle of heads
lift as the pennies sailed upwards, then bow as they dropped. She
could hear them laughing and teasing each other.

Wi's truck pulled in next to the wharenui. It had a canopy
over it and under the canopy was Aunty Anihera in an armchair
with blankets around her, there to welcome the soldiers. People
went to stand by the truck so they could talk to her.

Soon everyone began to gather close to the house. Kui and
some of the other old ones put their cloaks on and everyone
stood, holding their greenery. It was quiet, there were people at
the gateway and rain had begun to fall.

Then the grandmothers began to call the people in, asking
them to bring the sons home and calling to the ancestors. The
people came, calling back that they were bringing the sons, dead
along with the living. They were stepping slowly on the wet
ground. With them was a soldier like the ones she'd seen in

photographs and newspapers, or in the streets when she was in Wellington. His head and shoulders were bent so that his face couldn't be seen.

Halfway across the marae the group stopped while the crying and wailing of the grandmothers and aunties became louder and higher and went on and on. The women beat their chests and leaned forward, swaying from side to side, almost falling, and the leaves on their heads and in their hands waved and trembled. It was a long time before Nonny's family was allowed to take him to the seats under the tarpaulins for the speeches to begin.

When the speeches were over and the people came to hongi with them, Nonny lifted her up. He was smiling. He had red, popping eyes and smelt of rain. The sun had come out and people were steaming.

Later she went with the crowd of people to the urupa for the unveiling. From where she stood she could see the memorial stones for her father and Hori covered with feathered cloaks. The minister was beginning the karakia, and when Nonny took the cloaks away for the inscriptions to be read, the old ones began to mourn again. The wind was whipping at them, tangling the sounds together until all the sounds seemed to be part of itself.

On the way down the hill she could see men behind the tent bending into the steam, and she could smell the hot-earth smell of the hangi being lifted. The tent flaps had been opened and there were people hurrying to and fro.

twenty-six

Makareta and Mata have met. 'We returned from James Mahana's funeral,' Makareta said in her letter. 'He's a returned serviceman, the grandson of Keita's mother's brother. Aunty Gloria, Uncle Bobby and the kids were at home waiting for us when we arrived and Mata was there too. I forgot she would be there and went through the kitchen without noticing her. (Everyone else had come out to meet us.) Then I heard Keita come into the kitchen wailing, followed by Kui, and when I looked from the bedroom I saw Mata standing there, frightened-looking. I was surprised when I saw her, Mum, because you didn't say in your letter that she and I look alike. Perhaps you don't think so.'

But it was because of Mata's likeness to Makareta that I found her. When Anihera died not long after the end of the war, I stopped searching for Mata, believing that if she was still in Wellington I would find her one day — as I did, but it was nearly five years later.

So much death. I think I must be lucky to be alive. Men died in a war or as a result of it. Women stayed home and died in TB wards, or were taken from them to die at home.

Cissie left hospital and went to a sanitorium, where she was thought to be improving, but one night she was taken back to hospital with pneumonia. Ben and I had been with her only an hour before she died. I'd had the children for nearly two years by then and since they'd never been allowed to see their mother, they had become used to me. I was happy to have them after Cissie died and pleased that I had a good warm house for them to live in and a yard where they could play. Ben moved into Ministry of Works quarters at the place where he worked just out of the city and came to see the children when he could.

'Koro Day and Kui Dinah and their families came over to see Mata the day after we arrived home and I could see she was frightened of them too. They were crying over her, asking her one question after another in English. I don't think that she could understand their way of speaking English — "So you big, hmmm so." "So you just like you mummy. Got you grandmother name, hmmm." "Hmmm, that what clothes? So you shy." But they were talking to each other and to me in Maori at the same time. I don't think Mata had a chance of knowing what they were talking about. She speaks only English.

'I couldn't get used to her being here, standing without moving, looking nowhere and not saying a word — as if she was a new piece of furniture that had been brought in, or a post that had been shifted to a different place. My aunties kept telling me that I should give her some of my clothes and I did, Mum. I've found out that she's got a kind heart.'

My daughter comes to stay with me during the term holidays and I like to show her the city, wanting her to see what other children do, and to go to the places that city children like to go to — a circus, the Winter Show, the pictures, the zoo, the song and dance competitions, or to ride the dodgem cars. She likes to go to the pictures and seems to enjoy the other things we do, but I don't think she ever sees herself as a child who might take part in the way that a child does. She is more like another mother, taking Heni, Benny and Bonnie for holiday outings, enjoying the children's enjoyment and ending up with sore feet at the end of the day.

I think she prefers to stay at home and do some of the things she doesn't ordinarily do. At her home she is never allowed to do dishes, sweep floors or make anyone's bed apart from her own. She doesn't lay the fire, bring in kindling, help with the washing or carry water from the creek. Children are never left for her to look after, even though she has a way with children.

Outside the house by the chimney, there's an old kotukutuku bush that the Cat Lady planted. The small, pink bells are sparse among the foliage and the branches have been made brittle by insects that have eaten away the inside wood, leaving mainly the outer skin, the holey bark. At a touch it crumbles. I imagine the tree has a cat smell. Apart from the tree, the yard is only a lumpy piece of lawn, a brick path, a clothesline and a weed-filled dent where the air-raid shelter used to be. Makareta sits under the little tree sometimes with her back against the trunk, and I know she is missing Kui Hinemate and the old ones, although she never says.

'There was trouble at the funeral. Uncle Jimmy's wife's family wanted him buried up their end of the urupa, by Aunty Tui, but his brothers and sisters wanted him down in their part. Early on Sunday morning the cooks, who had got up early to get breakfast, woke us all up and said that two lots of diggers had gone up to the urupa — Jimmy's brothers and uncles on his side, and his wife's family as well. Grandfather Wi and some of the other men went chasing up the hill after them and barred them all from the cemetery. The last thing they wanted was two holes — inviting another death they said. And they made them all come back down to the wharenui, telling them that if they were going to argue they could do it in front of Jimmy before they put the lid on him.

'So they argued back and forth for half the morning, until Keita stood up and gave them all a good telling-off. She told them they'd all had their chance to find out from Jimmy what he wanted while he was alive. She told Jimmy off too. "You took long enough to die," she said to him in his coffin. "And could've spoken up and saved all this trouble." Then she told them they had to ask Jimmy's children what they wanted, and that whatever the kids said, that's what they would do. It took them a while to agree to do that, but in the end they did. I suppose everyone knew what the kids would say. Junior stood up and told us they wanted their father next to their mother, and that was it, that's where they put him. We had an interesting time there.'

Even though Alma is our good friend, Makareta has never become used to the parrots, and I notice that whenever we go to visit, Alma always has the birds away in their cages. 'Birds in houses,' Makareta says to me. 'Speaking people's language.' Then she'll say, 'Kui is the one who knows the birds' language.' And I picture her and the old lady walking along the creek tracks with the piwaiwaka turntailing about them as they go, all of them talking together.

There are pictures in my mind too, of Kui and Makareta at night with the lamp, Hinemate telling about all the things she has to tell, and of Makareta reading her school books to her or perhaps reading the letters that I have sent or the ones she is writing to me. Or I think of them unwrapping the parcels I send and making figures with the string, the old hands and the young hands dipping and diving like the fantails, making diamonds and double diamonds, woman that becomes man, kite, cup and saucer, butterfly, four brothers, Venus, thief, place of spirits, house of ghosts.

At other times I know she will be at different gatherings, whether it is for a death, a land discussion or a court hearing to do with land — there with the old people, sitting as still as it is possible to sit, watching and listening. I used to be concerned about the amount of school she missed because of the travelling she does with the old ones, who will not go anywhere without her, but I know now that in her schooling she is well ahead of her years. I worried once that her English would not be good because of being brought up in a house where English is not spoken, but she speaks English as well as the teachers that she learns from. There's no need for me to worry about her, except that old people die. I am not sure that my Makareta is prepared for that.

'That afternoon I went out to get Mata because the aunties wanted her to come and say goodbye. My other cousins were having turns riding downhill on a drum, and Mata had spent most of the morning watching them. As I went towards her I saw her rub something in the grass then hold it up to the light. I wondered what it was, and I also wondered which of us would speak first. Up to then we hadn't spoken to each other at all. "I found this marble," she said holding out her hand as I came near, "just there by the path." It was the first time I'd heard her say anything.

'It was where the old house used to be, the house that I've heard about but never seen, that Kui's brother made out of manuka and rushes. I've been told it had a dirt floor that they swept with a manuka broom, and that it was warm and comfortable. Keita was born there and it was there that the great granny died and Kui became Keita's mother. Things come up out of the ground there — green or blue glass, medicine bottles, bits of crockery, broken combs. Sometimes I find marbles there too — mainly bottlies or teapots, which I give to my cousins. But I have never found a marble like the one Mata held out to show me. None of us have. None of us have ever seen a marble like that, with drifts of smoke and ribbons and rainbows in it that trick your eyes, seeming to move. When my cousins saw it they stopped asking me to go and get bread for them and just stared. They didn't say anything about the marble, just stared and stared.

'Mata has a kind heart. I went to get bread, left them all there eating it and was just about to go inside again when Missy called me. She was dancing on the fence wires. "She give it to Manny," she called. "She give Manny the marble."'

I went to Alma's one morning and the birds were screeching and flapping in their cages. Alma was on the floor in the hallway, and at first I thought she was dead. I got her to hospital as quickly as I could, and on the way there in the ambulance she said, 'My sister had a stroke,' but her voice was faint and her speech indistinct. 'I looked after her. I don't want to be a burden to anyone.'

But Alma isn't a burden to me. She's my very dear friend, a lovely grandmother to Ben's children, helping me to care for them, knitting coats, jerseys and socks for them in Fair Isle or bright stripes, or making what she calls little odds-and-ends dolls and toys with her clever fingers. Before her illness we visited each other every day, and we had special dinners together on Sundays when Ben came.

Now in the mornings, after the children have gone to school, I go and help Alma to wash and dress and we have breakfast together. Then I tidy up for her and feed the parrots. There are only four now — Poppy, Winston, Tattersalls and Halfmoon. Halfmoon is the one that knows me. She's a small, green bird with a grey head, a bright pink band round her neck and bright pink eye circles. She has white, semicircular patches each side of her beak that can be seen in the dark. With her head on one side and her beak partly open she looks as if she could be smiling. I find myself wondering if we might be sisters, Polly being a parrot's name. In the afternoons I take Alma's washing home to do along with my own things, and in the evenings Heni takes her a meal. I've had telephones put into both our houses so that she can ring me if she needs me, but she seldom rings. 'Half of me is all right,' she says, 'I can make do with the good half, so don't you worry.'

It was when I was going to visit Alma at the hospital one day that I saw Mata from the window of a tram, sitting in a school playground. It could have been Makareta that I was seeing. It was Makareta's large frame and dark, plump face. The stillness was Makareta's as the girl sat, watching other children play, but Makareta does not have awkwardness and is not bereft. She has a river of hair that falls, touching the backs of her knees. Every strand of it has been touched and cared for.

The school was the same one that Keita visited when she'd

gone looking for Mata when Anihera was first taken home. And I knew that the orphanage nearby, which Keita had also visited, would be the place where Mata was living.

I went to the school the next day but was told that I wasn't to come on school premises inquiring about children. On my way out, a girl of about Makareta's and Mata's age came into the play-ground. I stopped her and asked about Mata, but she hadn't heard of anyone by that name. It was then that I realised that Mata would have been given a different name. I decided not to do any-thing further myself. Instead I wrote to Keita.

Keita received a reply to the first letter she sent to the matron of the orphanage saying that there was a girl fitting the descrip-tion in her letter, daughter of the man whose name she'd given, but that the father was now living in England and had arranged a legal guardian for the girl. The legal guardian, as was her right, the letter said, asked that no further correspondence be sent and no further contact with the girl be attempted. Keita kept writing but didn't receive replies to further letters until she wrote men-tioning Mata's land. Then she received a letter from the guardian saying that Mata would be allowed to go there for a short holiday.

I went to visit the guardian, Mrs Parkinson, soon after receiving the address in a letter from Gloria. I thought I might be able to visit Mata sometimes, take her out or bring her home with me for weekends. But I was told not to interfere and not to come there again. Mrs Parkinson was an especially pinched woman who looked as if she'd been out on a stalk all summer, rattling, with no watering.

'Keita gave Mata a photograph of Aunty Anihera, the one of when Aunty was a bridesmaid at your wedding. It was difficult to tell whether Mata was pleased or not, because her face is always so still, so expressionless. But I think she must have been pleased, because she kept going and getting it out of her bag and looking at it.

'I think you might be right, Mum, about wanting me to go to boarding school where I would be living with people of my own age for a few years. I might learn something — because I found it very difficult to talk to someone like Mata even though

I know my English is good. I just wasn't used to someone like her. I know Keita wants me to go away to school (her old school). To her, schooling is very important (and to me too, Mum). Keita doesn't think very much of our high school. I wouldn't mind going away if it wasn't for Kui, whom I don't like to be separated from even for a day.

'I've been teaching Kui to read and she's getting very good at it. She likes any books — storybooks, arithmetic books, school journals, newspapers. I read them all to her, translating as I go. She especially likes stories about different people of the world and about the constellations. She knows about the constellations from her old knowledge. I think it would be cruel to leave her now that she is so old, but I think Keita is determined. I think Kui might die without me.

'I said something to Mata about our urupa and Aunty Anihera's burial place. I could see that what I said gave her a shock and I felt sorry I'd said anything. She ran across the paddock calling to Aunty Gloria.'

twenty-seven

It was a hot night and Makareta was uncomfortable in her serge gym, long-sleeved blouse, blazer, tie, heavy black stockings and lace-up shoes. The new panama felt tight round her head and the elastic under her chin made her itchy.

For an hour they sat in the dark on the railway platform before they heard the station master coming. 'Ho,' he said as he went by them and in through the door. They could hear his noisy breathing. The station lights came on.

Soon afterwards they heard the train coming. They saw the big light beaming on to the track as it pulled in, squealing and steaming.

Aperehama and Wi went ahead of her into the train with the bags and pillows, and as Makareta stepped up into the carriage with Keita, Kui was beginning to cry again, her crying becoming a wail, 'Our daughters don't come back,' she was calling. 'Our children go, they never return.'

'She'll be all right,' Wi said as he and Aperehama stowed the bags and put the pillows down. The two men hugged her quickly then left the train as the whistle sounded.

The engine began to shoulder along, leaving behind the patch of light where, looking back, she could see Wi and Aperehama holding onto the old woman, putting a rug round her. She watched out of the window until they were out of sight and there was only the dark, passing countryside, the black paddocks and hills, the black shapes of houses and the occasional thin gleam of fence wires.

'I felt bad leaving her. From the window of the train she looked so old and so *small* that I couldn't stop crying. I couldn't help feeling that I was doing something wrong.

'She tried so hard to let me come, fussing round and getting me ready this last month — sewing all the labels on the clothes after we received the parcels from you, taking the hem up on the basketball gym so that it is now the regulation "three inches above the knees when kneeling". I felt sorry watching her, with her old eyesight, stitching such dark cloth, but we had to let her do it. The house gym, best gym, blazer and blouses were just right, Mum, and needed no alteration.

'And she decided I would need six pillows for the train journey so that I could sleep comfortably and not get my new uniform creased. (She's very proud of the uniform. So am I, even though it's so hot for this time of the year.) She made six new pillowslips with frills all round the edges. So we had to take six pillows with us. We were very comfortable on the train. (Also I was very glad to have the pillows for somewhere to hide my tomato eyes. Keita kept telling me not to cry, because my eyes would stick out like ripe tomatoes. They did.) But at the end of the journey we had a real struggle with our luggage. I don't know how Keita managed the pillows on her way home.

'The food that Kui packed for our journey was enough for smoko for a shearing gang. It cheered me up. At Taumarunui we had scummy railway coffee that was dark and hot and sweet.

(Scummy is a new word that I've learned. I don't know whether Miss Jamieson would approve of it.) I think of Miss Jamieson and Mr Davis, Mum. They were very good to me. I think of you too.'

'There, Daughter,' Keita said, nodding towards the window when she came into the carriage with the coffee. Looking out, Makareta saw a tall girl, older than herself, wearing the uniform, her short hair curling up under the brim of an old, yellowy panama. The girl was hurrying through the crowd with sand-wiches and drinks, laughing at someone who was calling from a window in the next carriage.

'You'll be home at Easter, home in May and August and at Christmas time,' Keita said as they settled themselves again. 'And you and Kui will be bending your heads over all your new books, talking about all the new things you've been doing. She'll have letters from you while you're away and she'll be all excited.'

'She's old now. She needs me.'

'Time goes quickly when you're old,' Keita said, pausing and watching out of the window into the dark for a while. Then she said, 'You have a good life when you have a good education. You marry an educated man and your life is good.'

Makareta sat up from the pillows where she'd been resting, almost asleep. 'Keita, I don't want to marry anyone.'

'Of course not, Daughter. Of course you don't, you're only a little girl.'

The Limited shot through the dark booping and huffing. People slept or moved about. The door clanked open at the other end of the carriage and the guard came through collecting the dishes and cutlery.

'Two girls from my school spoke to us when we got off the train. (We'd seen one of them on the station at Taumarunui.) The older one was a senior student called Raiha, the other was a fourth former called Puna. (They both had their panama elastic under their hair at the back of their heads, so I did that too. It was much more comfortable than having it under the chin.) They asked us if we wanted to share a taxi with them, but we had too much luggage, Mum. The driver couldn't take us all, so we had to get two taxis in the end.

'Most of the girls know each other (of course) and there was plenty of excitement as everyone started arriving. I felt nervous and very homesick but tried not to show it. There were girls leaning over the balcony calling to friends, and much kissing and hugging and talking about the holidays, exam results, families — and whisperings about the teachers, their new clothes, hairstyles, etc. Miss Green, the headmistress, is the one who has the nicest legs! Oh Mum, they talk about such funny things.

'There were girls to show us (the new ones) round, and to tell us what to do, and prefects checking clothing to see that it was all named. We are allowed to wear lisle stockings in the summer now, Mum, instead of these prickly, woollen ones. Do you think you could send me some, please? Fifth formers are now allowed to wear black nylons. I've been told that one or two of the girls at the end of last year drew lines (like stocking seams) down the backs of their bare legs and no one could tell that they weren't wearing stockings. None of the teachers noticed. There was a smell of sweaty suitcases, shoe polish, floor polish and soap on that first day — and something else. Girls!

'This place is so enormous that I'm having difficulty finding my way round. There's a long corridor with a dining room at one end and bedrooms at the other — dormitories. There are twenty girls to each dorm.

'In the bathroom there are three baths (with animals' feet), three showers and fourteen wash basins. There is plenty of water here, but even so, we are only allowed six inches to bath in (twice a week). There are flush lavatories, of course, noisier than yours, Mum. I'm beginning to get used to the noise of them.

'Being unable to sleep on the train, and on the first night in the dorm spending half the night thinking of you all and worrying about Kui, I was a wreck (new word) on the first morning. (I tried not to cry but there were sniffles and snuffles going on all round me, which kept setting me off.) Also there's such a lot of light here at night-time!'

In the mirror there was a girl with tomato eyes and awful hair. She put the mirror back into her dormitory bag, dabbed her face with her flannel and began brushing. But there was no time. Breakfast was in ten minutes, eight minutes, six minutes, the older girls kept reminding them. They'd been shown how to make their beds — mattresses flat and neat, blankets tucked and corners mitred, pillows turned so that the pillowcase openings faced away from the door.

Two minutes. Her hair wasn't done. It took a half an hour to do her hair — sitting on her special stool, Kui brushing down with long, slow strokes of the brush, talking on and on about the birds, the berries, babies, the relatives, the old ones, the ancestors, the kehua, the work, the walking, the dancing and singing, the sickness, the dreams, the wars, the stars, the waiting.

'You'll have to tie it back,' Raiha said. 'Here, give us your ribbon. Tie it back, just for breakfast. Do it properly after.' There was a bell ringing and everyone was going towards the door.

She hurried with Raiha along the corridor to the dining room, where they stood by their chairs waiting for grace to be said. 'Eat everything,' Raiha said, 'or you'll starve.'

'The first morning's the time you see all the red eyes at breakfast,' the girl next to her said as they sat down. 'You're not the only one.'

'Trouble with her hair,' Raiha said. 'Not enough time.'

'Give me one butter and I'll do your hair,' the girl said, and the others at the table laughed. 'Eat some toast, Makareta, if you don't want to starve.'

When they went back to the dormitory Raiha took the comb from her and ran the tip of it down the back of her head, dividing the hair and draping half of it over one shoulder. 'I had long hair too,' she said as she began plaiting, 'but not as long as yours. I got sick of it but I wasn't allowed to get it cut. So, know what I did? I chopped it with the scissors. Just one side. Gosh, Mum gave me a good hiding. Left me like that for two days. Showed me to all my aunties, who cried, and to all my uncles, who laughed. Then she took me to town to the hairdressers to get it cut, short like this. Easy. But Mum didn't like those hairdressers having my hair!'

Raiha's fingers moved swiftly down one side and then the other, then twisted the bands on and tied the ribbons. 'Got to hurry now,' she said. 'Things to do. Look on your list, see what you have to bring and I'll come back and walk with you. Put water on your eyes. Nearly bell-time, Makareta.'

Makareta moved the little mirror from side to side. Raiha's plaiting was tight and even. About her, everyone was busy brushing clothes, shining shoes, moving in and out of the washroom, staring at lists. At home Manny, Missy and the others would be running through the trees to school, along the track where the ferns were ticklish and cool on bare legs. And at school someone would mark the roll for the teacher, put new chalk on the ledge, inspect the duties and tick them off in the notebook as they were completed. She dabbed her eyes with her flannel. 'Come on,' Raiha said. 'Got everything?'

'It was so embarrassing that first morning, Mum, standing by my bed with my brush in my hand and realising that I had *never once in my life done my own hair*. I felt awful and it was lucky that Raiha so kindly helped me. That night I sat up in bed and practised brushing and plaiting. When the lights went out (eight o'clock for third formers) I was still practising. You should have made me do my hair myself Mum, when I came for the holidays, instead of spoiling me the way Kui does. But it's all right, I can do it now. I get quicker each day. We get up at half-past six and only have half an hour to make our beds, tidy up and get ready for breakfast. (We have porridge and toast for breakfast, and our own bits of butter. Girls swap things for butter.)

'There are points for the way your bed is made and for other duties too. At the end of the year there is a housekeeping cup. I'm in Kahikatea and have a green badge to pin on to my gym. The other houses are Puriri, Matai, Kauri and Rata. In two week's time there are to be house sports and I'm certainly not looking forward to that. You know what I'm like when it comes to sports — very uninterested and very lazy.

'Raiha is our house captain. She is also my "big sister" (every third former or new girl has an older girl to look after her) so I'm lucky.

'We have all sorts of stews for tea, except for Mondays and Fridays, when we have fish. Last Thursday at lunchtime we had something green. I think it was curried peas! Have you heard of having frog's eggs and dead man's ears for pudding?

'I've written to Kui twice, and I've had a letter from Aunty Gloria telling me that Kui is all right. She (Kui) has been over the hill visiting the other old ones so that she can show my letters to them. I can just see her walking up and down the hill tracks talking to the birds. And I can just hear the old ones, gossiping and gossiping, like old birds too. I hope that Aunty Gloria is not saying that Kui is all right just to make me happy. I've told Kui not to lift the water tins and that if she needs water she must use the little pot to get it out with.'

There were things not to tell Kui.

Makareta stoked the coppers as the water came to the boil, and Jenny and Puna came with the tub of clothes that they'd all been soaping and rubbing on the boards before rinsing and wringing. The girls began loosening the clothes and letting them into the boiling water. After this last lot had been boiled and put through a final rinse there'd be just the sanitary cloths to do. The Kui inside her was clicking her tongue.

She went over to the big wooden tub to help Trish, who had already started tipping water from the buckets where the cloths, already rinsed under the tap by those who had used them, were now soaking. The girls turned the taps on hard then began wringing the cloths ready for the coppers. By the time they'd finished Jenny and Puna had started lifting the boiled clothes out with the copper sticks and Tahi and Raiha were coming in from the clotheslines. Laundry duty was the most unpopular of duties, but Makareta preferred it to doing dishes or tidying the grounds.

On Saturdays they cleaned the school from top to bottom — something else she didn't write to Kui about. She found that she enjoyed getting into overalls, being part of a team and scrubbing down tables and shelves, wet mopping and polishing floors, cleaning the ledges, washing the windows with wet newspapers. She was getting better at it and found that if she talked inside herself as she worked, the tutting and chirking would soon stop. It was easy enough to tease Kui and make her smile.

'When we want clean clothes we line up at the clothing room and give our number to whoever is on duty and tell her what we need. Every afternoon we hand in our daytime ties and girdles and are given our dress ties and belts to put on. I've got an ordinary belt at the moment but have started making my taniko belt, which should be finished in a week or two. I'm doing a fern pattern, part of a leaf. I'm pleased with it. We have waiata practice once a week and I've learned some new songs and a poi.

'I'm all right, Mum. I like it here. I'm in the top class and not having difficulty with any of the work. Many of the girls are scholarship holders, like me. I'm pleased to be learning written Maori because I think that if I write to Kui in Maori she'll be able to read my letters by herself. I've taught her to read a little in English but I know she would find Maori easier. I'm sure Keita or Girlie will help her. Every Sunday at two o'clock is letter-writing time (compulsory), but it's not long enough for me. I have so many letters to write and you know how I like to keep writing on and on.

'Did I tell you that our English teacher has blue hair? It's from something she puts in the rinsing water when she washes it. The girls are so funny, Mum, with some of the things they say. But I quite like the blue hair. It matches Miss McAloon's blue eyes and goes with the clothes that she wears.'

twenty-eight

The headmistress rang me in the night because she'd had a call from Keita to say that Makareta must be sent home to be with her great-grandmother, who is dying. Miss Green wanted me to persuade Keita to let Makareta stay on at school for another two days so that she could sit her last exam. The Scholarship Board wouldn't approve of Makareta leaving before final examinations have been completed, Miss Green said. But Hinemate's dying is not something that should be kept from Makareta, even for a day or an hour. Also I'm sure the exam subjects she has sat already will be enough to get her through.

I have missed my daughter greatly over the four years since she started boarding school and has been unable to come to me for the holidays, but it is only right that she should have spent the time with her old people. There is time yet for me. Her letters have given me happiness.

I moved into Alma's house during the last months of my friend's life so that I could care for her properly. We have lived here since, Halfmoon and I, her only beneficiaries. Ben and his new wife are in the other house, and the children share themselves between us.

Now it is Hinemate who is going on ahead of us all. Makareta has sensed it already. Her letters during this, the last term of her school years, have been unlike other letters, as she waits, noting off the days.

'Time and silence, long silence and heavy time, wax and varnish smell of floors and walls, and windows open letting in heavy air. There's Mr Meihana in his shirt-sleeves with his tie loosened, his voice distant, low and heavy.

'I go over the work again and again but nothing changes. There is no more that I can find to do to help make tomorrow or the next day come, nothing saved that can be mixed with time, to lighten it, set it going, make it float and swirl, (except for writing to you, my mother, as I do at this moment). I think of rewena bread and ripe plums, watercress, ferns, the creek, the cool track, and birds. I think of Kui.

'Brown speckles on a creamy-coloured fountain pen are the colours of the egg of piwaiwaka that follow her wherever she goes, talking. Gold nib worn down on one side to accommodate language. How many words have I written — class work, homework, tests and exams, letters? (In Stephens' Radiant Blue, which reminds me always of Alma's eyes.)

'An exercise book, this last one before me, is filled with exercises and translations, ruled off in red. Red pencil is down to its last three inches. Other books and belongings are packed and ready.

'My room at home has a wax smell too. Rag mat. Patch quilt.

Faded wallpaper, a patched tear behind the door, sacking showing through. There's a burnt smell on the cracking windowsill, on the flaking paint. Kui will have waxed the door and washed the curtains (carefully because they're old and fragile).

'I've had a letter from Aunty Gloria telling me of Keita and Wi's visits up north. According to Aunty, not a word was said to anyone as to what the visits were about. I know Keita has land there, as she has in other places too, land or shares. She has land on all sides — her mother's, her father's, and when Kui dies there'll be that land as well. She says that the reason she has so much land is because she's the weed that survived the wars, the hard times and the flu epidemic. She was the one left to inherit. I've accompanied her on many occasions, as you know, to gatherings and court hearings, all to do with land. She's always fought to get the land tied down hard, and I don't suppose there's a pinch of dirt that has ever slipped through her fingers. I know that her visits away are always something to do with land.

'But Aunty Gloria seems to be worried that there is more to it than that. I feel that she is trying to warn me. She seems to be concerned about things that I would've thought forgotten long ago — to do with a promise between our family and the Te Waru family, of an arranged marriage.

'Of course our relatives up north have land adjoining Keita's. I can understand how the land could be joined, could be opened up and used if there was a marriage. Otherwise I guess not one family or the other will put a foot on it. Aunty Gloria said (more than once in her letter) that there are two things I have to remember about Keita. One is that she has plans for all of us, and the other is that if we don't fit in with her plan we won't be forgiven. She pleaded with me that if ever I went away from home I would always return. She said that what she and Anihera didn't understand at first was that they both had a right. Aunty Anihera belonged there just like any of us, just like Keita, and Aunty Gloria herself belongs there, just like any of us, just like Keita. It's not up to Keita to send anyone away. What do you think, my mother? I don't believe that Keita would do anything behind my back because I've always been part of everything my grandparents and elders have ever done. Marriage? I've no thought of it, no thought at all.

'Anyway I wrote to Keita asking about the visits up north and had a reply saying that arrangements were being made for my twentieth birthday celebration. It's going to be a big affair with relatives coming from all over the country. It's not what I want, but I suppose I'll have to have it now that arrangements have begun and promises have been made (of gifts of pork, mutton kumara, corn, etc.) I'd rather wait a year and have a twenty-first celebration if I have to have anything.

'All I want to do at the moment is to get my schooling behind me and go home to be with Kui until she dies. She has to see that I did come back as I said I would. (I suppose the idea of the early birthday party is because of Kui — hoping she'll still be with us then.) Later on I'll come and live with you, Mum. I want to continue my education or do some training. There's no work for me at home and I don't want to be a woman just walking in and out, useless, among the trees.

'Keita said in her letter that by the time of my birthday my land will be all fixed up for me. I don't know what to make of that, but when I go home I'm going to persuade Keita to let Aunty Gloria have her land as well. I think it's unfair the way Keita treats Aunty Gloria. Everyone at home has a new house except for her.

'After lights-out at night some of the exam girls put on their dressing gowns and take their papers and books along to the library. In the library they shade the windows so that the light won't show, and they settle themselves to study until the early hours (if they are not caught, that is). Sometimes I go with them, not so much to study but to finish my letters.

'I think of the long, white road, where, round the last bend, there is light from the lamp in the window. It is a sharp image, but one from a past time now that the electricity has gone through. If they need me at home they'll call. The bell, ringing, has a heavy, slow sound.'

*

So she is prepared, Makareta, for the death of Hinemate. I realise now that all her life she has been prepared for this time as she travelled about with the old ones wherever they went to tangi-hanga. She has a deep understanding of death as part of our lives, not that that will make her sorrow any less.

Last week I went out and bought a new pink dress, a grey duster coat, a rosy hat and spanky shoes, and was preparing to go to the prizegiving where my daughter would receive the top scholar awards. Now, instead, I prepare to go and say goodbye to the old mother. Makareta will already be on her way. 'Wake her now,' I said to Miss Green on the phone in the night. 'So she can catch the early train.'

twenty-nine

The old people waited in the meeting house for Makareta, who had gone home to dress for the birthday. Soon the visitors would arrive.

Everyone had been working for many weeks to prepare the marae and meeting house for this special day and now it was all done. Some of the verandah boards of the house had been replaced, straw from old nests had been cleared away from under the eaves. There was new tin covering the gaps in the roof and new paint on the maihi and the amo.

Although the day was fine there had been three days of rain earlier in the week and the men had spread straw thickly over the marae so that it would not be too wet underfoot when the guests arrived.

Inside the house the floor had been scrubbed and the whariki put down. The walls and ledges had been washed and decorated with ponga leaves and the poutokomanawa had been strung with flowers. The ochre-painted face of the ancestress, with its white-painted eyes, red lips, black, curling hair, that looked down from the back wall had been dusted and polished. The feather by her

ear had been repainted and in its whiteness it was flamelike, flickering in the dull light. The photographs at either side of her had
been taken down and dusted and hung up again.

There was thin sun coming in through the red and blue
window. It broke in soft, weakened colours onto the curling edge
of the whariki. There was a smell of damp and rot and paint and
polish. The old ones gossiped or slept as they waited. The
Daughter was surely taking a long time.

The children, playing out in the paddock, ran now and again
to the far end of it to where they could see the road, but so far
there was no sign of the visitors. Who? They didn't know who,
and the whispering, the secrecy of the old ones had told them they
weren't to ask. They ranged up and down with their manuka
hockey sticks chasing an old tennis ball. Their legs were bruised
and bleeding but the uncles and aunties, mothers and fathers had
been too busy to bother about that.

Earlier they'd helped to wash the potatoes, kumara and
pumpkin and to take the husks off the corn. They'd seen the
vegetables being stacked with the mutton and pork into the hangi
baskets, along with big tins of steam pudding, then watched the
baskets as they were put down onto the hissing stones. Once the
food was covered with the cloths their uncles had sent the dirt
flying off the shovels, heaping it so that no steam would escape.

At the cooking fires a heap of wood had been stacked and
some of the big boys were still chopping. Large pots sat on iron
rails over the fires and there was a smell of watercress and mutton,
and of eels that were smoking, white and dripping against the
corrugated iron erected at the back of the fireplace.

Although they'd been chased out of the tent, the children had
seen the jellies and trifles, lollies and fruit, the boxes of raspberry,
orange and lemon fizz, creaming soda, lemonade, ginger beer and
ginger ale. There were pickles and sauces being put into small
dishes, bread being sliced and buttered, cakes cut and covered,
bowls stacked ready for the hot food. They were hungry but they
knew it was a long time before they would eat.

There was beer for the party too, and some of the uncles had
started drinking it as they sat in the heat watching the fires, filling
jugs from a keg. After a while some of the old ones came out of

the house to join them, then the women from the tent came.

Everything was ready and they were all waiting. Even though Makareta was taking her time it didn't matter because it was all going to happen, at last. Old promises were going to be made good, but it wasn't to be talked about yet, time enough for that when everything was settled. Perhaps things had gone wrong in the past because people talk too much, so now they didn't speak of it, not even behind the hand.

But they were impatient to see this girl of theirs. What was keeping her? They wanted to see the new clothes and to watch Keita put the korowai and the greenstone on her. They wanted to see how the pendant would look against the lace blouse. Some said it was white lace, others said it would be cream or a pastel colour. Her hair would be brushed out, yes, and it would come down and over the korowai like another cloak. Makareta was going to change into another dress for the party because she had dresses galore. She had everything. Keita was going to build her a house on her land. If only Hinemate had lived long enough to see it.

Waiting. There'd been a lot of hard work, but for now the beer was good. The visitors had better be on time or their hosts might start on another of the kegs that were keeping cool in the creek. Any minute they might send a nephew to ask Wi if they could roll themselves up another barrel, and Wi wouldn't be able to refuse them.

They had all guessed what was holding the girl up. It was because Polly hadn't arrived and Makareta would be still hoping.

But why hadn't Polly come? Perhaps it was because there was something she didn't agree with. That would be it, because it wasn't like Polly not to be there. She should've been there days ago.

What was there for Polly not to agree with?

Here was the nephew with a new keg, Wi hadn't refused them. And after a while they thought they could whisper — about the young man being brought down for Makareta. A mokopuna of Te Waru, you don't say.

Over in the paddock the kids began to call, 'Kei te haere mai nga pahi, kei te haere mai nga pahi.' So the buses had been seen coming round the hill, but where was Makareta? The old ones were waiting in the meeting house where the ancient ones looked down from the walls. The feather cloak was ready, folded across Keita's knee.

Hah, but everything was all right now. They could all see Wi's car turning in towards the rear of the meeting house. Makareta had arrived just in time.

thirty

Missy touched the iron to make sure it wasn't too hot, then began ironing Makareta's blouse — the tucks, the frills, the ties. No trouble with an electric iron, no smudges to worry about. After that she would iron the party dress.

Bub rubbed Vaseline into the new patent leather shoes, over the tops and around the heels, the little heels — not too high, not too low. The shoes were already shiny but she wanted them shinier still. She was going to tell Makareta to wear her old shoes down to the wharenui so her new ones wouldn't get muddy. She would be the one to carry the new shoes for her cousin.

Gloria brushed the charcoal wool suit, hung it on the wardrobe door and lay the stockings and underwear out on the bed. Makareta would put on her underwear then they'd brush out her hair. Tonight, after Makareta had changed into her party dress, they could plait her hair up again. Everything was ready.

But Makareta was taking her time. Gloria went out to the washhouse to call her. 'I'm coming,' Makareta said. 'Can Bub make us a cup of tea?'

'I'll make it,' Gloria said. 'Have a quick cup. Then we have to get your hair done. We can't take long, Makareta.'

'Someone'll come for us if we're taking too long. If they see the buses coming they'll send someone over.'

She stepped out of the bath, wrapped a towel around herself, put her feet into a pair of sandals and crossed the yard to the house. As she went through to the bedroom she called, 'Missy, that dress is for you.'

'I've got a dress for your party, Makareta,' Missy said, following her cousin to the bedroom. 'Tonight after we've cleaned up I'll put it on.'

'It's not my colour. It'll suit you — a girl with yellow specks in her eyes and kehu hair. I want you to have it.'

'I'm too skinny and tall.'

'I altered it yesterday, took the darts in and let the hem down. See?'

'Mum . . .'

'If your cousin wants to give you a dress, Missy, then you can't refuse, but we better iron one of your other dresses, Makareta, for the party . . .'

'I like my new suit so I think I'll keep it on. When it's time for the party I'll take the jacket off so everyone can see the nice blouse that you've been ironing for me. I don't need two changes in one day, do I? Put it on, Missy, so we can see.'

Gloria made tea while Bub began undoing Makareta's hair and brushing it down. 'It fits me, it does,' Missy said, showing them the dress.

'I knew it would suit you,' Makareta said.

'Like a film star, Miss,' said Bub.

Just then Manny put his head round the door. 'There's a car coming. Looks like a taxi.'

'That'll be Polly, Makareta. You should know your mother wouldn't let you down on your birthday. Put your clothes on quickly now so your mother will be the first to see.'

Makareta put on her blouse and skirt, took her jacket from the hanger and Missy and Bub held her hair while she put it on. 'My mother's not coming,' she said.

'Of course . . .'

'I had a letter . . .'

'From Polly? Saying she's not coming?'

'Yesterday.'

'You didn't tell us. You didn't say.'

Makareta took the letter from her drawer and gave it to her aunt to read:

'I am very upset about something I have just found out about. I should have heard about it from you, Makareta. You are my own daughter and yet you kept this important matter from me that I have found out about from a stranger.

'I was visiting the hospital this afternoon and noticed an old kuia in one of the wards so I went to sit with her for a while. I found out that she was one of the kuia of the Te Waru family, the kuia Tarati. She told me that her people were bringing one of their young men down for an engagement to you. She didn't say your name, and didn't know that I was your mother, but as I listened to her talking I realised what she meant.

'It was wrong of you not to tell me. I'm very hurt about it. I was looking forward to the birthday party, thinking that afterwards, you, my daughter, would come to me at last, even if only for a few years.

'Kui Tarati said that everything had been arranged. The grandson would be brought down for the engagement, and when he and his people returned home the wedding would be prepared for. She talked about land.

'Makareta, I'm not saying it's wrong if it's what you want. Having someone chosen isn't a bad thing. Keita, Wi, the old ones, would've thought carefully, prepared carefully. You know their ways. But you didn't tell me. You said you would come to me one day and that there were things that you wanted to do. You have said you have no thought of marriage. I am more disappointed than I can say.

'I'm too upset to come to your birthday, Makareta. It was a shock to find all this out from a stranger, but I have to forgive you because you are my daughter. The money is for your birthday. I have gifts for you too but my heart is too sad for me to bring them or send them. One day I will give them to you . . .'

'Aunty Gloria,' Makareta said, when her aunt had finished reading, 'I'm going, the taxi is for me.'

Gloria began to cry, rocking herself from side to side, holding the letter against her chest, 'No, no, Makareta, you can't do this. You can't go, we'll all be shamed, you can't.'

Makareta sat down by her aunt. 'I can't marry someone, anyone, when I've got no thought of it.'

'Makareta, there'll be shame on all of us if you go. And if you go you won't come back. That's what Kui Hinemate always cried for.'

'I've been thinking of Kui all the time. She's been talking to me in her own way, and she's helped me to know that what I'm doing is right.'

'Makareta,' Missy said, 'it says in the letter you'll be engaged.' Missy's eyes were bright and her breath came in excited gasps. 'Then you'll have a wedding. It'll be beautiful . . .'

'I have to go.'

'No, Makareta,' Gloria said. 'You have to do what they want. They want to honour you, the two families together. It's not so bad. That boy has been brought up by his old people and his family won't let you down.'

'Makareta, Bub and I'll be bridesmaids for you, for your wedding.'

'I can't marry when there's nothing in my heart for it, when it's only my family who can touch me. I have to go.'

'Just for the engagement, Makareta, there's no harm. Then if it's not right, if it doesn't work out . . .'

'If it doesn't work out we'll all be shamed anyway.'

'If you leave now Keita will die.'

'If I'd found out sooner . . . Aunty Gloria, if you knew you should've told me.'

'I didn't know, Makareta. I thought there would be talk at your birthday but didn't know about any engagement . . . Makareta, the people will arrive soon . . .'

'If I'd known sooner I'd have gone sooner, but the letter came just yesterday. At first I couldn't understand it, because I really believed Keita when she said the celebration was for my birthday. I knew there was something in Keita's mind, and I thought perhaps I would come back one day, when I was older, when I was ready, to do what they wanted . . . But right now, I can't. When I finished reading the letter I was going to go to Keita and beg her to stop it, but it was too late. I knew the people were already on their way. I've waited until now to leave so it'll be too late for anyone to come after me. Soon the buses will arrive.'

'Just the engagement, Makareta.'

'If I could . . .'

Makareta put on her shoes. 'I'll come back one day, like you said, Aunty Gloria.' She picked up a small bag that she had already packed, and as she did so her aunt began to wail and cry, 'No, Makareta, I'll be blamed, I'll be blamed.'

'Kiss me, my cousins,' she said to Manny, Missy and Bub. She held each of them to her as they pleaded with her. Then as she turned to say goodbye to Gloria, her aunt brushed her aside and ran out calling to the taxi driver to go away. He started up the engine as Makareta opened the door and stepped in.

MISSY

thirty-one

Woman with
Obsidian eye
Made us mortal.

On the night we were born our mother woke with hard pain in her back. She'd had pain for most of the day, but because you'd dropped yourself down she felt light and energetic. We heard her singing, didn't we, as she scalded the milk, made bread, scrubbed the floor and the outhouse, washed the clothes and cleaned the tankstand down. Before dark she brought the clothes in from the line and stacked nappies and gowns, a blanket and towels ready on the rack over the fire.

When our father came home from work he wanted to go for Kui Hinemate right away, but she told him to wait so that Kui would go to bed and get some rest. They put our brother to bed and went to sleep themselves. I think that there was a flicker of fire in the grate and that the kettle was keeping warm.

The pain that woke her turned in her like a big wheel. Turning, turning, as she stared into the dark, then gradually weakened until it was gone. She woke Dadda then and asked him to go and get the great-grandmother.

Our father put on his coat and boots and went hurrying off with the lamp, the yard stones snapping.

Mama stoked the fire, stirring the embers, poking sticks into the grate, then made tea and set the teapot on the side of the stove — but in between times she leaned, gripping the edge of the table, talking to herself while the heavy wheel turned. She thought of our brother, Egypt, called Manny, who had been born in the night also, wrong way up and back to front, feet first and blue. Did you hear what she said as she leaned, her face so close to the table's face that her breath came, still warm, back to her? 'Won't die, won't cry,' she said. 'Not nobody.' Thinking of Keita.

Our mother didn't hate Keita, but knew her, understood what made her tick, believed that our grandmother would get satisfaction if it was known that our mother cried out, as though for the choice she'd made. She kept hold — for herself, for Dadda, for us, as though that could help her to understand something. As if it helped her to be.

Mama had her secrets when she was fifteen, writing secret letters to our father overseas, being in love. Then when Dadda returned from war in the hospital ship she ran away to Wellington to be with him. She had no money and nowhere to stay. Dadda's relatives took her to live with them until it was almost time for him to come out of hospital, then they gave her money and sent her home.

But she was in love and didn't go home at all, stepped off the train somewhere up the line and returned. Dadda's family tried to make him send her away because she was only a child, they said. Do you see her? Our mother, in her skimpy dress and coat, her old shoes, a piece of stringy ribbon tying back her bouncy hair. He wouldn't send her away. She wouldn't go without him, naughty girl.

So the two of them were put on a train, but not to come home here. They went to our father's parents' place, where they lived until Manny was due to be born. Mama wanted to come home then because there was really no room for them at our other grandparents' place. There was no chance of work there for Dadda.

She hoped that Keita would accept them when they arrived, but Keita shut the door on them and they had to go and stay with Aunty Kahu and Uncle Pop.

However, Keita arranged a wedding, since, according to her, our mother was no good for anything else, and when it was over she said, 'You married this man and now he'll look after you I'm sure,' and went home. Our parents slept at the marae that night and the next day walked over the hill towards Uncle Pop's place, in love with nowhere to go and not unhappy. At the top of the hill they looked across and Dadda pointed and said, 'There's a house for us,' and they went running and shouting, Mama too fast with her round, round stomach, Dadda stumbling, laughing after her. To here.

They came dancing in to spider webs and dry fern. There was only one room then and no floor. Beetles dropped on them, pieces of wall fell away and they couldn't stop laughing. They started cleaning with a manuka branch, sweeping the dirt floor and brushing the cobwebs away. They made a bed of dry fern when they'd finished, took off their wedding clothes, spread them and dropped, rolling together.

The next day they went to Aunty Horiana's, whose land this house is on, and asked if they could stay here. Aunty Horiana's grandmother, who was still alive then, said, 'You have it because you've got a right.' Think of them scratching here and there for boards and old nails to fix a floor, finding stones for a fireplace, patching holes with pieces of tin. Before Manny was born Dadda found work on the roads.

'All right, my darling,' Kui said when she arrived. 'Our baby's the right way up this time.' That was you she was talking about. She didn't know about me.

You came headfirst into a circle of lamplight above a pad of paper and towels over which our mother squatted — tiny, translucent, chicklike. Blood pulsed close under your skin and your cry was thin and indignant. You began to breathe, your limbs tightening, mucus running, as Kui held you in a small world upside down. When our mother bore down again the whenua dropped onto the towels, our whenua.

Kui helped Mama onto the bed and tended to her — washing and rubbing, pulling and pinning the binding cloth — and when that was done she stooped and spread the placenta, took the lamp down to look closely at it. That was when she found out about me, saw the signs, but she never spoke of me, I don't know why. She put our whenua, our blanket, aside for burial and I listened to your indignant crying, Missy, thinking that the indignation could have been for me, your brother, your twin. If Kui had spoken there could have been a tear for me perhaps, at least a word or two.

*

'Around Maleme,' our father said, 'fighting around Maleme. Some died there, some wounded, some taken. Twenty-eighth didn't get right in. By the time we got to Pirgos there were too many of them. Enemy. Came in on troop-carriers, gliders, down on parachutes, in hundreds.

'Well, getting out of there, keeping in the shelter of the bamboos and the olives, that's when I got it. Boom. Both legs and a hole in the side. Nothing. Just a hot feeling in the legs but couldn't get up, couldn't move.'

Our mother was sitting in bed holding you against her shoulder. Kui was asleep by the fire. There was a candle. 'Why?' she asked. 'Why now?'

'Passed out,' he said, 'and when I came to, the firing's stopped. Blacking out. It was getting dark and bodies all around. Blacking out, coming to, blacking out, coming to. And in between times I hear my name, someone calling me, whispering. I know it's brother Rere but I roll myself over, drag myself into the bamboos so he can't find me because I don't want him carrying me. I think if he carries me he won't make it back. Up and down the grapes he went, round the bamboos looking at all the dead ones, seeing if it's me.'

'In the night, in your sleep, you talk,' our mother said. 'But only in your sleep — and once when Manny was born. Why? Why now?'

'In the middle of it I think of a baby, that's why,' he said. 'I was laying there thinking it's nothing, to die, blacking out, coming to. But in the middle of it there's a baby, like in a dream. It's a little new baby, like my brothers and sisters I seen born, like this new little missy we got. My own baby it is. Like telling me, don't die.

'So I just waited, listened.

'Just on dark and there's no one calling me, no noise, no one moving so I pulled myself along, a little bit, a little bit, coming out of the bamboos. And when I get out he was there, Rere. He knew I was there somewhere. Not among the dead, so I must be there somewhere. He waited until he heard the bamboos jingle and he knew. He chucked his gear away, tied my legs and put me over his shoulder, swearing. "Leave me," I said.

'But no. Off he went over the stones and the rough, carrying, but most I don't remember. We holed up now and again and once when he put me down I looked and saw he's covered in blood, head to toe, as if it's him who got it. That's what I keep getting in my dream. Our brother covered head to toe in blood of mine. Blood moving, running, like coming out of him. My blood, him bleeding it.

'We made it back to Platanius but I don't remember much of that.

'Then when I came back home and got the news that Rere was dead it was the worst day, the worst day of my life. He carried me, saved me, and now he was dead . . .'

'Not from carrying you. Later in Egypt he died . . . another country.'

'He was laughing, telling about me hiding, about him hiding from me. Should've left me there for a Crete girl to find, he said.'

Our father took you and tucked you into him — you along with the skimp, the scrap that was the me that had rubbed into you, but he didn't know about me. You, us, against him, quiet, quiet. Then he said, 'Now Hori.'

'Hori?'

'They were all up getting ready to go to Horiana's when I went to get Kui. Just heard about Hori.'

'Hold your baby, Bobby,' our mother said. 'It's why you came back. It's why you come out of the bamboos. You come out of the bamboos for your kids and me. Pretty, see, and sleeping.' She'd have said that of me too if there'd been blood enough, if I'd followed you squealing into the patch of yellow light. Pretty, see, and sleeping.

The next morning, as dawn came, our father took our placenta, our blanket (which held the only sign of me) wrapped in paper, and buried it where baby blankets go.

But there's a spritish trace of me that has curled itself in to you. If Kui had spoken there could have been a story about me.

thirty-two

It was fingernail
Fire
That set the world
Ablaze.

You walked with Makareta in your new clothes on your first
day at school, Manny up ahead dipping, dapping. Mama had
made you a skirt from a dress and a flour-bag blouse with a green
button on it. You had a real pair of pants from the shop, clean
fingernails and a rag hanky. I would've walked with you,
would've had new clothes.

'You have to say, "Please may I leave the room," if you want
a mimi,' Makareta said. 'Don't say mimi at school.'

'Why because?' you asked.

'It's a rule.'

'And any kids talk Maori to you,' Manny said coming, going,
turning himself, 'you got to run away. Headmaster hit you with
a big strap.'

Then listen to you howl, sitting bang on the track, mouth as
big as a fire door. 'Mama, Mama. Wanoo go home. Wanoo-oo.'
Missy Sissy. Our brother skedaddled, disappeared into the trees.

'Don't listen, don't listen to him,' Makareta said, pulling you
by the arm. 'Get up or you dirty all your new clothes.' And that
got you up, shut you up, because you liked the clothes. 'There's
a nice teacher,' Makareta said, brushing you down. 'Miss
Jamieson. Pretty dresses, beads and earrings, stockings and high
hells.' Then Manny appeared again, shunting his breath, putting
his face to yours, 'It's a Pakeha,' he yelled and down you went
again, listen to it, bawling to beat thunder. 'Look what you did,
Manny,' Makareta called as he ran, ran, gone.

She coaxed you with bread and jam, wiped your eyes and
nose and told you about the books that there were to read, the

slates there were to write on, the stamps for good work. 'There's blackboards and desks,' she said, 'a stick with a hook to open the windows, an alphabet, a photo of the King.' Your mouth shut onto the bread and jam, your eyes sprang open and you let Makareta take you by the hand. 'It's not a real Pakeha, it's Miss Jamieson,' she said.

'Hey, Missy, you come?' kids called as you went in through the gate. 'Missy, you five? Headmaster got a big strap.'

Into a big room where your eyes saw, from floor upwards, the high heels, stockings, pretty dress, beads and earrings. Red, red lips, smiling at you. Listen to it, your heart, flippity flipping. Red lips speaking to Makareta, 'Tell me your cousin's name.'

'Maleme Karoria Tatua,' Makareta said. I would have had a name, Pirgos or Platanius, if I'd squeaked, if there'd been enough blood for me. Manny was jumping from foot to foot saying, 'My sister, my sister, she five.'

'Take her to Mr Davis to enrol, then show her the lavatories,' Miss Jamieson said. 'Egypt, you stay here and explain where you've been for a week or more.'

You crossed the playground with Makareta to the other room where a yellow-haired man was making chalk lines on a board. Makareta gave our mother's note to him. 'Good morning, Maleme,' Mr Davis said when he'd read the note, but you didn't answer, Sissy Missy, eyelids down, mouth shut tight, feet pushing hard into the floor. 'Is this Egypt's sister?' he asked. 'Can she talk? Does she understand English? She was meant to be here two weeks ago.' He put our mother's note on his desk and turned back to the board, where he began writing in loops and sweeps between the lines that he had drawn. 'Take her back to Miss Jamieson,' he said. 'Tell her she has to come to school every day.'

Out by the steps Bessie was ringing the bell and Makareta took you and stood you in line with the primer children. Manny, behind you, bumped you in the back and you began to walk, following the kids to the foot bath, where you all swished your feet as you went through, coming out at the other end making footprints on the concrete to the door. You all wiped your feet backwards, forwards on a scratchy mat, crossed the floor making footprints footprints to the big mat where you sat down. 'Good

morning,' is what you all had to say before showing your hand-
kerchiefs and fingernails.

'Good, Maleme,' Miss Jamieson said about the handkerchief
and fingernails. I would've had nice fingers, a hanky to show,
would've sat straight with my arms folded, hands tucked, one up,
one down. 'Good, Pirgos or Platanius,' she'd have said to me —
pretty dress, beads, earrings, lipstick. Lipstick! You reached out a
hand to hold Manny's arm, Miss Sis, and he dug his elbow hard,
shoving you.

Then Miss Jamieson began talking about something, asking
something but you didn't know what. Kids were shooting their
hands up to be chosen. Miss Jamieson chose Junior, who went to
the front of the room, where he stood facing you all. He had to
stand up straight, put his feet together, keep his hands by his sides
and talk to you. 'Our father and our uncle they goan up the hill
to kill a pig,' he said, 'and they kill a pig. They burn it and cut
it and hanging it up in the big tree any questions?' Hands, hands.
'How big it is?' Tati asked, and Junior stretched his arm as high
as he could to show how big.

Hands.

'Our sister gone away in the train any questions?' Tuahine
said.

'Where she gone?'

'I don't know, any more questions?'

'How big the train?'

'I don't know, any more questions?'

Hands, hands. Our brother Manny stretching, flicking his
arm see, eyes like eggs.

'Egypt?'

'Our mother got a dead baby,' he said. 'Our father bury it by
the other dead baby, any questions?'

'How many dead baby you got?'

'Two, any more questions?'

'How big it is?' Manny held his hands apart to show the little
size, then sat down.

He was telling about something that had happened just a few
days before you were supposed to start school. Mama had been

sewing the skirt, pulling string from the flour-bags and boiling them for your blouse.

But first of all mention must be made of Suda Bay, the name given to our brother Chumchum, Chummy, Chum, who was next born after you and me. You and Manny were under the table eating a potato when Chummy drew his first scrawny breath, both of you too young to remember. After Chummy there was a named and buried one, a girl, who you saw briefly one morning when you woke, before the box was closed. That made five of us including me.

You were playing with Chumchum down the bank when you heard our mother calling, but you pretended not to hear. You were watching for the kids coming home from school. After a while you noticed something different about our mother's voice, something not angry, which made you curious. So you took Chumchum's hand and went up the bank into the yard, where you saw Mama at the woodheap sitting on the chips, her back against the chopping block. 'Go and get Kui Hinemate,' she said, but you didn't want to go, stood with your feet planted wanting to know why. 'Mama's sick,' she said. 'Go on, go and get Kui.' Standing, standing, wondering how long before Mama got wild, sent you flying–running with a smack, but our mother didn't move. 'Tell her Mama bleeding,' not moving, not picking up a stick to smack with. Then Mama lifted herself and you saw that the woodchips were covered with blood. Everywhere blood, wasting wasting, blood that could have been for me. 'Chopped?' you asked.

'From in Mama's puku,' she said. 'Run and tell Kui.'

So you ran crying along the track, Miss Tissy, through the long grass, the sourgrass, the puha, the poroporo and the nettles. Running, running, to the end of the path and round the side of the hill from where you could see our grandparents' place such a long way away, nettled legs burning.

You made your way downhill, carefully at first, but the steepness of the slope set your legs going faster and faster, too fast for themselves so that finally you went headlong, over and over, landing in the cold grass yodelling. But there was no one to hear.

Got up and made your way alongside the creek, through the wiwi, across the paddock looking for Aperehama or our grandfather, hands and knees bleeding, bleeding, wasting.

No one along the fences or in the paddocks, only the high grass and the ghosters. You were yelling for Mama, yelling for Kui.

No one at the sheds or in the gardens, no Aperehama, no Wi, no Keita, no Kui. 'Kuuii, Kuuii,' you called, and she came out onto the doorstep shading her eyes. 'Is that you, little daughter Maleme?' she said.

'Mama sick.'

'Come to Kui.'

'Mama sore bleeding.'

'You're only as big as the wiwi, daughter Maleme. I'll tell Keita about Mama, then you can take me.'

Near the house you heard our mother call in a voice that was for dead people. She was still sitting on the wood chips and was rocking backwards and forwards, holding Chumchum against her with one arm. With her other hand she held something wrapped in a cloth. Kui put her face against Mama's face and cried in a way that was for dead people, then took the bundle. It was Mama's dead baby wrapped in a piece of material that she'd torn from the bottom of her dress.

You helped move everything out of the kitchen into the yard while Kui and Keita prepared the bedroom. The outside fire was lit and Wi and Aperehama were cutting meat and preparing vegetables. People were arriving.

Once our mother was settled Keita went out to the woodheap and began cleaning up where Mama had been sitting, sprinkling water and scooping all the woodchips and wrapping them in paper. Blood again. She sent you to ask Aperehama to cut flax for her and you went with him, holding the lamp.

You watched as Keita stripped the blades of flax and began making a basket. And when it was finished you watched her put the wrapped woodchips into it, along with our brother's blanket, and hang it in a tree. But where was the basket, sweet-smelling

and green, to take *our* blanket to the ground? It had been newspaper only for you and me.

It was quiet after that. You went to sit with Makareta by the
fire, hungry. There was meat and watercress cooking but
everyone was waiting.

A long time later you heard Dadda singing and wanted to run
and meet him but you weren't allowed. Everyone stayed by the
fire while Wi went down the bank carrying a lamp, and not long
afterwards he returned with Dadda. You, Manny and Chum left
the fireplace and went to Dadda, holding a leg, a coat, a hand.
There was noise and crying again.

He took the baby from Mama and began unwrapping it, our
grandmother Keita holding the light down low. Baby had his nice
clothes on by then. 'Little brother,' our mother said in a tired way.
(No one had said that of me.) 'Keep it, Mama,' Manny said.

'He's dead.'

'Us hold?' So you each had a turn at holding the brother, who
was real but didn't move, real but made no sound, his face smaller
than a hand. If there was a time for Kui to mention me, that could
have been the time, but perhaps she had forgotten me by then.

You went out to wash and have kai, and later, when you
went back inside, Mama was asleep with the baby beside her. Kui
and Keita were seated on boxes on either side of the bed and their
thoughts had gone back behind their eyes.

It was just daylight when you woke. Dadda was out in the
yard nailing a box. The fires were still going and people were still
there with their blankets. Once the box was finished everyone
came into the house while Dadda put our brother in it.

While our father and some of the others were away at the
urupa Kui had to wrap Mama in cloths and tie her titties up. Stare,
stare, Missy. You liked pretty Kui with her old face, big hairy
spot by her nose, long skinny arms. She had white plaits with two
of Makareta's ribbons on them and wore a black dress that nearly
touched the floor. Her feet were long and wide and she had
yellow bumpy toenails. Had to bend her head down to get in the
door. 'What you got a big spot by your nose, Kui?' you asked,
Miss Nohi.

165

'My brother put it there,' she said. 'Swapped it from his chin onto his finger, then onto my face, singing the wart-swapping song. He tried to put it on my nose but I moved my head.'

'Should put it back on him, Kui.'

'It only came there years and years later. My brother had gone to war by then,' she said.

When you heard Dadda, Wi and the others coming back along the track Kui went out to call them. Keita and our mother followed and Mama was saying, 'Tell them put the shovel away, Kui. Don't let me see the shovel.'

They'd named our brother and buried him by our named sister, in the place where babies go. Mama was sick with milk and bleeding, and it was two weeks after our birthday that you finally got to school.

When the older children went to their desks to write on their slates, Miss Jamieson snapped a piece of green chalk in half and gave a piece to Billyboy and a piece to you, sending you to draw on the boards. You made a circle with two eyes, and from it drew two long legs. You were pleased with that, made another and another until there was a family, and a baby in a box. Even though you didn't know it, I think one of the smudges you accidently made could've been the me that is rubbed into you. Behind you, Miss Jamieson walked up and down saying, 'Sit up straight, feet together, "four arms" on the desk, don't write with your nose.' You looked round every now and again wondering what it was about. There was a rolled-in-a-ball sock duster that had a loop of ribbon sewn on it, which hung by the board on a nail.

After lunch you all stood by the basins, where you had to dip a finger into a saucer of salt and rub round and round and up and down on your teeth to get them clean. You had to spit and wash your mouths, being careful not to waste water. I would've had teeth, beginning to loosen and wobble like yours. The older kids had toothbrushes and were spoken to for flicking at each other.

In the teacher's book was a boy with magic beans. He had a hat and a jacket, long pants and flash boots, and when his mother threw the beans out of the window a beanstalk grew to the sky. You thought of having boots and clothes like that, beans like that, climbing to the sky where there might be a chook with golden eggs. But there could be a giant up there as well, you thought, in big boots, fee-fumming and chasing.

After the teacher had put the book away you all sang *Swing low sweet chariot, Comin' for to carry me home.* There was a stove in the room but no wood, and you wondered where Miss Jamieson cooked her kai; no bed and you wondered where she slept. You wanted a mimi but couldn't remember the words.

'Bigger than trees?' you asked Makareta on the way home.

'No giants,' she said.

'Where they are?'

'In the giant country I suppose.'

The track narrowed and Makareta let go your hand walking ahead of you. You followed close behind, close behind, reaching, touching. 'Where it is, the giant country?'

'Nowhere.' She stopped where the tracks joined and sent you off home through the short cut. 'Wait for you tomorrow,' she said. Off you went, running running, through the giant trees, Hei Ha Hei, like Maui scooting from fire that the angry tipuna had sent to chase him. Hi Ha, Missy!

Mama was burning a needle in the fire and Chummy was starting to yell. Piece of white cotton hanging from the needle from when Mama sewed your dress.

'There's a kid with magic seeds,' you said.

'There's a kid with dirty clothes,' Mama said, 'and a rip in her sleeve.' True, Missy, look. Covered in green chalk, tear in your blouse from scatting too fast through the trees, mud marks from the morning when you'd sat yourself down on the track. 'Climbed up to the sky,' you said.

'No school for you if you get your things dirty and torn. Needn't think we got plenty of water to wash your dirty clothes.'

Mama held Chummy down, our brother squawking worse than a stolen hen, opened up his foot with the needle and began pressing the poison out. 'Get me kawakawa Manny. Missy, get a bowl.'

'And teacher got chalk for me and Billyboy,' you said, returning with the bowl.

Mama bathed the foot, covered it with kawakawa and tied it
with a rag. 'Walk on your heel, like this on your heel,' our mother
said, showing Chummy what to do. You wished you had a sore
too, wrapped in warm leaves and a rag, walking on your hell.
'Which Billyboy?' she asked.

'Henrietta's,' Manny said. 'Five, like Missy.'

Our mother sat on a box, put tobacco on a tishy paper,
licked, rolled, nipping the dangles from each end, lighting from
between the teeth of the stove.

'And a song,' you said.

'I looked over Jordan and what did I see?' Manny sang, and
you laughed because Mama knew the teacher's song and joined
in:

> *Comin' for to carry me home,*
> *A band of angels comin' after me,*
> *Comin' for to carry me home.*

And our father knew it too. You ran along beside him carrying
the tin. I would've raced you for it, snatched it, looped my fingers
through the little wire handle and carried it home. Dadda put his
hands out to the trees and sang

> *If you get there before I do,*
> *Comin' for to carry me home,*
> *Tell all my friends I'm comin' too,*
> *Comin' for to carry me home.*

You followed him up the bank to the house. 'A desk, a blackboard, chalk,' you said. 'A chair, a book, nice dress, high heels.'

'Red mouth too?' our father asked, bending over laughing by
the fire. 'Like Wi's dog been worrying sheep?' Dadda made you
wild.

That was your first day. School was for you, you thought as you
went out and rubbed and rinsed your clothes, hung them on the
line and poled them up high. Later in the dark you unpegged
them and ran from the sky giants, the talking animals, the dark,
the ghosters. Our mother put the clothes on a box by the fire so
they'd be properly dry by morning.

thirty-three

One who lives in the moon
Controls the blood's flow.

School was for you but there was always something to keep you away — your clothes, your hair, getting water, helping Mama, raincoat.

At school you'd found out that there were things you were supposed to have. A raincoat was one of them. Look at you, running along the tracks to school on wet days in a sugar bag, one corner of it tucked to the other to make a hood. See, throwing it into the bushes before you go in the gate because it's not what you're supposed to have.

A bed like the one in the reading book, a pillow, a tablecloth, a pencil for a note from your mother, a toothbrush each, an apple, toast, a glass of milk.

Supposed to have right answers too, good reasons, as Miss Jamieson said when she asked where you'd been for two weeks, a month, two days.

Reasons like — sick, burnt, toes cut off. But it was Jacko who had chopped off a toe and worn a big bandage to school for the teachers to see. It was Tama who had a shiny neck, a burnt off ear, a scarry arm. And it was Tati who had gone to hospital and stayed there for almost a year.

Also there were some things not allowed, especially to do with kai. Big kids waited by you in the shelter shed at playtime to see if you drank all your malt milk — wanting to ask for it, but they weren't allowed to ask. Teachers became angry if you asked for milk or kai, or if you gave your kai to anyone. But at home if you kept kai to yourself you got a good hiding. There were words not allowed too — kai, taringa, piss, poaka, bugger.

And lies. Why have you been away? Where have you been? Helping Mama. Was it lies?

About little sister Keita, called Bubba. The tuakana and teina must all be told about and remembered otherwise how can I be counted?

'You're stopping home, Missy, that's that,' our mother said, but you didn't know why. There was water in the tank and Mama wasn't sick, hadn't been sick for a long time. It wasn't raining, you had clean clothes for school and there was nothing walking in your hair. Then a thought came to you as you watched our mother pick up the water tin, stop and lean by the door. 'Getting another dead baby?' you asked.

'Getting a sore ear if you don't clear up and get the dishes done,' she said going out with the tin. Manny was pulling wood across the yard.

When Mama came back in you looked to see what mood she was in but it was difficult to tell. She was sweating and hurrying. 'After that go and get Kui,' she said. So it was right, you thought. Mama was getting another dead baby. 'Don't play, Missy,' she said as she went out frowning.

You speared a piece of soap with a fork, swished it in the water and started washing the plates. You'd nearly finished when Mama came in again, wet from washing clothes. Sweating. 'Get her now,' she said. Her hair was wild and she was trying to brush it back with her soapy arm. Her dress was torn but she had a pin holding it across her stomach. She stood in the doorway, bigger than the door.

Kui Hinemate cut the loaf, gave half to you to carry, and you followed her across the paddocks and up the rise to the track. Then you walked together towards the house, where you thought you might see Mama with her baby.

No. Mama was at the line hanging the clothes and Kui went inside, put the bread on the shelf and began stoking the fire. You thought the bread might stay there until Dadda came home crying. Manny had started chopping, standing on a branch, cutting, cutting, tossing cut pieces on to the pile.

'Take these out for your mama,' Kui said, giving you a blanket and picking up towels. So you went out and helped Kui to spread the blanket in a shady place past the clothesline. But Mama didn't sit. Instead she walked. Kui lay down on the

blanket. 'Look after our fire, little Maleme,' she said with her eyes
closed. 'Make Mama a cup of tea. Get bread for you and your
brother.'

Hi ha!

'Manny,' you called as you returned to the house. 'We're
having bread,' and he put the axe down and went running to get
butter and syrup from the outside safe.

When you'd eaten the bread you made tea, and you and
Manny went out carrying cups in one hand, bread in the other.
Mama was crouching on the blanket looking down and Kui was
getting something from her, talking, then holding it up. Mama's
dead baby. You hurried, slopping and spilling, past the dripping
washing.

Kui had it by the feet and its mouth was opening and shutting, screaming. Ugly. Red, ugly face, dribbles, arms that moved,
tight hands. You dropped the bread and tea, turned and ran.
Ahead of you Manny was jumping down the bank, throwing the
cup onto the wood heap, chucking the bread. You could hear Kui
Hinemate laughing.

In the house the two of you sat against the wall holding on
to each other. 'Silly,' Mama called. 'Come and see. Little sister,
come and see.'

'A baby, not dead,' Manny said, jumping up, egg-eyed, and
you went out with him to where Kui was giving the baby to
Mama.

When our father came home you all ran to meet him, Manny
ahead because he'd been born feet first. Then Dadda went running
home fast on his short legs and you all crowded round as he
picked up the bubba who could move her head and twist her
mouth, who had to have a nappy on her bum, a bandage on her
puku, a dress and blanket to keep her warm.

After Dadda had put the baby down, he took his rabbit gun
from the corner and stood on a box to get the bullets from the
ledge.

Sometimes you Manny and Chum went with him just as it was
getting dark and you'd sit on the hillside as the rabbits came out
to feed. Dadda would lift the gun carefully and look along it while

you sat without breathing. The shot would zing out and you'd hear the dull knock of it hitting, watch the white leap and drop of the rabbit and the white-flashing run of the others, zigging and zagging away.

You'd run, wanting to be the one to pick up the dead-eyes rabbit with its twitching legs and ears, to be the one to carry it by its warm back feet, but it was always Manny who was there first. After a while, as you waited, the other rabbits would come dawdling back, nibbling, twisting their ears.

At home Dadda would hang the rabbits upside down in the tree while he sharpened his knife. He'd cut quickly round the feet, slit down the legs then pull the skin down, cut the neck and pull the head and skin away. Headless, skinless, pink rabbit with lumpy, dark blood where the neck had been chopped. You would look for the red hole in the head behind the big eye, talking about the bullet and the blood.

Dadda leaned by the lamp to put the bullet in, then went outside and shot up in the air so that everyone would know the new baby, not dead, had been born.

And that made seven.

thirty-four

Red earth woman
Your children are crying.

There were two coming along the road a long way off. One was our mother, one was the cousin. Slowly. They had a bag.

'Shush, Bubba, Mama coming,' you said trying to stop our sister's grizzling, 'Chumchum, Mama coming, Manny, Manny,' you called. Chummy came running but Manny had gone. There was mimi down Bubba's legs and the dust had stuck to it. Her dress was wet and she had a mucky face, sticky hair and a bleeding sore on the back of her head. You tried brushing her down.

You watched Mama get under the fence wires and hold them apart so that the cousin could get through with her bag. For a while the two went out of sight, then you saw them coming across the paddock, and as they came towards you up the bank you heard their voices and the sound of manuka swishing, and you and Chumchum grabbed Bubba by the arms and ran with her, hurrying to the tankstand to hide from that new voice, that cousin. Our mother called from the yard but you didn't answer, and when Bubba started grizzling again you told her to shush, shut up.

When Mama and the cousin went inside you came out from under the tankstand and crept along the side of the house until you found a hole in the wall. You put your eye to it. 'Uglee,' you said, moving back so that Chummy could see. He eyed in through the hole then put his mouth to it. 'Uglee,' he whispered, 'uglee, uglee.' After a while our angry mother called to you to come inside to do this, do that.

'Only me been looking after Bubba,' you said as you went in. 'Bubba done mimi, Bubba done tutae.' Then you had to run out to get the washing off the line because Mama was stamping. After that you had to take Bubba's nappy, running with it to the dunny, where you shook it over the hole until the lumps loosened and dropped, back again to put it in the bucket under the tank-stand. 'In trouble, you,' you called to Manny who was coming along the side of the house.

'Got tuna,' he said, which meant he wouldn't be in trouble at all, bloody bugger.

'Good, good boy,' you heard our mother say.

Then Mama and the cousin came out. Mama pointed the way to the dunny and the girl walked along the track, walked silly.

'Mama, Mama, Manny never look after Bubba, only me.' Sore-face Missy.

'I heard you getting smart to your cousin,' Mama said.

'Run away and played.'

But Mama just waited by the path for our cousin and told you to show her where to wash, which bowl, which water to use.

So you showed her the basin, water, soap, towel, pointing there, there, there, there. Grizzle-guts. You watched our cousin's face redden, watched her slow eyes looking at this and that and her slow head moving this way, that way. Wondered if she'd had a pie and a raspberry drink on the train.

And later, when our mother dished out the eel and potato, you still had the hump, throwing your eyes round to see if she gave Manny and Chum more than she'd given you. The cousin had a big lot and didn't know how to eat properly. 'Maluna, I love my silver belly tuna,' our father sang about the eel.

After tea you got into bed crying and calling for Bubba, not wanting the cousin in your bed. Also you knew that our mother didn't like you. Only Manny and Chumchum had been allowed out in the dark playing ghosts instead of getting the wood in. Only Manny and Chum had been allowed to get changed by the fire. Bubba was in Mama's bed, sucky-noise Bubba. Bubba, cuddle and warm. You moved hard against the wall as our cousin got into bed beside you.

Mama went outside with the dish water and you heard the water swish across the grass, heard the bowl rattle against the side of the house as Mama leaned it. Dadda was out there too and you could hear the two of them whispering. You poked a hole in the paper that covered the wall cracks, pulled it back, put your eye to it but it was too dark to see. Mama and Dadda were out in the grass whispering and breathing, whispering and breathing, the grass whispering too. Whispering and breathing, breathing, breathing.

thirty-five

You went along the bank with Manny and Chum to a place where the creek was wide but shallow, turning the stones, peering into the mud until the water cleared, picking out koura one by one. Picked them up behind the heads, holding hard into where the pinchers joined so you wouldn't get nipped. And when the tin was full you came out of the water and tipped them on to flattened rushes in a clear place where Dadda had chopped the manuka down.

When you had come there with him in the weekend this place had been your house. There had been a roof of trees then and you hadn't been able to see the sky at all. 'My house,' you'd said, going from room to room, but Manny and Chummy hadn't taken any notice. Instead they'd watched Dadda stoning the axe, spitting on the stone, sliding it over the silver eyebrow of the axe. Quiet house with a wet-tree smell.

In your house you'd watched Dadda swing the axe back and down, cracking it low into the tree's leg, jigging it out again, swinging back, then hitting again, making a red smile in the leg of the tree. Cut, cut, fast into the smile. The tree cracked and Dadda had pushed it with one hand so that it fell, swishing down through other tree branches, hitting the ground, tossing and rolling. After that when you'd looked up, there was sky. Your house with all its walls falling.

You'd helped Dadda to drag the branches out into the clearing and he'd sent you all home with them. Returning for more, you'd passed him bringing the trunks on his shoulders. His face and clothes were wet, his neck was tight like a bundle of bull-rushes, he had bits of tree in his hair and he was lifting his eyebrows at you.

'Manny, Missy, Chum,' our mother called, and you ran along the tracks thinking of scaring May with the koura. There was something you wanted to ask Mama about Dadda.

'Yaar,' Manny shouted, poking the tin under our cousin's nose then taking a koura and chasing her with it. Our cousin ran, leaving Bubba to cry, running to Mama in the creek holding her clothes tight round her. Mama was wild with all of you.

Later you helped Manny to cook the koura, dropping them into the water, where they quickly turned pink. You watched as the colour deepened and when they were red enough Manny moved the tin to the edge of the fire with a stick and toppled it. There you all are, picking, cracking, tossing from hand to hand, scratching for tiny bits, huffing and blowing, looking through your eyelashes to see if May will eat, but she won't. Soon gone, and you're hungry still.

'Mama, Mama, is it paying day?'

Mama was picking up the water tins and starting up the hill. 'Bring the watercress,' she said.

'Is it paying day?'

'Yes.'

'Dadda coming? When . . . ?'

'How would I know?'

You picked up the watercress and followed after her. 'When?'

'Keep quiet. Shut up about Dadda,' she said.

That night you all sat up in bed waiting, counting to a thousand so you wouldn't fall asleep before bugger Dadda came home, but kept losing your way in the numbers. 'Pinch ourself,' Manny said. So you began pinching yourselves, and each other, to keep awake. After a while your fingers loosened, nails wouldn't dig, eyelids dropped. You went to sleep criss-crossed over one another like a bunch of scissors.

'I'm as free as the breeze,' our father sang, dancing into the yard, but you were all eyes-down on comics, wouldn't hear, wouldn't see.

I can do as I please
What's to stop me and why
Open road
Open sky.

And as he danced chewing gum began to fly everywhere. That brought all your eyes up, brought you to your feet. You left the comics and went running about the yard picking, picking, calling don't swallow. Don't swallow chewing gums or they stick on your rungs.

Ringa ringa pakia,
Waewae takahia
Ringa ringa i torona
Kei waho hoki mai.

Our father arm slicing, hip cutting, dancing on his bandy, silly legs.

MISSY

Turi whatia
Hope whai ake
Hei hei
Hei ha.

thirty-six

Old woman
Rotting
Gave an enchanted
Bone.

At the top you climbed on to the drum, looking down the long slope, wondering if you could. You spread your toes, gripping the drum's curved surface, bent your knees and worked forward to the edge.

Over.

At first you had it, walking it down, toes through to heels, thrusting the drum, getting faster, eyeing ahead down the slope, looking out for the holes and stones and ridges, riding them, beginning to fast foot on the rocking drum. But the worst bump was coming up fast. Could you?

You hit and flew — outwards, sideways. Smacked like a board against the hard hillside.

It was like night and day coming and going, star time without breath or sound. There you were pulling for breath, like fighting a way up from a deep creek hole, like reaching and pulling the water surface down over you, pulling, pulling, until at last you gasped, until at last your ears caught sounds. 'Ha ha, Missy. Sweeta like-a lolla.' Hear it?

When at last you sat, pulling your knees into the circle of your arms, Jacko and Manny were both spreadarmed over the drum, arguing.

Over in Keita's yard the aunties and uncles who had come to

see Mata were passing tobacco, lighting up, laughing, talking, yack yack yack, talking Maori. 'Missy,' Makareta had said in the icy school playground, 'don't tell the teachers about Kui and me.'

At the beginning of winter Mama had fixed a cardigan for you — darned the elbows, sewn on buttons and rolled the sleeves up. On the morning of the hard frost you'd done up the buttons and unrolled the sleeves so that they dangled, covering your hands, then you'd gone running through the stiffened grass and poroporo to the top of the bank, flapping. No hands.

From the bank you'd seen the white paddocks and the icy banks and ridges, and across the first paddock, like a chain, were Manny's footprints. He was running over the brittle ground with his white breath streaming. You saw him stop at the beginning of the school track, hopping from foot to foot by the creek, bending, picking up stones.

You ran, with your own white breath pouring about you, Chumchum behind you, slapping his arms, hissing, calling out to you.

At the creek Manny was dropping rocks on the glass ice, which shattered like windows, and you watched him pick up a large ice piece, melting, dripping, and take a bite of it, cold eyes shocked and feet dancing. Eating windows. Hotcold. You stepped red-footed onto the hotcold ice, found a jagged piece and bit. But back along the track there were others coming. Jacko and Alamein.

You, Manny and Chum ran with your ice and hid in the hard ferns. 'See you, Manny; see you, Missy and Chumchum,' Jacko and Alamein said as they came. They were stepping carefully and their eyes were going from side to side, but you knew they couldn't see you.

When they came near, the three of you ran out, knocking Jacko and Alamein down and putting ice down their necks sweeta like-a lolla. Jacko got you too, clapped his ice onto your ear, held it there, while Manny, Alamein and Chum rolled together yelling in the iced grass and ferns. Then you all jumped up and ran to school with your knees and feet cracking, bleeding onto the white ground.

At school the kids were jabbing their heels into the frozen puddles or skidding on the grass. The apple and plum trees were holding out hard, white branches, sills and ledges were ice crusted and kids were running their fingers along them, shouting and licking.

You waited by the gate for Makareta, who you could see coming with Kui Hinemate. 'Kui, there's ice frost,' you said when they came near.

'And naughty children have been playing in it, getting wet and cold,' Kui said, speaking in Maori, but you knew what she was saying.

'Speak English, Kui,' Makareta whispered in English. 'You're not allowed . . . '

'Your dress is wet and torn, your cardigan is muddy and your legs are bleeding. Your mama's going to smack you, I think.'

'Kui, Kui, the teacher will hear you,' Makareta said.

'We're not in school, Daughter, not even inside the gate. I'm not coming in to school, only going to do business at the post office on a frosty morning.'

'Kui Hinemate, Kui Hinemate,' Jacko and Alamein called from the fence. 'Kui Hinemate, there's ice frost.'

'Don't get wet, don't get cold,' Kui Hinemate called back, not in English.

'They'll hear you, Kui. You're not allowed.'

'Maybe that's right for you, Daughter, but this old woman speaks her very own language wherever she is, wherever she goes. Otherwise who is she? Now goodbye, Maleme; goodbye, Makareta. Don't be angry, Makareta.' You said goodbye to Kui but Makareta hurried away without looking at her or speaking.

The lawn in front of the classrooms had become a mud patch where children had been sliding, the branches of the fruit trees were hung with melting drops and the ledges were steaming. The bell was ringing and the kids were beginning to make their way through the cold, cold footbaths. 'Missy, don't tell the teachers,' Makareta had said, because she knows what a tattle-tattle you are. 'Don't tell the teachers about Kui and me.'

*

You stood, brushing the grass and sticks from your clothes and watching Manny come down the hill slope, thrusting from the knees, his eyes scooping forward seeking the rocks and bumps, his feet riding the drum and riding the space above it. Over the big bump he went, knowing it, flying away then landing again on one foot, two feet, hammering down the last slope to the bottom. You would too, next time.

Everyone was hungry and you looked each other over to see who should go and get bread. But you all had torn clothes, you were all bleeding and knew that any one of you would be in trouble if you went anywhere near the mothers and grandmothers. After a while you saw Makareta and Mata coming and as they came near you began asking Makareta to go and get bread for you.

Then the cousin, Mata, reached out an arm and opened her hand, and in her hand was the best marble.

There were no words for the marble. You all stared at it, stared, stared, and after that turned back to the drum, hungry, silent, waiting for bread, each of you holding a marble in your eye.

Makareta went back to the house and returned with bread, and when you'd finished eating you lay down in the grass, sore, wishing for more.

Then you sat up again because something was happening. Mata was reaching out and her hand was opening. Manny was reaching out and his hand was closing. No breath or breathing, no hungry or sore. In his hand. Manny had the marble.

Tell. You climbed up onto the fence. 'Makareta, Makareta,' you called. 'She give it to Manny.' Makareta, about to go into the house, stopped and turned. 'Makareta, she give it to Manny. She give Manny the marble.'

thirty-seven

At Little Marble Path a few small children were firing stones into the holes left by those who were more expert now and had gone on to Big Marble Path. The patch of ground was bare and hard and the trunks of the two big manuka trees were rubbed and smooth.

Big Marble Path led in among bushes and was wide in some places, narrow in others. The way was covered with smoothed-out holes, old and new, of hundreds of games played with bott-lies, teapots, chinas, steelies, stinkies and stones. Hear the rules — funks no funks, throws no throws, eye-drops no eye-drops, spans no spans, bully-toas no bully-toas, bowls no bowls, clears no clears. Ground packed hard, scooped, mounded and furrowed. Feet slapping up, down, up, down.

Hear also — liar, thief, cheat — in one language or another.

Bessie was the one trying to win the marble from Manny out on the longest range with the rule being No Nothings. Jacko was in charge of the start line, which was scratched in the dirt with a stick, one step further back for each game.

Bessie had her foot on the line, long front teeth hard over her bottom lip, no nothings, no nothings. Green and white marble rested on her forefinger, thumb-flicker sitting behind it.

Eyes. Watching for the funk, but only the thumb moved. The marble arched, dropped, shooting forward over dips and mounds and furrows halfway to the hole.

Manny — not with the best Mata-marble, which was the one they were really playing for — but with his second-best orange and white china, flicked hard and straight.

Followed her into the hole, then they were away, up and down Big Marble, up and down, up and down. Then off onto the narrow track, rough and stony, no clears no nothings. Until Manny dropped near enough for Bessie to try — No Funker, Far Flicker Bessie, but not so dead-eye. Nearly time for the bell.

Would she? No. Away again, back and forth, back and forth until Manny dropped close again, not too close, bell ringing.

Eyes half closed, long teeth biting, no funks no funks, flicked and missed. Manny was close enough.

Pinged her and picked up his marble, then Bessie upended him with a kick in the ankles. Bessie picked up her marble and ran.

You walked with Makareta, happy that Manny (which meant you, all of us) still had the marble. The others hurried past, Manny after Bessie calling, 'Keep your stink marble,' in the language not allowed to be spoken.

'Stick it up your bum too,' Jacko called.

You could see Mr Davis waiting on the steps as the bell jangled. 'Speak English, speak English,' Makareta hissed as they went by.

'Keep your stink marble,' Manny yelled in English.

'Stick it up your bum too,' Jacko called.

thirty-eight

Titama, Titama.

On the night of the concert you went out to the tankstand and told Mama that Aperehama would be coming to get you in the truck. Mama smiled, lovely Mama, wet, shivering, wrapping the towel round herself, putting her feet into old shoes. 'Good,' she said.

You stepped into the bowl, tucked your dress up under your armpits and began washing down. Hair there like Mama's, fluffy, curly. You squeezed the cloth against your stomach and watched the water run, slicking the little curls then running down your legs. Legs blotched from old sores, ugly. But you had a pretty place between your legs, pretty to touch. Your own little titties too that you liked. You dressed, pulling at the skirt, which was

too short even though you'd let the hem down as far as it would
go.

Mama was sitting in the yard with the scissors, her hair
brushed and parted. 'Cut some of these bits off, Missy,' she said.
You could hear Dadda singing across the paddocks and Wiremu
and Rapata were running to meet him.

About the two running brothers.

Wiremu was born the year after our sister Keita called Bubba.
He was named after our grandfather Wi. Rapata came two years
after that and was named after Dadda. You were their little
mother Missy on the days when our mother was too weak to lift
or carry. The blood, the blood! Nine of us altogether, if only you
could know.

'I told him not to get himself rotten,' Mama said as you began
snipping at the hair, standing back every now and again to see if
it was even.

'What you doing?' Dadda said. 'Dolling up?'

'I told you not to go getting yourself rotten.'

'Don't growl, my Glory.'

'You can stop home, that's what.'

'What what, my Glory?'

'Let him come, Mama,' you said.

'I told you. This morning I told you it's your daughter's
break-up and don't go getting yourself rotten.'

'Leave him, Mama,' Dawn Daughter, Dawn Daughter tying
the two together. 'Just as silly as him, Missy; that's what.'

You finished cutting and began rolling the hair and pinning
it up at the sides. You drew the rest back into a band, divided it
and combed it round your finger to make ringlets, like Dotty
Lamour's hair in *Road to Rio*, a film that had made you all laugh
though it was really about love.

Everything, everything was to do with love.

Now that there was a bus, and when there was money, you were
able to go to the pictures held in the high school hall on Saturday
nights. Sometimes there'd be a double feature — two long films,
all about love, which was what you liked best. On most nights
there'd be shorts to watch first — old newsreels, cartoons, serials,

also singalongs you could all join in, following the little ball that bounced in rhythm from word to word as the lines came up on the screen. Songs about love. But it was the main picture telling its story of love you waited for — of love found, love lost, love found again. You believed in love.

Cowboys saved townspeople from cattle thieves and death, snatched women and children from under the feet of stampeding cattle, walked into bar rooms and pulled card cheats up by their collars, threw themselves from horses onto fast moving trains to chase bad men over roofs and through carriages, between the wheels of trains. But it was to do with love.

Sailors and pirates had battles at sea, up and down rigging with their swords clashing. Or on land, in fine clothes, swords were drawn in velvet-curtained rooms and fighting ranged up and down stairways, across balconies, round pillars and poles, because of love.

Tap dancers and singers made their way to Broadway but nothing was more important than love. There were thieves and highway robbers saved from their bad lives by love. Even Mickey Rooney found his love. And when the picture was over and 'The End' scrolled on to the screen to music that was all about love, you always remained seated until there was nothing nothing more and the lights went on.

Gordon, the picture man, would pack away the projector and films, take the screen down, then he and his family would begin sweeping the hall. One night you'd asked Gordon when he was going to get another Alan Ladd picture. 'Alan Ladd, that's your heart-throb, is it?' he'd said. 'They say he's a bit short at one end. Has to stand on a step to kiss the ladies, or lean off of a horse.'

As you waited on the verandah with the primer children you could see Miss Jamieson at the piano, swaying a little in the light of two lamps held by Chum and Billyboy. You listened as the first notes of the mazurka sounded, picking in and out among the old reeds and boards of the meeting house before joining together filling the spaces, sweeping upwards, finding ribs and rafters. Then the notes came down, dispersing, until there was only one left. The people held themselves still for it, let it cling to them, then whistled and applauded. You walked the little children round to the side entrance and lined them up for their items.

'Send them in, Maleme,' Mr Davis said. He was wearing his dark-blue suit and a blue tie you thought might be new. It matched his eyes.

One day when you'd taken a message over to his house, Mrs Davis had been sitting on the back steps knitting a pullover, and not long after that Mr Davis had worn it to school. 'I said four o'clock, Maleme,' he'd said, returning to the classroom on that pullover day. 'You were supposed to go home at four.' You kept your head down, kept on writing, even though you'd wanted to look at him. Like Alan Ladd, only bigger, and would've looked all right in cowboy trousers, boots, chaps, gun belt, fringed jacket, big hat. On wet days he wore a floppy cloth hat to school.

You finished the line you were doing, numbered down, ruled off and put the work on the desk in front of him as though it were a prize. Sometimes the punishments he gave made you feel like laughing. 'Don't forget,' he said, 'cans for you tomorrow, extra duty on cans.' But he'd had a stranded look when he said it, as though he didn't believe. The new pullover was blue like his eyes.

It was Jacko who had called you Missy Can-can because of the number of times you'd been given extra duty emptying lavatory cans. After school one day you'd gone to the lavatories for the first can and taken it to the end of the playing field where the boys were digging the trenches, but listen, 'Missy Can-can, Missy Can-can,' listen to Jacko. You were tipping the can when he said it. If you let him get away with it, it's who you are, Missy. You climbed through the fence, ran right round the edge of the playing field and climbed back through, went up behind him and shoved. Good, my sister. Up to his shins, pitching sideways. Hi Ha!

Coming out of the classroom behind you with a bundle of books, Mr Davis had said, 'Can you get these keys, Maleme, and lock the door,' jingling keys on his little finger under the pile of books. You unhooked them, locked the door. 'Drop them in my pocket please.' Then he'd asked, 'What do you do . . . when you're away, when you don't come?' A question trapping you. Not a little girl any more, too big not to answer. 'We don't want them knowing our business,' Mama had said. But Mr Davis hadn't waited for an answer. 'You'd better go,' he'd said. 'You were meant to go at four.'

You ran out of the gate, listening to your feet echo on the pumicy ground. *Not so smart/cause Gloria/Is not in love/With you.* Which was nothing to do with it.

Nothing.

But you were pleased to have escaped the question.

The bleeding. Someone had to get water and wood on the days when Mama couldn't walk or lift or carry. Someone had to lift the babies when she wasn't strong. Someone had to bring the bucket, wash the cloths and clothes. 'It's only you can help me, Missy,' Mama had said, her voice just a whisper.

It was time. You tucked the pois into the top of your piupiu, started the song and led the seniors in for the final items. The audience, recognising the tune that came from the dark, began to applaud, and as you moved into the light they joined in the singing, watching every movement and every expression to see if eyes, faces, hands, the click clicking of the skirts matched what the words and voices told, as one song moved into another. You caught a glimpse of Dadda leaning in through the window, knew Mama would be wild with him for singing so loudly.

People watched and began to applaud again as the canoe formed, the poi balls making white waves beside it, white birds above, taking them on long, long journeys.

But they became quiet when you and Tati walked out into the space at each end of the canoe and started the long pois circling, held breath as your wrists secured the rhythm and your feet and hips began to turn, head and eyes shifting, watching the turning balls. 'Hey Missy, hey,' you heard our father call as the clapping and whistling broke out all around you — you and your big teeth, smiling.

On the way home in the truck Manny stood on the tray and sang 'Bid Me to Love' like Mrs Davis, then 'Dayo' like Harry Belafonte, everyone joining in. His feet moved as though he was riding the drum,

MISSY

Come Mr Tallyman,
Tally me banana.
Daylight come
And I wanna go home.

E rua nei aku ringa
E rua nei aku ringa
E rua nei Baba Lou.

You took your new pen out of its box, hooked it to the top of your blouse and pressed it against your chest, your heart. Blue as the sky. You and Billyboy had been given the pens as farewell gifts from the school committee and Mr Davis had said good things about you when he presented them, things that made you feel lonely and strange.

The beams from the headlights cut through each other and picked out the bumps and dips as the truck footed round the hills. 'Dark moon,' our father sang and everyone else stopped singing because they wanted to listen to his voice.

Away up high up in the sky,
O tell me why,
O tell me why,
You've lost your splendour.

The song hadn't got to the top of the hit parade because of 'Love Letters in the Sand', but you'd liked it better. Your light withdraws. Is it because I've lost my love?

Mortals have dreams,
Of love's splendid schemes,
But they don't realise,
That love can sometimes bring,
A dark moon, Baba Lou-a,
I hear you calling, calling,
Calling for me,
E rua nei aku ringa.

I have two arms, Baba Lou.

thirty-nine

Y ou followed Rahera onto the bus on your first day of high school and suddenly found yourself sprawling in the aisle with Billyboy on top of you. Everyone in the bus was laughing. Manny, coming in behind, grabbed the boy who had tripped you, pulled him to his feet by the front of his shirt and punched him out of the door. The driver turned in his seat, put his foot into the middle of Manny's back and sent him flying out too, turned back, slammed the door and drove off.

Noise. Some were laughing, others shouting, swearing, telling the driver to stop the bloody bus. But he drove on, clicking his chewing gum, swinging the big wheel this way and that travelling the winding road.

At school the driver took you to the headmaster's office along with Billyboy and the swearing cousins. 'I won't have it,' the headmaster shouted. 'You pa kids and you mill kids fighting in the bus on the first day.' He was oversized, red and spitting, with ears that might fly him away. 'Thistles,' he said. 'Report at lunchtime and you can dig out thistles. Next time I'll cane the lot of you.'

You and Billyboy were put into 3C, and Alamein told you that the pa kids were always put into 3C. 'It's the bottom class, the dumb class,' she said. 'Teachers don't like 3C.'

You'd looked forward to starting high school, having shoes, having new clothes. And you'd liked the idea of having new books and coloured pencils to make maps and diagrams with, like the ones Makareta had shown you in the books she'd brought home from boarding school.

But much of the time in class seemed to be spent copying work from books or the blackboard, work that you didn't understand and that was never explained. If you tried to work neatly someone would lean over and blob ink onto your book. You always had to make sure you got them back, otherwise how could you be you? After a while your books and the books of the others in the class began to look like the half-used books that Manny used to bring home — blotted, smudged, the edges of the pages scuffed and grey and swollen.

Our brother Manny didn't return to school after being kicked off the bus. He was fourteen and a half and Dadda found him a job on the roads. He saved money and bought slippers for Mama and sometimes at night our mother would put them on and sit holding her feet in front of her. When she went to bed she'd put the slippers away in a box under the bed where she kept her wedding shoes. Ha, you were jealous about the slippers, wanted to work and have money so you could buy something for Mama too. And Manny was putting money in a tobacco tin, saving for a new house, he said.

One lunchtime in the second term you were watching the older girls practising basketball when the sports mistress asked you to fill one of the places. Afterwards she told you you could be in the team if you had black stockings and basketball boots. Hi Ha! Basketball was for you. All afternoon you could think of nothing else but how you could get stockings and boots.

That was the day you found out that if you sat at the back of the room, kept quiet and pretended to write, then nothing would happen to you, and that if you didn't hand your book in at the end of the lesson it wouldn't be asked for. And from that time onwards you spent much of your time in class copying words of songs into your hit parade book, or writing the names of singers, decorating them with loops and swirls and coloured pencils — Elvis, Patti Page, Cry Johnny, Frankie, Louis, Debbie, Harry, Pat Boone. In your own world, Missy.

By the end of the afternoon you'd worked out what you would do.

After school you didn't get on the bus to go home. Instead you went out the back gate and ran the five miles into town to wait across the road from the pub for Dadda.

He didn't see you at first, not until you walked up beside him smiling your best and taking his arm. 'Dadda, I'm in the basketball team,' you said.

'Hey, my Missy.'

'I need money for stockings and boots.'

He laughed, putting his hand into his pocket. 'Look at this,' he called to one of his mates. 'My daughter come to take my money before I swallow it.'

'That's the girl,' his mate said.

'In the basketball team. Shoes and whatnot.'

'Good on you, girl.' The man raised his eyebrows and crossed the road. 'See you in there, Bob.'

Dadda pulled out a ten-shilling note and some coins. He gave you the note and you pick, pick picked the coins off his hand and went running. 'Hey, what about my beer money?' he called. 'Little bitch tart, worse than your mother.' Laughing as he crossed the road.

Mama was angry with you at first, until she realised what a good idea it was. 'Every pay day,' she said, whispering with the wonder of it, 'you can go and get the money and do our shopping. I can go down Keita's and ring the shop to get the order ready for you.'

So once a week you'd go into town, and after you'd done the shopping you'd go to the pub where Bessie had a job as a kitchen hand. It was a warm place. Pay night was the busy night and the boss didn't mind you coming in if you wanted to help. You could make tea and toast for yourselves as long as the work was done. The pub was meant to close at six but it never did. It was always eight or nine before Dadda and Nonny came out and you started for home.

There was a fourth-form girl called Ama who had a scrapbook of film stars. Some of the pictures and stories had been cut from magazines but she had autographed photos too, which she'd written to Hollywood for. At lunchtimes on the days when there was no basketball practice you and Ama would sit with your song and star books and talk about the songs you liked, the pictures you'd seen, the film stars you were in love with. Even though Alan Ladd was still all right, Johnny Weismuller, Hedy Lamarr and Margaret Lockwood the wicked lady were your favourites at the time.

At home there was some excitement because fundraising had begun for the new marae dining room. Every Saturday night there were card evenings and socials, and once a month, dances were held in the local woolshed. You'd be there helping to sweep out the shed, cover the walls in ferns and decorate one of the shearing stands where the band would play. Outside, a tent would be put up for the beer drinkers. And lights would be rigged up on poles — the way men do it — with leads running everywhere. You all learned to step over connections and duck under loops of cords. If you tripped or tangled yourself, all the lights went out. All very 'behind', according to Tuahine.

Tuahine was Billyboy's older sister who had gone to the city to work. She came home telling of the films she'd seen, the dances she'd been to, the good times she was having. Jingly Tuahine. See her? She had clothes, hairsets, money in her pocket and lived the life of a movie star, it seemed.

But still she always turned up to the woolshed dances, in her cerise or burnt-orange clothes, her hairsets, bright lipsticks, nail polish, three-inch heels and dangly earrings. She was the one who got you all rock 'n' rolling, laughing about it, telling the band their music was old and 'behind'. You followed her everywhere.

One night you were standing together under the light at the corner of the woolshed and looking across to the tent where the uncles were standing with their backs to you. Her three-inchers were sinking into the ground and she was throwing her arms about to balance herself and she yelled, 'Hell's teeth, butcher knives. All dressed up for the dance, big boots and butcher knives,' and sat down in the sheep dung and laughed until she cried. You laughed because she laughed — not because of the sight of our uncles bending their elbows, dressed in bush shirts and boots, their knives strapped round their middles. 'They'd die, they'd die,' she kept saying in amongst her laughing and crying. And you knew that 'they' were the city people who owned cars and radiograms and modern clothes, who saw all the latest films and lived the life of stars. You began to dream of having a share of all the up-to-date things, all the fun and excitement of city life.

Sometimes Tuahine brought friends home, along with cars and engagement rings. Ponty? He didn't fit your idea of 'star', in spite of his royal-blue suit, suede boots, string tie and sideboards.

He was little and old-looking. Manny and Billyboy were better, you thought.

He could dance though, rock 'n' roll like nobody's business, no matter how old the music. One night Tuahine threw the engagement ring at him in the middle of a dance and it fell down through the spaces in the floorboards. The next morning, when you were all cleaning up, she was under the shed crawling about in the sheep marbles, crying and looking for the ring. Her man was stretched out asleep under the pines and his boots were gone.

She found the ring and came up to help pull the ferns off the walls. 'I'm in love, I'm in love,' she was saying as she bobbled along dragging the fronds. 'Especially with the ring and the car.' You thought of being in love too, living the life of a star.

When you turned fifteen you took a job at the hotel. You liked the big kitchen with its wooden benches and big sinks where there was endless running water. Under the benches were shelves with curtains across them where all the pots and bowls were kept, and up above the benches were cupboards full of dishes. There was a special bench for salt and pepper shakers, sauce bottles, sugar bowls and butter dishes. There was an electric stove as well as a big wood stove that kept the place nice and warm. It was winter when you left school, and it was good to arrive at work in the mornings and walk into the warm room.

Not far from the job was the Moonbeam dance hall, which was an old pavilion in town that had been painted and hung with streamers, coloured lights and a spinning mirror ball — not a lot better than the woolshed apart from the mirror ball. But to you it was an exciting place, a star place, a place for music and dancing and love. The men in the band wore cowboy outfits that sparkled and played music on instruments that gleamed — even though they were no better to listen to than the home-grown woolshed band. The music was still out of date, according to cousins from the cities.

At the Moonbeam you danced with your brothers and cousins and were in love with everyone else, dreamt of being danced away and kissed in moonlit gardens by someone glimpsed over Manny's or Billyboy's shoulder, who could look like Audie Murphy, Elvis or James Dean. Mortals have dreams.

On some nights the band leader would offer the microphone
to anyone who wanted to get up and sing. It took you a long time
to do it, but one night when your dress was all right and you had
new shoes, your feet took you to the stage steps, stepped you up.
Then you began to sing and every other sound stopped. When
you'd finished everyone clapped and clapped for you.

Your job was to rinse the plates and stack them ready for
washing, scrape and soak the pots and oven dishes then take the
bucket of scraps out and tip them into the bin for the pig man.
The dishes had to be put away and the woodbin kept full. And
when all the pots and pans had been washed you would help
scrub down the benches and mop the floors before Mrs O'Keefe
came back with the shopping.

It was a good job where you could save money. You thought
you would keep the job until after Makareta's birthday, then
you'd go and stay with Tuahine in the city, be a singer, be a star.

forty

The mists of morning sighs
Rise

You ran in the dress that Makareta had given you, calling to
her as the taxi moved down the wheel tracks. Bub was
behind you and our mother stood at the top of the drive, pressing
her hands to her chest.

Makareta was looking out of the back window of the car and
her hand was up by her face scarcely waving. The hair you had
just been brushing filled the frame that was the window.

When the car reached the road you stopped running, watched
until it rounded the corner leaving only the surging dust. 'I'll be
blamed, I'll be blamed,' our mother was saying.

Then, in the distance, there was another disturbance of the
dust. 'Buses, buses, Mama,' Manny said. The visitors were

arriving and you had all been left with the shame. There was nothing left to do but go and tell Keita, and everyone, what had happened.

'What is it, Daughter?' Wi asked Mama when you arrived at the house. 'I see she's not with you.'

'Gone,' our mother said, weeping and moaning as she told Wi what had happened. Men at the cooking fires were looking across, wondering what had gone wrong.

You crept into the house with Mama and Wi, a house suddenly quiet, eyes going from Mama to Wi and back again. You listened to our grandfather greeting the dead who belonged to the house and to those who belonged anywhere, then greeting the living before telling what he had to tell. You listened to the silence that followed and to the breaking of that silence as the women began to wail and cry. Our grandmother moaning, beating herself, let the korowai that lay across her knee slide to the floor. You saw Uncle Nonny, who had come from the cooking fires, standing at the door looking shocked at what he saw. 'Kua tae mai nga pahi,' he said.

Buses. The visitors would be getting out of them and waiting to be called in. Mama, beside you, waited, trembling.

'You did this.' It was Keita standing to accuse Mama. 'You before, now you again. It was you. You sent our granddaughter away, you and her mother between you. Planned this between you, thinking nothing of our shame. You could have been the honoured one yourself once but you didn't want that. You wanted that useless husband of yours instead. Now you've sent our child away out of spite, and left us with the shame.'

Keita wailed, clutching her chest as Wi and Aunty Henrietta took her by the elbows to sit her down.

Who would help Mama?

Koro Paora rose to his feet and talked about what had happened, about the visitors, who they were, why they'd come, telling everything, to give people time. 'We don't want to keep them waiting too long,' he said. 'But before we call them we have to decide what we will do, must find our own peace first.' He sang his peace song.

After that the house was quiet again, waiting. Mama, beside

you, was still trembling. Who would help her? Keita, opposite, held the cloak against her, her nostrils wide and her face drawn and pale.

Everyone waited and only the eyes moved.

You stood. The eyes shifted to you, and words, that at the moment of standing had been only a thought, were coming from you, shocking and loud. 'I want it to be me,' you said.

You waited, but there was no movement, no sound, so you said, 'I want to be the one,' and remained standing with no more words to say, knowing you must not sit down even though our mother's hand had reached to sit you.

Stood in the centre of the circle of eyes, not knowing if the people would sit you down or sing for you. Quite still, no matter how loud the heart. And not heeding the feeble voice of me reminding you of your dreams. The singer, my sister, what about the singer?

Waiting, for them to see, understand.

Waiting to know if they would sing for you in your yellow dress, standing where the light slanted in through the window. Behind you were the pale face, the flickering eyes of the ancestress, around you the silence of the house.

Watching.

Grandmother Keita, a movement of the head.

Then Keita stood, unfolding the cloak and came toward you. You stooped so that she could put the cloak round your shoulders and press her nose to yours. You remained there holding the eyes, while Keita returned to sit down. The people sang for you and you were the one.

You were taken out onto the verandah with the old ones, where the women started to call and the visitors stepped on to the marae where the straw had been spread.

Bringing someone for you.

At first you saw only his feet, which was all your lowered eyes could see, feet in polished black shoes walking forward with all the others through the sticking straw. The callers brought the visitors closer, and when all the feet stopped moving, you listened to the wailing of women that occurs when family meet family.

The feet turned and the group went to the seating that had been arranged for them.

It was during the speeches of welcome that you heard his name for the first time and still you had seen only his feet. Even so, you knew you could love.

As the speeches went on through the afternoon you were glad of the cloak about your shoulders as a cold dusk settled. Our mother, beside you, whispered, 'I'll help you, Missy, if you can't love.' But you knew you could love. 'Keita's been there,' she said. 'It can't be just anybody. They have to honour you.'

'Where's Dadda?' you asked.

'Drunk. Asleep. Manny and Nonny tossed him in Aperehama's car.'

The speeches ended and the old ones drew together to cry with each other and with you. Then his nose was pressing against yours. You saw that he was dark and solemn with a broad face and a wide body. His eyes were black-brown and he had lashes like brushes, eyebrows like brooms. His hair was thick and wavy, black and Brylcreemed.

Later, seated together at the table, you wondered what you should say to him. That morning you'd been someone different, a girl, full of the excitement of preparing for a party. Now you had chosen yourself to be a woman, to be the one. You wondered if Hamuera knew that it should have been someone else sitting there beside him. So much had happened that it was difficult to believe that only a few hours had passed. 'Did you have long hair before?' he asked leaning towards you. So he knew. All the eyes were on the two of you. 'Aunty Billy, the one with white hair, was telling me about someone . . .'

'My cousin, Makareta,' you said. 'She ran away this morning.'

And he laughed. You wanted to look at him but there were too many eyes. People were passing food, putting food on your plate that you couldn't eat. There were songs, gifts going from family to family. 'It could have been Zac,' he said. 'The one down the end there, older than me, but I'm the one keen on farming.'

'So they made you be the one.'

'They asked me,' he said. 'I agreed.'

As the meal ended you saw Mama talking hard to Dadda, who had just come in. She took him to greet the old people, then brought him to you and Hamuera. 'What do you think, Son,' he said to Hamuera after they had greeted each other. 'About having a boozer like me for a father-in-law?'

'Shut up, Bobby,' our mother whispered at him.

'Well you know, you know, he might like it. How do you know he don't like a few beers.'

'Keep quiet.'

'Yes, my darling, my Glory, don't growl . . . You see, Son, yackitty yack in your earholes night and day and so on. See, Glory, what you missed? You could had one of them instead of a drunk, shot-up bastard like me.'

'Should've too.'

'What you think? What you think, Son? What you think of my beautiful daughter here?'

'I think I'm lucky,' he said. There was a smile on the solemn face. You were glad to be your new self then, knew you could love.

When the clearing up had been done all the guitars were brought out and there was singing and dancing all night long — all the aunties getting Hamuera to dance with them, giggling, teasing, prying, gossiping, while his family danced with you. Late in the evening our cousin Tuahine danced up to you. 'How about you?' she said. 'Supposed to come to Wellington, you. Who's going to room with me now? Jeez, have to find me a man.' You knew you were saying goodbye to dreams, but still there was love.

MAKARETA

forty-one

My cousin Mata has walked into my life. We have lived in the same city for more than thirty years and yet our paths have never crossed during that time, I being incarcerated in my tower in one part of town, she being state-owned in another. Tonight by street-light our eyes met and knew each other.

It's many years since I travelled in the city buses. I had sold my car the day before, and after a late night at a farewell given in my honour I was waiting for a taxi when the bus came along. I liked the idea of a night bus ride during this, my last few weeks of living in the city. I was the only passenger.

Had I been in my car or in a taxi, perhaps there would have been no encounter. I stepped off the bus and hurried up to the house, knowing that from here I could observe the whole long sweep of road and know which direction she was taking.

She had walked since early morning, crossing suburbs, walking the streets, following many tracks and pathways as though searching for something — but she sought nothing, literally. She had only what was in her pockets and wanted nothing more.

Sought nothing, but our eyes found each other, which is an irony. I can give her some of what she has longed and waited for, but is now seeking not to have.

I need her. She has never been needed before.

She still has the same square body that we both had when we were girls. She has the same short, curly hair, turning grey now, the same sad and innocent look, the nervous hands that hold or pick at the sides of her clothes, the eyes that are unsure where to look. They are family eyes, and our eyes knew each other.

I love this city, the hills, the harbour, the wind that blasts through it. I love the life and pulse and activity, and the warm decrepitude. And I enjoy the work that I do which takes me into many forums. There's always an edge here that one must walk which is sharp and precarious, requiring vigilance. But I have decided it is indulgent to live here alone. Missy has been calling me home. Home has been calling me home.

I was twenty when I arrived red-eyed at Polly's. It was my birthday. She was in bed asleep and I tapped a shilling on her bedroom window to wake her. The taxi that I had taken from the railway station was curling away on the road behind me and the night was quiet and cold. Polly had been crying too. I got into bed beside her and told her all that had happened that week and that day.

I have never stopped loving my first home, but even though I missed it I have never been afraid of the city. I could often feel excited by the shops, the noise, the lights, the strange, waiting people and the hurrying — but it was a long time before I felt part of it. There was an angled hardness of buildings and a brightness that made me ache sometimes, an underfoot beat that burned the strength out of me. My cousins of the cat house smoothed their way through town like cream, wove in and out of traffic, stood loose against posts, pillars and walls and could disappear and reappear between one footfall and the next.

At first I thought of going to university, but there was a doubt, a feeling I had that I couldn't understand at first.

'Leave it for now,' Polly said. 'Leave it for a month or two. It's too late to enrol anyway. Let's just enjoy ourselves, Daughter. Give yourself time.'

It was good advice, because after I'd had time to think about the circumstances in which I'd left home, I realised that university was something I'd thought of because it would be acceptable to Keita and the family — something that could perhaps lessen the hurt for them of what I'd done. It could be seen as a reason, apart from the true reason, for me leaving. But it wasn't something I really wanted for myself. It was too clean, too easy. I wanted to try myself out.

When I asked Polly what she thought Keita and the family's reaction would be if I went nursing, she said they wouldn't like it. 'They won't like their puhi washing strangers,' she said, 'touching the heads of strangers, carrying pans, touching the dead. They'll think I've put the idea into your head because it's something I would've liked myself, something I could've done if I'd had a chance. I don't want you to do it because of me.'

But the more I thought about nursing, the more I wanted to do it. One of the reasons I'd left home was because I was never allowed to do anything there. In a place where everyone else worked hard I had never been allowed to work, never been allowed to dirty my hands. I'd been loved and given everything, and now my mother had used the word 'puhi' — the cherished, virgin daughter. I realised the aptness of the word as I looked back over my childhood and realised that I had been brought up as a special daughter, for an arrangement with a special son. I would've done it for them if I could, and felt an enormous sorrow when I left them all with the burden of shame. When I received a letter from Aunty Gloria telling me what had happened after I left, I was full of love for Missy, love and gratitude.

Once I had decided on nursing as a career, my mother wrote to her sisters in Auckland, both of whom had been nurses. They came down to see me, to get me ready they said. Aunty Nui gave me her nurse's watch, which had been to war and all, and Aunty Lex went out, bought material and made a linen bag for me. They had badges and photos to show me and all the advice in the world.

'Trying oneself out' wasn't an acceptable reason for becoming a nurse, I soon realised, but by the time my interview came round I had some sense of nursing as a vocation and was able to answer, adequately, matron's question as to why I wanted nursing as a career. I wanted to care for the sick, I told her, I wanted to serve humanity. Once I had made the utterance about caring and serving, I had no difficulty in making the ideology my own.

I was the oldest, at twenty, of the intake of probationers.

On our first day we gathered in the sitting room to be given our room numbers, linen numbers and allowance chits for shoes, stockings and studs. We were all watching each other, but I think I must have been the most watched one. I was the oldest by a few years, but I felt much older. And I was the most different, being Maori, and having plaits that wound round my head three times. We were all strangers watching each other, but mostly what I saw when I looked about was that everyone seemed to be watching me. The next day we went to our first class.

I liked the work and the learning, the strict routines, the uniforms and insignia and the way of life. Boarding school had prepared me for some of it. I liked the people that I worked with, including those who had authority over us, but had no particular friends. Boarding school hadn't prepared me for that. I seemed to be always set apart, people stood off from me. It was rumoured that I was a princess. 'It's because you look stately,' Polly said. 'And because you're Maori and you're top of the class. It's hard for them to understand that, a Maori being top of the class, that's why they have to make you a princess.'

So nursing was my vocation. I loved, most of all, to work in the wards, attending to the needs of the patients, although it was difficult for me sometimes. I was lucky that I had Kui Hinemate beside me, or inside me, or wherever it is that she speaks to me from.

First of all there was her disapproval to deal with, but I'm a daughter who has always had her own way. I had to make her know that this was something I really wanted to do. After that she helped me.

When there were things that felt wrong for me — touching the dead who were not my own dead to touch, shifting the bed of the dead into a ward for the living, handling the linen of the dead and depositing it with all the other linen without any clearing, preparing the room where someone had died for someone else to come into — she helped me to have the right karakia to say and to do my own cleansing. They were the customs I had observed so well as I journeyed about with old ones when I was a child, everything that Kui Hinemate and the grandmothers had taught me that would keep me safe during my life. But I did them surreptitiously. Being thought a princess was enough, I didn't want any more rumours circulating about me.

So it was a double life, as my life always has been in the city, but it became less difficult as I understood it more. It's an absorbing and interesting life as long as you are certain, and as long as you keep hold of who you know you are.

There were other areas of difficulty for me. Maori patients

would see me, perhaps just as I passed by, and would call to me or send for me and want me to attend to them. They would want only me to touch their heads or attend to personal matters. I longed to do what they wanted, and sometimes did, but the hospital was a place of territories that were strictly and jealously guarded.

I was twenty-nine when I married Mick. He was thirty-six and had been married before. He came into my ward after an operation followed by complications that nearly cost him his life. It's easy for patients to fall in love with those who care for them. Sometimes it is fleeting, over once the patient has gained his strength. I wasn't one, myself, to fall in love, even though I often searched in my heart to decide on what was compassion and what might be love.

About two weeks after Mick left the hospital he rang and we arranged to meet. I was looking into my heart. We went to a cabaret and I felt relaxed and happy with him as we danced or sat and talked together, and at one stage he reached out and touched my hair and I allowed his hand to rest there and his fingers to drift through a loosening strand. That's when I knew that I would marry him. It is my hair that has linked me to all those who have ever loved me, and only those who loved me, and whom I loved, could touch my hair.

We married at the end of that year. It meant an end to my nursing days, there being no true place for a married woman in the profession in those times. We bought this beautiful house, here in this inner-city suburb of beautiful houses — a house on three levels, with many rooms. It is large and spacious and I have a view of the wonderful harbour. Also it is private and enclosed and I have surrounded it with the trees and ferns of home, but it is an indulgence now that I am alone.

Our twins, Michael and Kate, were born the following year, and while they were little Polly came every day to help me look after them. She was an important part of our lives. The children were her life.

I enjoyed those times at home together when the twins were little, but also there were events taking place that were exciting. 'It's all our people, on the move,' Polly called to me one morning as she stepped out of her little car waving the morning paper. Michael and Kate were five by then and had just started school.

She was talking about the Maori people assembling at Te Hapua to begin the Land March that would bring them from the top of the North Island to Parliament with their Memorial of Rights. 'Not one more acre,' she called up to me as I came out onto the balcony.

This was a different Polly, a more flamboyant, eccentric Polly than the one I remembered as a child. She had put on weight and always dressed in bright clothes. It was as though the parrot house had somehow worked its way into her and shown her the brightness of herself. On the other hand, I suspect she had always known the brightness that was within her.

I was beginning to hear over radio and television, and to read in the papers, some of the things I'd heard talked about as a child — Raupatu, Te Tiriti o Waitangi; also the Native Land Act, the Public Works Act, the Town and Country Planning Act, the Rating Act, the Counties Amendment Act and all the laws that had been passed that gave Pakeha authorities power to seize or obtain Maori land. 'Not one more acre' had become the catch-cry of the land marchers.

We followed the news every day as the marchers progressed down the island, and when they reached the outskirts of Wellington for the last part of the seven-hundred-mile journey, we decided we must join them. We put our raincoats and a bottle of drink into our car and drove out to meet them, leaving our car and joining them just as they came down the street from the marae where they had spent the night. There were people coming from all directions to join. It was exciting. There were people I hadn't seen for years, some from home, some I'd gone to school with, some from nursing days, some whom I remembered from going here and there with Kui and my grandparents when I was a child.

We moved at a much faster pace along the motorway than I thought we would. There was a sense of purpose and strength, feelings of exhilaration and euphoria. We walked under a washed sky, to one side of us the green, rolling hills covered in new spring grass. On the other side cars went by, the people in them sometimes acknowledging us with a wave or a toot of the horn, while others, with averted faces, showed their scorn or hostility.

Polly and I were near the end of the column, from where we could see the front marchers a mile ahead of us. But we were all like one, a whole. The broad back of us undulated and swayed with the dips and curves of the road. There were times of quiet and times of singing, the songs coming from the front and being picked up row by row, and as we went down through the Gorge our voices echoed off the hillsides. It became overcast, and when we arrived in the city rain began. Beside us on the road the cars and trucks swished through the wet, and the front of our formation turned up the street to Parliament, where we all eventually assembled and the Memorial of Rights was presented.

That night our house was full of people who needed to wash and rest. We cooked a big meal and had extra mattresses and blankets brought up from Polly's so that people could sleep. It was a night of singing and talk and stories, one of many such nights, because it was from that time that I began to be involved in the many activities and movements of the people in our determination that our existence, culture and values be recognised — that we as a people survive and have authority over our lives. It may have been the beginning too of what eventually led to the break-up of my marriage.

Everything I did during those years Mick seemed to support, and I know we really did love each other. I know he really cared for Polly and valued the time she gave to the children. He had a business to run and I supported him in it, I think, in every way I could. I accompanied him to the right social occasions and knew all the right things to do and say. I organised dinner parties and felt at ease in any company. I was interested by any company.

At the same time I was aware that I was an oddity in the various circles. Exotica of a sort. But I was untroubled by that and found it an interesting challenge to fit myself in to whatever the occasion. People were careful, or careless, when they spoke to me, but the careful and careless alike had an awareness of me, a certain wariness, because there was a whole otherness to me that was beyond their comprehension. I did not exult in this, and nor was I troubled by it. Polly thought it was funny. 'If you're a princess,' she said, 'that must make me the queen.'

The outward signs of the distress of our people were there in the streets. For years we had been told through statistics and through the media of our lowly position, our poverty, our bad health, our underachievement, our unemployability and our criminality. We didn't need to have these things spelled out to us, because we were living them, or living next to them every day. They were the things I'd seen and heard talked about when I was a child. Now our sorrow, our powerlessness and our destitution were out there in the streets for everyone to see.

There in the streets groups of men terrorised each other, brutalised the women that lived with them and caused fear wherever they went. They were the beaten, the hollowed-out of our people, the rawakore, the truly disinherited, where nothing substantial was inbuilt and nothing was valued or marvellous — where there was no memory, where the void had been defiled by an inrushing of anger and weeping. No one had loved their hair. Or, if sometimes they were not the disowned and disinherited, then they were those who had learned to look at who they were in distorted mirrors, had seen awry reflections of themselves and had become traumatised. And their stories of self-hatred were told in their foulness and self-defacement, their maiming and their havoc. They guarded what was left of themselves with weapons, high walls, and dogs.

There were children too, mauled and ravaged, committing slow suicide with petrol, pills and glue. Pretty children in large coats who inhabited the subways, doorways and pathways of the town. None of us could be unaffected by them and no one was blameless.

But we were up and walking, up and talking because we needed our own answers. We were the ones to know the missing pieces that had to be salvaged and reclaimed before they became irretrievable. I think Mick understood these things too, because we talked often about them, but perhaps he didn't feel the same as I did.

My life became extremely busy, my knowledge of our language and culture being needed everywhere as we sought our own solutions. There were issues of land, language, health and

welfare, money, work, education, customs and culture to be discussed, promoted and worked on. And I began to hear our language in places where I had never heard it used before, in places
where I never thought I would hear it. I began to see our rituals
and ceremonies used in unusual ways and places, not always in
ways that I thought the old people would approve, and sometimes taken over by people who didn't understand them and who
had their own agendas — which is another theft, another
treachery. Sometimes, for all the work we did, the hopes we built
up, the results obtained were mere dressings that covered ever-
deepening abscesses.

There were those among us too, building their own empires,
who postured and posed and traded on the mystique of being
Maori, and there was, therefore, a need to challenge, expose, con-
front — the way that women often do, not that women were
always the blameless ones. As a people we had our own con-
voluted minds to straighten out, our own anger to deal with, our
own priorities to set, our own hakihaki, our own mortiferous
sores to tend to.

Double everything.

There were frustrating times and good times. There were
times when I was away from home for days on end, times when
Mick and I saw each other as one arrived and one departed from
an airport, but I felt the importance of the work I was doing. I
had been given knowledge, understandings in my childhood that
I knew I must share, yet all the time there were obstacles —
because culture is deep. It is deep. Even the remnants or the memories of it are deep. It is not something that can be adequately
explained to those of another culture, but neither should it need
to be explained, I think. It only needs, at the least, to be allowed,
to be let be, to be trusted. But there was, is, fear out there, fear
that is difficult to allay and difficult to comprehend. Polly said,
'They think if our children are taught their language we'll all have
to cook in a kerosene tin on an outside fire again and we won't
be able to count our own toes.' My beautiful mother.

One afternoon she came with the children to pick me up at
the airport. 'I've ordered swings and things for the yard and I'm
having the fences done,' she said, 'then we're going to have a

kohanga at my place.' It was a bitter Wellington day with wind blasting from the south. She was wearing a red poncho with a black fringe and a knitted hat of Rastafarian colours. She looked like the sun. Michael and Kate were nudging each other and making eyes at me as we made our way to the luggage claim. 'About eight kids,' she said. 'Bonnie and me.' All the exhaustion that I had been feeling from work and travel fell away from me as she outlined what she had in mind.

It was ten years or more since I'd heard, with some surprise, the demand, by a small group who were being labelled radical, that Maori language be taught in the schools. I was even more surprised at the anger and controversy that these demands engendered in some circles, because I couldn't think how it would hurt or harm anyone if our children learned to speak the language of their parents and grandparents. I could only think how good it would be. I could only think of the hollowed-out amongst our people, the disinherited who were the truly poor, and of what we must do to make them whole again, what we must be allowed to do for the sake, not only of ourselves, but of everyone. I was incredulous that many people, some of them our own, would see this as detrimental, retrogressive, even sinister.

I attended the national gathering of elders held at Parliament where discussions were held on the various aspects that affected our people. I had been invited even though I was not an elder. The promotion of our language was discussed eagerly, and we talked about commitment, leadership, training programmes, the setting up of language boards, and of the language needing to be given official recognition and equal constitutional and legal status to English. It was painful to me to think that we were asking for official recognition of, equal status for, a language *in its own homeland.* How could that be? And this state of affairs, regarding the language, seemed to epitomise all that had happened to do with our land, our lives and our culture — having to ask, having to fight to retain what was our own and that belonged nowhere else in the world but here.

This didn't dampen the optimism of the group, however, and the following year, at a similar gathering, proposals were put forward for Maori language pre-schools to be set up. It was an exciting time with these kohanga springing up all over the country, and people having renewed hope that our language, through our own initiatives and via the little children, would revive and survive after having been suppressed for so long.

So I became excited over Polly's idea of a kohanga at her place and I helped her to set it up, remembering all the stories Kui Hinemate had told me, all the songs she'd taught me and all the games we'd played together. I realised with some sorrow that I had not taught these things to my own children. Nor had I taught Michael and Kate our own language, and at fourteen years of age they were wanting to know why.

Why indeed? I had as a child, or at least as I saw it, kept my life at home separate from my life at school. At school I saw my first language as something to be ashamed of, something that should be kept secret, a wrong, punishable thing — even though another part of me told me that it was language, and all that went with it, that gave me to myself, made me know who I was. And I realised later that having that knowledge, that security, that sound base, allowed me to reach out and to know that I could do anything else in the world that I wanted to do.

But my life had a different focus once I started work, and by the time I married Mick I hadn't spoken my first language for more than ten years. I remember him being really surprised when he found out, after several years of marriage, that I had this other tongue that was part of me, this other self that was also me, a whole other imprint. He was surprised and interested, and believed in me. That's what I thought. He came to understand that I was someone with the knowledge and upbringing that would enable me to take initiatives in the new activism. It seemed that way.

When Polly's kohanga had been running for two years she became ill and we persuaded her to have the children moved to another venue, where she could go as a helper two or three times a week until she was better.

But she didn't get better. Not long after her kohanga closed she was diagnosed as having cancer. She wanted so much to live, fought her death in a way I have never known anyone to fight, and took every treatment with real hope. Despite what I'd seen all through my working years, despite what I really knew, I hoped too.

She stayed on in the little cottage — the parrot house — for as long as she could. It was a comfortable house, which she had had renovated and modernised after I had come there to live. She was active for as long as she could manage, and liked nothing more than to take Michael and Kate to town on a Friday night. This was something they'd done together since the children were little. She'd buy clothes for them that they didn't need, and of a brightness never seen in a suburb such as this. They'd buy a packet of fish and chips each and eat from a hole torn in the paper, then go to the pictures or any circus or fair that might be on. The children were her life. She spoilt them.

When she could no longer cope on her own we brought her home and gave her the best care we could. It was during this time that Mick left. I suppose it was too much for him having Polly there, but he never said. He had agreed that we should bring my mother home and had always treated her with love and respect. It was the unhappiest time of my life when he left. I did love Mick and I did need him. I have never thought of love as not being forever.

I showed the children how to care for their grandmother and let them tend to her as much as they would, not wanting to deprive them of her dying.

Before she died she said, 'Take me home to Mum and Dad and Cissie when I go.'

It hurt me badly to hear her say that, and she saw that I was hurt. 'Remember that your home is not my home. Your turanga-waewae is not my turangawaewae, although mine is also yours. You must remember I only lived there a little more than five years, and remember I was only married to your father for two or three years.'

'But it's my home,' I said. 'It must be yours too.'

'It could have been my second home if I'd decided to stay, but you know how it is. I ran away from there.'

'They'll want . . .'

'No, my daughter, they won't ask for me. Or if they do it will be out of respect for you, and only because your grand-

parents are no longer alive. If Keita was still alive she wouldn't
let them ask for me.'

'What about me?' She didn't answer. 'I only have one home,'
I said. She wouldn't look at me. 'And when I go back there to
live, you won't be there, with Kui, Keita, Wi, the others who've
gone.' She wouldn't look at me, wouldn't answer because there
was nothing she could say.

And it was as Polly said. Her younger brother and older sister
came to live in the house with us during her last days, and as soon
as she died my Uncle Mat began preparations to return her to
their turangawaewae. I rang through to Missy, begging her to
bring the old people down to ask for Polly. They came, but as
Polly had said, it was out of love for me. Our elder made a long
and proper speech of it, giving his oratory the prestige of movement, gesticulation, haka tawhito and waiata tawhito, reciting the
whakapapa, explaining all that was already known, about my
father — who he was and who I was. He did all that in the living
room of this mansion in the suburb of mansions, where nothing
like it had ever been done before. There was no dishonouring of
me, no affront to my mother's family, but the gist of it was that
there was a place for my mother where my father would have
been buried, had he been brought home. There was a place for my
mother amongst her husband's relatives if her own family would
allow it. If her own family allowed it, her husband's family would
take her with them and she would be honoured as one of their
own. He told them of my strong desire for my mother to be
buried in our family burial place, where her descendants would
one day go.

He asked, but I had wanted him to demand, even though
demanding wouldn't have made any difference.

My Uncle Mat was brief in his reply, but it was not because
he wished to be curt. It was because speechmaking was not his
usual role, and also he was taken unawares. He thanked Nonny
for the honour to his sister of wanting to take her to the turanga-
waewae of her husband's family. He said that their own home
marae was already being prepared for her homecoming and that
they were all depending on him to bring her there. He couldn't
go away without her. He spoke of their love for me and reminded

me that my mother's home was also my home.

We sat in silence for a time after Uncle Mat sat down. I knew there would be no further plea. It was as Polly had said.

After a while Nonny stood again and said that our home marae was also being prepared, and that Polly must be taken there for a day and a night, to allow those who knew her to farewell her in a proper way.

So that is what we did. It may have been incongruous for this neighbourhood to have an arrival of old-model cars and vans, and a large group of mourners crying on the footpaths, the very elderly being assisted through our gateway and up our paths by the younger ones. The people may have looked shabby in their best-pressed black, their headscarves, their shawls, blazers and bomber jackets. It may have been quite shocking to those living round about to hear the karanga that called my mother's family, my father's family and the groups of friends into the house, and the calls of sorrow and acknowledgement as the groups filed in. It may have upset neighbours and passers-by perhaps, or it may have intrigued them. It comforted me to see the people coming up through the trees.

We took my mother back home for a day and a night before moving on to where all her family waited for her at her own place. I had to be satisfied with that but I found it difficult.

I thought Mick might return when she died, at least to pay his respects, but he didn't.

It was after Polly died that I decided to sell the house. Michael and Kate were eighteen by then, both in their second year at university but not wanting to continue there. They are alike to look at, both tall with dark hair and dark eyes, but with a paleness of skin that always reminds me of Kui Hinemate. They are different in what they want from life. Kate has always wanted to travel, Michael to go back home and become a proficient speaker of our language. So they have gone their own ways. I receive letters from Kate from different parts of the world, and letters from home from Michael. He is living with Missy until I arrive, and is spending as much time as possible with the elders. Also he is working very hard at a hydroponics project that he and Manny have set up there. It's an effort to make employment, to help us be in charge of ourselves and what we do, because it is an age of unemployment, and in this, our people, as always, are the ones hit hardest.

At first I did not intend leaving the city, despite messages from Missy that I was needed at home. I only wanted to sell the house and buy a smaller place. People are on the move these days and it is easier to keep a finger on the pulse living here. There are meetings all over the country as Maori people attempt to take their lives into their own hands, shape their own destinies. Brave people are demanding of government departments and through the media that our culture and language have recognition in the various institutions, even though it is an injustice, an absurdity, for a language and culture to be pleading its worth in the place that is its home.

There is work in the city that is important — information that needs disseminating to help people understand their history and their lives, help them to know that the position of powerlessness they find themselves in is not through any fault of theirs, because they, and those before them, have fought bravely throughout many years. They need to know that. They need to know that our truth does not appear on pages of books unless it is there between the lines. Our truths need to be revealed. But on the faces the truth is written, on the scarred and broken faces, in the sick, disabled bodies, in the dreamless, frightened eyes.

People need to know that there has been a massive robbery. There's been treachery, and they, the victims, are receiving the punishment day by day. Loser pays. If they have not fought bravely, or at all, it is because theft has been complete and includes theft of will to fight, theft of will to survive.

Survival, for those who could still will it, has been a groping in the dark. It has meant a dulling of memory, of the senses, of thought, of emotion, a loss of identity, as people sat at conveyer belts labelling tins, at machines fitting pockets into trousers, as they shovelled coal, rolled roads, cleaned sewers, washed floors, wet-mopped plazas, buffed corridors, carried wood and water, day after day and year after year until there was little left of themselves, little left for the children. Yet it was all meant to be for the children.

Or there was only anger or sorrow left, which became drunkenness or insanity. The lullabies were lost because lullabies take a long time to sing and there has been no time.

There is work to be done because people need to know of the tactics that were used to destroy the economic base of the people, of the weight of legislation by which land and resources passed from their control. They need to know what the yardstick is that they have been measured by in schools and workplaces, which found them always wanting. They need to know there is a health system that endangers them, sometimes puts them in risk of their lives, an education system that withholds knowledge, blunts understanding, erodes self-esteem and confidence. They need to know that people have fought bravely in the past and that they can fight bravely too.

Also it is time to revive the song, written by one of our most-loved composers, that tells us to beware of government welfare, which will control and enslave us and which will quiet our voices.

Yet it is difficult. What is there to live on now, for many, if it is not welfare? How do people become self-reliant when the wherewithal to do it has been robbed from them piece by piece. Should people struggle on and on blindly, each generation emptying itself out more and more, sacrificing their children? Because it is not as though there is nothing owed — yet it is more than money that is owed. I was brought up by my old people to be a keeper of the culture and a holder of the land. I could look upon that as a privilege. On the other hand, I could look upon it not as a privilege but a right — a right that others, through circumstances, have been denied.

My work around the city, around the country, is not always with Maori people. It is concerned with explaining to others, teaching, negotiating — though I've come to see now that my energies must go to my own. There is no time for everything. I love the work that I do, but I am tired.

The Treaty of Waitangi is a covenant that must reside as the base on which our society builds if there is to be a just society. I heard about the Treaty as a child, and knew it to be a treasured thing in the minds of those who spoke of it, an agreement on which the people, in spite of treachery, still based their hopes.

Now the Treaty, and all the issues surrounding it, is being discussed in Parliament, in government departments, in schools, but when you look at what the discussions lead to, you find no significant shift, no real change. You find instead deceit and procrastination as the different authorities pay lip-service while awaiting a change in emphasis, a change in government perhaps, a declining of the curve.

Yet some Pakeha people, those with pride, are genuinely seeking. These few are coming to understand that what they can do in the interest of justice is to know themselves, to understand their own true history, which also does not appear truthfully on pages of books, to understand the promises made on their behalf, to break their own silences, to search out the true meaning of racism and injustice, for which they are responsible only if they are inert. The seekers, the honest seekers, those taking measures, working out what can be done, are proud people who act from a base of self-worth, humility and dignity. They do not feel threatened, but challenged. They know they need not feel ashamed or guilty, because they are claiming their own, true heritage and their lives are honourable.

I'm tired. It's burn-out time, time to go home. Perhaps I will be able to rest there for a while, but perhaps not. Our home marae have become focal points again as people attempt to return to self-sufficiency and to regain self-assurance and self-love. There is a lot of work yet to be done. Missy has told me that it's not enough to send Michael up there with hydroponics, that I must come myself. There is knowledge I have been given that I must share in order to help people to be whole and strong.

I'm pleased to have Mata here. It means I don't have to send for Michael to come and help me, or to bother Heni and the others who have their own work to do.

Mata packs the household things lovingly, almost as though she knows about love. She's neat and careful and systematic in her wrapping and packing, says that wrapping and packing were the first jobs she had in the place where she has worked since she first left school. While she packs I sort and arrange my papers, see my lawyer and the land agent. Apart from that there are the many phone calls, the letters that come every day with requests for me to attend meetings, seminars, conferences. But I know I must rest for a while.

We're gradually getting everything packed away into three different lots — one lot to go to family at the parrot house, one lot to the cat house, and one lot to be stored until my new house is ready.

Now there is Mata to consider. I want her to come home with me to her land. Aunty Gloria has said that I must persuade her, mustn't take no for an answer. But all that she has agreed to so far is to assist me home. I cannot get her to agree to stay. She wants nothing, she says, which is what she has always had. I keep waiting for a change in her, waiting for something to happen. I don't want her to walk away from here to walk forever. Gifts are meant to be given, and one day returned. It must be her turn, again, to hold the coloured marble.

MISSY

forty-two

I was sixteen when I stood in the house, a year and a half out of school and three years from barefoot. If there was a little voice that spoke to stop me, I didn't hear. If the nudger nudged I was unaware. The girl in me was star-struck and in love with love.

Even so, when I think back to that time, I know it wasn't the romantic heart that stood me, although it was the romantic heart that, as always, took over. If I pare away at the whole mixture of emotions of that brief time from when Makareta showed us the letter to when I stood in the house, I know that the first movement — a silent drawing-back of a bare foot in the silent house — was made in defence of Mama.

The people in the house that day waiting for the visitors, but first of all waiting for Makareta, were mainly old people. Most are dead now, but thirty years later the story is still told and the events of the day are still talked about.

The dress that Makareta gave me was full-skirted, made of yellow taffeta, and had a goldish look because of an over-layer of off-white nylon. It had been raining but the sun was beginning to shine and I stood into it as it splintered through coloured glass onto the bleached flax matting.

Well, whatever the mixture of colour and light, it is said that my aura was golden — words used as if it is a miracle being told. They say that as they watched I grew taller, that my girl's body became the body of a woman, that as I waited the korowai came and placed itself around my shoulders, and that after a long time of standing while visitors waited at the gate, I sang an ancient peace song in the old language. One of the kuia saw a moko on my chin carved in the same pattern as the one the ancestress wore. I know that the old ones see the ancestors in different ways and in different places, and that they often see them in the young. This house is a place where the tipuna are seen by the ones who have the gift of seeing.

The woman in me knew that I could be the one, knew I could be who the people wanted me to be. If they sang for me, I belonged to them. If they sat me down, I was free to go to the world and the stars.

But I wanted them to claim me. I had no doubts at that moment. I was calm and unafraid as I was taken out onto the verandah, as I watched the feet coming through straw and as I sat through the afternoon waiting to see who it was, above the knees, being brought to me.

After that day Hamuera and I saw each other only twice before we were married. It wasn't that the families wanted to keep us apart, just that the time went so quickly and there was so much to do.

About a month after our engagement I was taken up to meet his great-grandfather, who hadn't been well enough to travel at the time they brought Hamu down. Before that I'd never been further than our little town, so it was a weekend of excitement for me, of trying to look right and be right, and of receiving all the advice in the world. It was a time of being with the old ones and all the sitting, waiting and listening that that involves. While Hamu and I sat holding hands, the old ones talked and laughed around us, commenting on how we looked together, teasing us one moment and in the next moment referring to us as the taonga, the treasures of the people.

At the time I waited patiently but listened with only half an ear to the old people, being aware all the time of Hamu beside me, thinking about what we might say to each other if we had a chance to be alone. Now, at this time of my life, I would give anything to listen to the stories that we were told that weekend about all the different taumau marriages that had taken place, or to remember the people who told them, but I was in love, full of love, sure I knew what it meant.

The only other time that Hamu and I saw each other was when the koroua died and we all went to his tangihanga. We were the dreamed-of couple bringing the families together at last. Eyes, all the eyes were on us, knowing everything.

It was when Hamuera first wrote to me that I began to doubt. He's a quiet man but his letters were talkative and clever — so schooled, so spelled, so neat, I thought. They reminded me of Makareta's beautiful schoolbooks and I began worrying that I hadn't been to school very much, remembered that I was from the 'C class' and that it was really Makareta who had been brought up to be the one to marry Hamuera, not me. Makareta was beautiful too — so dark and smooth-skinned, so gentle and *meant*.

I believed in love, the song kind of love, the movie kind, where two people are meant for each other. There you are, the woman. Somewhere in the world there is a man who is meant for you. You will meet and fall in love because of fate. It is destiny that unites true love. I began to doubt that I could be the one when it was Makareta who was meant.

And I began to have dreams in which I saw myself as Makareta. I had her dark face, her round, black eyes and thick black hair, which covered my back like a blanket. But in the dream I was both Makareta, whom I could see, as well as myself, unseen. The me that I couldn't see was in love with the me that was Makareta. I could hear the unseen self saying, 'Makareta, I want you to come home.'

In another dream I stood naked, knowing that somewhere there were clothes for me. I looked everywhere for them but found only newspapers or torn blankets, which I wrapped about myself. Keita, in the dream, said, 'No, no, you haven't found them. Go back and look for your clothes.' So I peeled the paper and cloth away, which had become like a layer of skin and saw that my legs were bleeding. They were full of holes out of which my blood was emptying. Mama was there saying, 'I didn't mean it, Missy. Missy, Missy, I'll wind you.' And she sat on the red ground and began tearing strips from her skirt, bandaging my legs and saying, 'When you take them away all the scars will be gone.' I would wake and think of leaving.

At first it was the letters that caused the doubts. Then it was seeing the houses go up that made me look into my heart.

After the visitors had gone Keita arranged for houses to be built on the adjacent land. It was land shared by the two families and now that the two were to be united it could be used.

It was tough land, swampy at the road's edge, then rising to scrub and manuka. Further back were sharp, tree-covered hills and heavy bracken where wild pigs and deer had done their damage.

Keita was used to hardening her heart. Her love for Makareta, her pride in the upbringing that they'd given to their special daughter, were still strong, but because of what my cousin had done Keita put love and pride aside and hardened herself. It was easy for her to do, like knotting sixpence into the corner of a handkerchief and tucking it up a sleeve.

Keita was only a small woman but she knew how to be big. Hamuera's family was giving a son, someone strong and good-looking, someone who had been away to school. His family had promised cows and a tractor as wedding gifts, and Keita had no doubt in her mind that our own family was being honoured by them.

Also she knew it was time to forgive. Not that our mother and father were deserving, not that they hadn't done wrong as far as Keita was concerned, but she'd been let down by Makareta, who had been given everything. I was looked upon as the one who had saved us all from shame.

So even though I wasn't the one who had been brought up to be the link between the families, Keita knew that the family had been pleased with me. I felt it too. She knew that Hamuera's elders had realised I wasn't the intended one, and knew that they would have found out that I hadn't had much schooling and hadn't been brought up by the old people. They would have made their own enquiries, an old cousin talking to an old cousin behind an old hand. There'd been a lot of whispering. But because they'd said nothing, hadn't accused Keita, hadn't taken Hamuera and gone home, my grandmother knew they had accepted me as their new daughter.

I wasn't beautiful like Makareta. I was skinny and toothy and scarry-legged with multicoloured hair, but they saw me differently. Tall like the tipuna, with eyes like Ava Gardner, they said — ancestress and actress! And I was poked and prodded and peered at. Even so, the hardest-slitted eyes on me, then and after that, were Keita's.

I'd saved us from shame but still Keita knew the Te Waru family had something up their sleeves if anything went wrong — something to accuse us of. She could leave nothing undone to make sure that Hamuera's family continued to feel that the arrangement honoured them.

Our mother needed a good house. It wouldn't do for Hamuera's family to see where their new daughter had been allowed to live. So there would be a new house for Mama and one for Hamuera and me. There would be room for my brothers and sisters to have houses too, as long as there was enough work nearby for them to be able to keep on living here, because even with the new land being opened up there still would not be enough for them all to make a living from it.

Keita went to town and arranged the loans, then let it be known to everyone that there was land to be cleared, a swamp to be drained, sites to be levelled and fencing to be done.

From then on the main talking point was the wedding that was to take place, the houses that were to be built, the land that was to be brought in.

We had work.

Before the end of winter everything had been planned. Gardens were extended so that extra corn, potatoes, kumara, pumpkin and cabbage could be planted. Grass seed was sown in the spring after the frosts had gone. Those who were home during the week spent what time they could cutting the scrub on the new land and taking it to stack in the paddock where the cooking fires would be, and where the marquee would be set up for the wedding. They cut posts and trimmed battens for new fences. We cleared bracken and dug out thistles.

In the weekends everyone went on to the land, taking rolls of wire, nails and staples to do the fencing, or they set about the task of removing stumps from the ground. And when the first roughness had been worked out, one of my uncles came with a tractor and discs to break the ground ready for sowing.

Keita and Gloria set up a cooking place and cooked wild pork and vegetables in the big pots for the workers, made paraoa parai in the camp oven and kept the water boiling for tea.

After much of the clearing, fencing and sowing had been

done, sites were levelled for the houses, and when these were ready the builder and the materials arrived.

I watched the foundations being laid, the framework going up, the weatherboards beginning to cover the frames, and seeing all this was what had me doubting. I wondered how all of this could be for me if I wasn't the one meant. I had doubts when I looked into my heart.

But it was when the houses were nearly finished that Mama became ill, and for a time I couldn't think of anything else but that. Ever since I was a little girl Mama had been my responsibility.

One afternoon Keita came into work and said that Mama had been taken to hospital. By the look on my grandmother's face I thought Mama could be dead.

And when I went into the ward, into the whiteness and the stillness of the room, a question came from me in the language I'd never before spoken — 'Kua mate a Mama?' — a question too terrible to be asked in English. 'Still with us,' Keita said, not in English. 'We have to sit and wait and pray.'

We waited — Dadda, Manny, my grandparents and me — now and again reaching to touch Mama's colourless face, her black hair spread on the white pillow, the sheet-white hands. And when the nurse asked us to leave at the end of visiting hours, Keita told her that we had to stay and watch. 'I'm afraid you can't,' the nurse said. 'But if you like, one or two of you can wait in the waiting room?'

'One or two will stay,' Keita said. 'The others will wait in the waiting room.'

'I'm sorry but you can't stay in the wards.'

Keita didn't answer, just turned away from the nurse and gave her attention to Mama.

'I'll get Sister,' the nurse said and went, her white shoes squealing in the corridor.

It was before the sister came in that Mama's lips moved. 'They come,' she whispered. Keita leaned towards her. 'Send them away,' she said. 'Tell them to go and not come back. Tell them now.'

'I'm afraid we have our rules and you'll all have to leave,' the sister said as she came in.

'We're staying by our daughter,' Keita said.

'If one or two would like to wait in the waiting room we'll be checking Mrs Tatua every hour. We'll keep you informed.'

'Someone will stay.'

'Rules are rules, I'm afraid.'

But we turned back to Mama as her lips began to move again. 'Gone,' she said.

'Good, Daughter. Good. Don't let them back.'

'I'll tell you what,' Sister said. 'Hubby can stay a while as long as the rest of you will go. If hubby would like to sit quietly in case Mrs Tatua wakes . . . as long as there's no trooping backwards and forwards in the corridors.'

We left Dadda and I went with Keita to the waiting room while the others went to our relatives' place to sleep, and after some hours of waiting Keita and I took off our shoes and went along to the ward, where Dadda was sitting in the dark. 'Shifted her hands,' I said.

'Shifted her hands, opened her eyes, said nothing,' Dadda said.

'Never mind, she saw you,' Keita said. 'If you weren't there, if I let those nurses send us all out, Gloria would wake up and think she's in heaven.'

Our father's sorrowful face loosened and he laughed, and in the dark I saw Mama move. Her eyelids flickered but didn't open and her lips curved into part of a smile. 'See there,' Keita said. 'If we'd all gone out my daughter would have listened in the dark, heard nothing and said to herself, "Huh, this heaven's a quiet place,"' which was enough to make Dadda laugh to wake the dead. Our mother's smile widened. 'Shush, Dadda, coming with torches,' I said.

'I'm afraid no one's permitted in the wardrooms after lights out,' one of the nurses said.

'Sister said the husband could stay,' Keita said. 'But my son-in-law and my granddaughter are going now. I'll stay so that my daughter can see somebody when she opens her eyes.'

'Hear that?' Dadda said as I went with him along the corridor. 'Son-in-law. First time I've heard that from her. Ha ha, my daughter, it must be you that's bringing your father up in the world. Ha ha, son-in-law.'

At work next morning I turned on the big taps, beating the soap shaker until the water foamed. Doors were opening and shutting, trays were coming in, dishes were being scraped and stacked, trolleys rattled, cutlery slid on the trays. Hospital sounds, but the smells were different. Voices.

'Where were you?' Lootie asked.

'Up at the hospital,' I said. 'My mother . . .'

'How bad?' Lootie swung the stock pot up.

'Collapsed at home, bleeding.'

'Mmm. They took her womb out, I suppose.' She pulled the skins off the onions with a long knife, leaned back from the fumes squinting. 'I got a cousin lost her womb. After that she change into a man.' The skinless onions rolled on the board and she halved them with swift chops, diced them, lifted the board to her shoulder and shunted them into the pot. 'And they give her blood, I suppose . . . ? You got to watch them with that blood. They can give you a Chinaman blood, a Japanee blood, a white man blood, a black man blood, or any blood all mix up together. After that you don't know what you going to change into.'

I plunged my arms in and out of the water, pulling the dishes through, Lootie droning beside me, thinking of Mama. But there was something that Keita had said in the waiting room in the middle of the night that was nothing to do with Mama. 'When you stood in the house you had no doubt,' Keita had said, seeing into the corners of me. I hadn't known how to answer her at first.

'I hardly went to school,' I said.

'You're talking about that other one, your cousin. All her going away to school didn't help us. She ran off and gave us no thought.'

'And I wasn't the one meant.'

'Huh, meant. If you're not the one meant your Aunty Anihera and your mother wouldn't've done what they did. If you're not the one meant your cousin wouldn't've gone away. If you're not the one meant it wouldn't have been you standing in the house with the words coming from you without a doubt in your heart. What you have to know and remember is that your marriage is for the people, like mine was. When I married your grandfather we had seen each other just once, but we had been promised since we were children. We were brought together when I was nineteen. Three months later we were married and it was up to the two of us to make a success of it. We did our best because we had to. It was for the people, and if it went wrong it meant the people were wrong. The people had the responsibility of us. At that time I knew nothing about the land, but I had to learn. It had to be me because there was no one else left in our part of the family of my generation. Now you have to learn too. We gave your cousin all the knowledge, gave her everything, but she turned her back on us. You have to know that you and Hamuera can't be wrong. If it goes wrong, then it's all the people that are wrong. The people, all of us, have the care of you.'

So we were like an investment or an insurance policy, I suppose, but I didn't think of that then. We were being given everything, being cared for in every way and nothing could be different from that. There could be no going back, because it was what they all wanted, what Keita wanted, what Mama wanted.

It was what I wanted too. I knew I could love. My doubts were no match for that. It is now, on looking back, that I understand these things more fully.

'The girl's stacked up,' Lootie said. 'Got them done and cleaned up. Clean up again today if you want to go. If Bigboy let you.'

It was a wedding for everybody, and everyone had work to do and decisions to make in preparation for it — except for me. I was told my part would come on the day — to wear the dresses (because there were to be two wedding gowns, one arranged for by Keita and my own family, the other by Hamuera's family), to say the words, to sit at the centre table, be the one.

All I knew was that the dressmakers were busy, bridesmaids and groomsmen were being chosen from all the families, food was being promised from everywhere. The meeting house was being renovated, the grounds levelled and drained and trees and flowers were being planted. Everyone was discussing mattresses, bedding, sleeping spaces for the hundreds of people who would be our guests. And they were talking about water, water, water — and wood, of course. I had my job to go to, letters to write, Mama and the family to look after. None of the arrangements were for me to worry about.

When the day came I think I managed to be who they all wanted me to be, though some of the memories are indistinct now. I was carried along on words — called words, words spoken, words sung. But what I remember most was the happiness of the old people. After the ceremony the big whariki were brought out from in the house and spread on the ground for everyone to put their gifts on. And the kuia and koroua in their best wedding clothes stepped out of their new shoes and sang the old songs, danced the hula, did the pukana, laughed and played. They were like tekoteko coming dancing off the boards of the house with spread fingers, sharp elbows, their paua eyes coming to life with brand new whites showing and centres glinting, faces stretched and mouths turned down. Making it real.

After the wedding we were sent away in Hamu's brother's car with the middle tiers of both wedding cakes in boxes on the back seat, to visit relatives who had not been able to attend.

It took three weeks to see everyone, and everywhere we went we were treated like important people because of the ancestors and the land, but I didn't realise it fully then. Rooms were made comfortable for us, special food was prepared and we were given money and gifts to help us on our way together.

And when we arrived home again our house was ready for us. Our new cutlery, crockery, pots and pans had been unpacked and put in cupboards. Curtains were up and cupboards were stocked. At the back of the house there was a newly built chook house with six black hens and a bantam in it. Everyone was there when we arrived and we had an all-night singing party in our new house.

We were given everything and it made the old people happy. It was for all of us, now and forever, they kept saying. They said it was like the old times.

What we had after our homecoming was hard work. Even though we'd been given so much and there was always help when we needed it, it was hard. We had dry stock at first and there was land to bring in, fences to make, clearing, ploughing and planting to be done. Later we built up a milking herd. It was hard work then and it's hard work now. But I always knew how to work hard. I liked the way it felt to work hard around my house and on the land. I was ready for that. I was sure.

But what I became unsure about was the one thing I'd never doubted before, that is, love. I believed in love and was certain I knew what it was. But I suppose it was because of the circumstances of our coming together that I needed assurance that Hamu and I had married for love — my idea of love.

All the eyes were on Hamu and me. Mama, Keita, the old aunties and uncles all poked and spied, all had their own ways of talking to us, reminding us.

I don't know if the eyes found fault with me, but I know all my family loved Hamu. He worked hard for us and had knowledge of what to do on the land.

But he's a quiet man and it was hard for me to understand that at first. He didn't talk much. And in a way I didn't want him to be so good at things, so solid, so loved by the family. I think I wanted him to be like Dadda instead, silly and singing, and what Mama called 'useless'. I wanted him to tease me with loving words, the way Dadda teased Mama.

I could remember the times when I was a little girl when Dadda would wake us in the night with his crying. Mama would have to shake him and hold him. And she'd light a candle and go out into the kitchen for a cloth to wipe his face with. She'd talk to him until he'd calmed down, then he'd say things to her like, 'Where would I be without you, my Glory, what would I do?' After a while the two of them would sit up in bed and Mama would roll them a cigarette each. She'd light them from the candle then blow the candle out. There'd be a sweet candle and smoke smell and we'd see the two cigarettes, like two burning eyes, glowing in the dark.

We knew that Dadda thought Mama was the most beautiful woman in the world. He told her. He told everyone. He had songs for her full of all the love words, even though Mama used to say they were only silly drunk songs and she'd rather have six-pence and a bag of flour.

Or what is love? There is the love that you both know, where excited feelings make your skins tingle and the black centres of your eyes enlarge, as though you let each other into yourselves through your eyes. Your bodies are together and you have him inside you with your skins riding against each other and you put your mark on each other. Is it love? Apart from each other there were times when you could doubt it. Apart from each other you could be not satisfied with words, or entering or marking. You could want to lay the other open, want to eat the heart, suck the eye sockets. Is it love? I wanted to know that Hamu couldn't live without me. I wanted words from him that would open him.

Or is love what others see, what they all watch for in faces, in eyes, what they listen for in the words you use, the things you say, as if they're watching it all happen on a screen? These were the thoughts and doubts that came from the child in me.

And the eyes watched for other signs too — watched for little children opening doors to visitors, kids finding eggs or carrying an egg hidden in the hands, babies sucking their toes. They watched me for difference or change and they analysed dreams. But it was nearly two years before I became pregnant with little Gloria, and it was Dadda who had the dream. 'I saw them. Two,' he said, 'wrapped up tight and sleeping.'

He believed all along that I would have twins. 'Where'd the other one get to?' he said when he first saw baby Gloria through the window of the nursery in the hospital where she was born. 'Looks like a ten-bob note,' he said, and I thought how silly and funny my father was. Then when I looked at my baby again I began to see that it was true. She looked just like ten shillings. I was glad to have Dadda there to make me laugh.

The girl that I was had been frightened going in through the big doors in the middle of the night with broken waters and scarcely time to wave to Hamu and Mama before the doors shut behind me. I followed the nurse with the suitcase into a hot room where my particulars were taken down and my clothes were taken away.

I was unprepared for having to have a standing bath supervised by someone I didn't know, who was no older than myself, and then to be stretched out on a narrow bench to have her shave me, the razor first of all sweeping round and over my big stomach as though I was being peeled and sliced, then scratching and scraping between my legs until all the hair was gone and I was an egg, ready to crack. I was glad of the pains as they became stronger, that distracted me from all that was happening.

I was unprepared, when taken to the theatre in the early hours of the morning, to have to lie on my back while strangers pushed my knees up under my chin and a mask was held over my mouth and nose. I pushed the mask away, I pushed my baby down, heard myself scream, unprepared for the sound of it, felt myself breaking in two. Then little Gloria came, my own wet baby, into the hands of strangers, but I don't mean to say they were unkind. At last she was given to me, but there was no one there to see her except for kind strangers.

And when baby and I had been attended to we were wheeled away from each other in opposite directions. I wasn't prepared for that. Back in the ward I couldn't know if it was my baby or someone else's that I heard crying every time the door to the nursery opened at the other end of the corridor.

That night I woke in the dark and thought of the placenta, wondered what had happened to it. Where was the little parcel wrapped by Kui Hinemate, or the basket made by Keita, for the whenua to be buried in? I tried to sleep. It was best not to think of such things.

In the afternoons sometimes Mama and Keita came to visit, or Lootie or Bessie from work. In the evenings Hamuera came. My visitors were allowed to go and see little Gloria through the nursery window, as if window-shopping. They'd give baby's name, then a nurse would wheel her, in a wire cot that some other baby could have died in, close to the window where they could see her head and part of her face. She was wrapped in every baby's blanket and there was a note on a pink card, stuck to the bed with sticking plaster, which gave her name, her weight, her date and time of birth.

Sometimes my visitors would come back into the ward

looking uneasy and I would know they had left baby Gloria turning her mouth for food.

They'd stay until the bell rang, then go tiptoeing out, not wanting their best shoes to put specks on the waxed floors, not wanting sounds to go from themselves along the corridors or for eyes to look at them as they went. Outside my window they'd turn and wave but not speak, as though they didn't want their words falling into the pansies and forget-me-nots for the birds to find — as though they didn't trust these birds who made their nests from whatever they found in one place or another.

There were little pills that were given to us every morning that gave me stomach pains. I found a little hole in one of the bed rails to put them into.

Samuel was born a year after little Gloria, and Tina a year after that. Each time I went into hospital I tried not to remember too much.

We've been through the good times on the land, and the bad. It's been hard to afford machinery, which seems to be necessary but it cuts out people. Mostly it's been a struggle, but we all eat. People are heading back in these hard times and we have to find new ways, as Manny and Michael have done with hydroponics, as Hamuera has done by contracting, while the children and I work the land. Mama Gloria has always helped us — looked after the children when they were little, made a vegetable garden, prepared meals for us.

I think Keita was happy before she died. She kept saying during her last days, 'We're all still here.' And so we are. That's all I can think of for the days ahead, that we'll be here keeping hold. It's what Hamu and I have been given to do. We all have to survive but we want more than just surviving, that's what Makareta has always said. We want the best of everything for ourselves and the children, everything right for them, but I don't know yet how we will make that be.

I never thought there could be anyone else like Keita, but after Keita died, Mama Gloria became the new Keita, stubborn, determined, keeping us all on our toes. She misses Dadda, as we all do.

'Fifty-nine is my ripe old age,' Dadda said when we brought him home from hospital. There was so much wrong with him that the doctor said it was easier to tell what was right. His legs and hips had given out, he had pain in his stomach, his liver and kidneys weren't functioning properly and his heart was playing up. We had turns at sitting by him, singing to him, happy enough for him to go when the time came.

As for the young ones, they seem confused, or some do, eating health food, smoking the taru kino and drinking top shelf. The old people say their confusion is because their whenua have gone down the slush hole with all the tutae and the rubbish, instead of being buried in the ancestral places where they belong. I think they must be right, or that must be part of it. These are some of the things I wanted to talk more to Makareta about. These are some of the things she and I have already discussed during our long telephone conversations.

Anyway, some of the young parents are bringing those ways back again now. Good on them. They're bringing their babies' whenua back from the hospitals, not too scared to ask for them. They treat the hospital as if it's their hospital, brave young people. They're giving their children the ancestral names, staunchly. It's good that they want those things back again, or it's good that they want to do things their way, because they have many needs. There's been a lot lost to them.

I think the ancestors or God have made a mistake taking Makareta. It's such a waste when the kids, all of us, need her so much. She's got the knowledge of the old people. She has their language and their stories and the lovely kuia ways that children love, even though she's not the age of a kuia yet. Also, she has the knowledge of new ways of doing things that are all right, comfortable for us, or she knows how we can change these things to make them comfortable and acceptable. It's not sticking to the old ways that's important, she said, but it's us being us, using all the new knowledge our way. Everything new belongs to us too.

But she's dead. We're waiting here to call her home and it makes me hurt and sad.

I had an angry thought when I saw the group getting ready at the gateway to bring Makareta in. I had to stop myself from thinking it, because I know it's not right to send bad thoughts to people arriving. I looked at our cousin Mata, whom I haven't seen for nearly forty years, and wondered why it couldn't have been her instead of Makareta being carried home. What use are you to us, I thought, then put the thought aside.

After that I turned my pain back to Makareta. 'You come home to us like this?' I said as they brought her through the gateway. Because ever since Polly died I'd been asking her to come home and build a house on her land. We needed her here. But she liked her life in the city, liked her work there. I know it was important work and we were all proud of that. She was well known all over the country, as well as in other parts of the world, for the work she did for our people — the advice, the help, the knowledge that she was able to give. But it wore her out. She could've rested here. We'd have cared for her, treasured her, the way we always had.

She sent Michael to us instead, telling us it wouldn't be long before she came too.

Her coming was only a month away when she rang to tell me that she'd found our cousin Mata. Mama Gloria had been dreaming about Mata and saying that she'd never turned up the way Keita always said she would. 'Her land's here,' Keita would say, 'so one day she'll come.' I had a picture of Mata's expressionless face in my mind, her outstretched arm and the magic marble.

But it was after she left here that Mata began to be a more real cousin to us. She was talked about often, even though her name was hardly ever spoken. They called her 'Anihera's one'. The old people, whenever they met, would ask Mama Gloria, 'Have you heard any more of Anihera's one?'

My mother would tell them about Keita writing to the woman who was Mata's guardian but not getting any reply. Gloria had tried writing directly to Mata but her letters were never answered.

After a time people stopped asking, and Keita and Mama Gloria stopped writing the letters, but now and again we'd hear Keita say that the land would bring Mata back one day.

Now Mata is bringing back to us the one whose place I stood in when I was sixteen. Makareta has never told me if she thought it was what I would do. She's never told me if it's what she hoped as she watched from the window as the taxi pulled away that day. I never asked.

But I think I did right. If I had other dreams, if there was something else, some other part of me, what does it matter? If love is different from what I thought, what does it matter?

It was up to me before, it's up to me again.

I think we've done all right, Hamu and me. Our as-is-where-is marriage is just as good as any do-it-yourself, pick-your-own. Better than most, I think.

MATA

forty-three

I didn't mind the hunger or the tiredness as I walked. I was glad of it, happy to have feelings that were only from hunger or fatigue. I wanted to walk forever, liking the night and the black road, not minding the sore feet, the aching body, pleased to be one of the street people. Somewhere further on I would have to sleep, but would do that only when I could walk no more.

The road ahead of me began to rise and curve and every now and again a vehicle approached. I would see the lights ahead of me at the bend, or hear the noise of the engine behind me, and I'd quickly cross to the side of the road to wait on the footpath until it had gone by. I don't know why I had chosen to walk the middle of the road, but perhaps it was something to do with words that were going through my head — 'middle of the road, middle of the night, middle of nowhere'. I had picked up the beat of them, needing words churning through me that would keep thinking away. I guessed it was already past the middle of the night.

It was when I arrived at the bend in the road that I heard someone call my name and, looking up, saw a woman standing on the footpath. 'Mata, over here,' she said. I wanted to walk on, wanted not to hear, wanted to keep on doing what I was doing and not be distracted from it, because I had made up my mind. I had instructed my feet. But my feet turned. I put them into shoes and crossed to the footpath. 'Remember me?' the woman said, 'Makareta, the spoilt one, when we were little girls.' She took my hand, put an arm round me. 'This way,' she said. 'My house is up here.'

We were at the beginning of a long driveway lined with shrubs and trees. There were low ferns on either side, shielding lights that lit our way. 'I saw you from the bus,' she said. 'I knew it was you and when I got off the bus I hurried up to the house because I knew I could watch you from there. I thought if I tried

241

to walk back I might lose you.' I didn't answer her. All I could think of was that I was doing something I didn't want to do.

The drive became steeper and Makareta turned me onto a narrow path that led through trees. 'It's quicker this way,' she said. We went over a little bridge under which I could hear water running. There was a bush smell that I could remember from a long time ago. We continued on up a series of stone steps until we came to the house where a light shone over a solid wood door. 'This is where I live all alone,' Makareta said. 'But not for long.'

We went into a hallway where Makareta took off her shoes, so I took mine off too, remembering something about the taking off of shoes from that long time ago. We walked on deep, white carpet into a lounge where a dog stood and put his nose to me. He was white and shaggy too, just like the carpet. 'It's all right, Hipi, this is our cousin Mata,' Makareta said. She arranged the cushions on a chair and I sat down into the deep comfort of it. I hadn't said a word since we met and sat there feeling my grubbiness, my shabbiness, my dullness, my ugliness, my shyness. I'd wanted only to walk. 'A cup of tea first,' Makareta said.

It was a high-ceilinged room where I sat, with polished beams and large windows. One wall was lined with shelves of books and had a built-in sound system and television, and a cabinet that I guessed would contain music and video tapes. Wall lights lit up paintings that almost covered the two remaining walls. In the paintings were wooden figures that had been brought to life. Their dark faces stared out as though their hearts were broken, and there were patterns that curled in on themselves, or out from themselves in colours of feeling, strands woven into them as though they came from trees. Other patterns wove in and out into a flow or a clenching. There were birds that seemed to be people, and people that seemed to be birds. In some of them, people walked on long roads with banners flying.

As well as the lit pictures there were carved figures that were not lit, some large ones standing in shadows against the walls and smaller ones here and there on the shelves.

Makareta came with a cup of tea that she put on a little table by my chair.

'Thank you.' My voice sounded bruised and strange.

'And then a bath. I'll run a bath for you,' she said, and went away. I repeated the words of the room over to myself — beams and windows, lights and shelves, books and pictures, colours and patterns and faces — to keep myself from thinking.

The bathroom was spacious and mirrored and the bath was warm and perfumed. I thought Makareta would leave me but she didn't. She took soap and a cloth and began washing me, letting the warm water run down over me. I felt ugly and shy, but there was nothing I could do or say.

When Makareta had finished she went away and came back with satin nightclothes, wool slippers and large towels, which she left on a bench for me. By the time I had finished dressing she had a meal ready. It was poached fish, with lettuce, tomato, little beetroots and warm bread rolls. She had set it on a special tray for me with a white napkin and silver cutlery. I'd never thought of such things. She had her own tray too and we sat down in the armchairs with them on our laps. 'I'll have just a little,' she said.

Later she took me to the bedroom where I was to sleep. She turned the bed covers back for me, helped me into bed and tucked me in the way a mother does. I didn't want to want it, and I couldn't speak. 'In the morning,' she said, 'you can tell me everything that has happened to you since last we met, or tell me everything that has happened to you since before that.' I could feel my eyes closing.

What I told her the next day was mainly about the waiting. First of all waiting for my mother to come, and then after that, waiting for there to be someone for me, a mother, a friend, a child, someone to love me that I would love. I had waited and wanted — until at last I had decided that I wouldn't wait any more, wouldn't want anything but what I already had, which was myself, shabby and ugly, my name, my little photo in its frame, my own two feet to walk me.

I talked and talked as I had never talked before, in a way that I didn't know I could. It was as though the walking, the thinking and the not thinking, had jolted the tongue inside me. I told her all that had ever, or never, happened, wanting to talk on and on. I had come away so as not to want, so as not to be sitting waiting, yet here I was reaching, letting all that had waited and waited inside me pour out. I had found someone, even though I hadn't looked for her, someone who treated me closely, as though I was part of who she was. I remembered that a long time ago she had given me a dress and shoes.

Then I remembered that I wanted not to want.

I stopped talking and took out the photo of my mother to show her. 'This is my only piece of luggage,' I said. 'I want to walk away before I find myself wanting more than this. I'll walk, and either I'll keep on living, or I won't.'

She sat down beside me and put her arm round my shoulders. 'I need you,' she said. Strange words. I had never heard them spoken before. 'I'm tired and I need your help. I'm selling up and moving back home and there's all the packing to do, all the things to sort out. It'll take three weeks, perhaps four. If you'll help me I won't have to call on Michael or our cousin Missy, or anyone else. And if you come with me you won't have to walk any more.'

'People go away,' I said, 'or they die.' I don't know why I said it. 'I don't know people for long, then they go away, or they die.' I listened to myself say it in my own flat voice, my own unfeeling way.

Then I decided I would help her. She had the house to sell and communications to make with the children's father. She had papers that she wanted to go through and arrangements to be made with her lawyer. She was in between cars, had sold one and was waiting for the delivery of another, more suitable for out in the wop-wops, she said.

She went about doing what she needed to do and I began the packing.

It was a house of beautiful things, some of which she wanted to take with her, some of which she wanted her cousins to have. I used to dream about houses but never houses like that. I used to dream about belonging in a house with my own family. I'd have pictures in my mind of rooms and furnishings, windows, cupboards and fireplaces, dishes, glasses, knives and forks and things. I'd go over them in my mind. But I always had trouble seeing my family, picturing a family for me. The figures in the houses were always shadowy. They were borrowed families, people that I'd seen through a window or on a train, and I was trying to make them my own. Sometimes there would be just me and my mother, whose face I couldn't remember. I would build a house around us and this mother and I would sleep in each other's arms.

Makareta spent most of her time in her office sorting books and papers, or, once the car arrived, out seeing lawyers and land agents, while I worked from room to room wrapping and packing. It was a house of many rooms, which I worked steadily through. In the late afternoons I would walk to the shops for a few supplies, then come home and cook a small meal for us. If I hadn't been there to cook, I don't think Makareta would've eaten at all.

In the evenings we talked, and each day I looked forward to that. Nothing had matched it in my life. I was unafraid about enjoying those times together because I knew that they would soon end. I had made up my mind to give myself to the task that was to be done, and at the end of it I would go on my way.

Sometimes Makareta talked about a house for me, on land she said was mine, but I didn't really listen. I knew just to accept for now that we were together, that something was happening to me for now, fleetingly. I knew not to want, not to have dreams — to have just myself and wherever my feet would take me. My life was not something that mattered.

By the end of three weeks everything was done, everything was packed and labelled. I was sorry when all the work was finished. The labels read — Back Home, Cat House, Parrot House. New owners were to move into the house in two weeks' time. Makareta tired easily and often rested in the middle of the day, but apart from that she looked well and cheerful. She was big-boned but not fat. She was beautiful.

Often I would hear her on the phone talking to her son Michael or to Missy, discussing houses and land, and me. She was looking forward to going 'back home', and the house that she had arranged for was almost completed. She had a deposit for me too, for a house she said, but I couldn't think about that. Whenever she mentioned it, it drove me silent. There was a cousin with a bulldozer who would clear the site for the house as soon as I said yes. 'Tell me yes,' she would say. 'There's no one to live on your land but you. There are children you can give it to if you want, later. But for now tell me yes. Say you'll go and live there, to let the people know you, especially the ones who knew your mother, because there are people there who grew up with her, who remember her. Do it for them. Aunty Gloria tells me I have to make you come home, so say yes. If you want a child to inherit your house and your land, the old people will tell you who.' I had learned not to want a house with or without a family inside. How could I? How could I want when I had given up wanting? None of this made sense to me.

She talked about the old lady often, the granny who looked after her when she was a little girl. 'She's by me,' she said. 'I can't see her, but sometimes she leans on me, sometimes she tickles my arm letting me know she's there. I hear her talking into my mind. When I'm lonely I talk to her, or when I need to sort something out. I was lucky during all those long nightshift hours when I worked as a nurse because she was there. I don't know how I would've managed without her. And when I'm needed back home she sends me there. I was home when Wi died, I was home when Keita died, because she let me know but I don't see her . . . Michael's the one, she said, "the one who sees." "Who's there?" he'd say when he was little. "Who's there with an old face?" I'd tell him, "That's Kui Hinemate who looked after me when I was a girl."' I thought Makareta was a little strange from some of the things she said.

I was sorry when all the packing was finished. The walls looked different without their books and pictures, and the house seemed emptier without the eyes of the carved figures looking out from the corners and down from the shelves. But still it was a beautiful house, surrounded by dark green trees. Through the windows, through the trees, there was the blue and white harbour, and at night the sea of orange and yellow lights.

Makareta arranged for the Cat House and Parrot House boxes to be collected, and before going to bed I shifted them into a room close to the front door for the carriers who were to come the next morning.

That night I couldn't sleep, but lay awake reminding myself not to want, telling myself that all I had was me, my name, a photo, my two feet, and that there was nothing else that was anything to do with me.

After lying awake for several hours I got up and walked about the empty rooms, reminding myself that this was a stopping-off place, a rest on my journey to nowhere. I wasn't unhappy, liked the thought of nowhere, of emptiness, of not wanting. It meant pushing away hope that sometimes comes, and trying to think of nothing, finding ways of not having thoughts. I decided to make myself a hot drink and sit and look through the windows, through the trees, for the last time.

When I passed Makareta's room someone was in there, someone I remembered from a long time ago, and even though it was dark I recognised the old lady who had looked after Makareta when she was little. So I went into the room. The woman didn't look up or speak, but stood with her hands in front of her, palms upwards, looking down at Makareta. Makareta's eyes were open and she was looking at the woman.

Then I noticed the other people. The room was full of them. They were shadowy. They were old. But even though they were shadowy I could see that some of them looked like her, Makareta, or like me. They were rustling and shuffling and seating themselves.

I moved over closer to the bed, but I could see by her stillness that Makareta was dead.

That was all right because people go away, or they die. I went to the kitchen and made a cup of Milo. I sat by the windows drinking it, looking out, then I went back to my room. After a while I went to sleep.

I woke next morning to the doorbell ringing. It was the carrier who had come for the Cat House and Parrot House boxes.

When he'd gone I showered and dressed in my own old dress. I put my own two shoes on my feet and sat down and ate an orange and had a cup of tea. I tidied the room that I'd slept in and took the photo from the windowsill, then walked out of the house and down the long drive and stood at the gateway deciding which way I should go, waiting for my feet to walk me. But my feet stood still, then they turned me back.

There were things to do when someone died. The dead don't just disappear to heaven, I had to remind myself of that. There were things to do, but I didn't know about them. I remembered Makareta saying, 'Tell me yes. When I go home I want you to come with me. Gloria's expecting you. Your cousins are expecting you. All the ones who knew your mother are expecting you. They want you to stay and not go away again. Tell me you will.'

I'd found it hard to answer her. But when she'd said, 'I need you. If you come I won't have to send for Michael, or anyone, to help me,' I'd said I'd go with her. She'd hugged my stiff body and thanked me. Then she'd said, 'We'll see about the rest when we get there.'

Now she was dead so there was no need, but there was still something that I should do. There were things to do when someone died, but I didn't know what they were.

I went into the room. The old woman was still there by the bed, but the others had gone. Nothing about that night or morning seemed strange to me at the time, but I felt that my life was changing even though I didn't want it to. I had stopped waiting and hoping. I had tried to walk away but my own two feet had turned me.

'What will I do?' I said to the woman. She sat plainly visible in the chair by the bed but didn't look at me, looked only at Makareta and didn't speak.

So I sat in the chair on the opposite side of the bed and tried to think. I thought of going out to the footpath and finding someone to help me. I thought of knocking on someone's door. Then I thought of the one person I knew who would help me, who would know what to do. I rang the wharf and asked for Sonny. I didn't know if he still worked there. I hadn't seen him for ten or more years. The man who answered the phone said they would give him a message to ring me. I waited there by Makareta because I thought that might be the right thing to do.

It was an hour before Sonny rang back. It was difficult trying to tell him all that had happened. I heard my flat voice asking if he could just tell me what to do. He said, 'I'll come up after one o'clock. I can knock off at one. What's the address?' The address was there on the slip of paper that the carrier had left. I read it out over the phone.

It was about three o'clock when he arrived, along with two elderly women. I stood in the doorway as they came up the drive. It seemed the right thing to do. They pressed their noses on mine, and cried, clutching my stiff shoulders. Inside the house Sonny introduced me to the two women. 'This is my wife Mata,' he said to them and I was surprised. I'd forgotten we were still married. We'd had nothing to do with each other for many years.

We went into the room where Makareta was, and as we went in, the two women began to call in their own language. It was strange to me. Makareta's granny had gone. When they finished Sonny stood by the bed and spoke in the language that I didn't know he had.

The women sat down then, one on either side of Makareta. Sonny took my elbow and led me out. 'We have to have a wash,' he said. 'Then we'll find out what we have to do.'

I remembered something about washing from a long time ago — when I'd found out that my mother wasn't an angel flying. As we'd left the cemetery Aunty Gloria and I had washed our hands. She'd washed her face and dabbed her eyes as well.

'We have to ring the family,' Sonny said. 'The ones close around, so they can come here quick and take over.'

'I don't know any,' I said. But then I remembered the carrier's dockets with the Cat House and Parrot House addresses and the two phone numbers on them.

Sonny rang one of the phone numbers and a little girl answered. She gave him her father's work number and Sonny was able to get hold of Benny, Makareta's cousin, and tell him what had happened. Some time later six people arrived. The two old women went to the door and did their strange calling. The group of cousins and their father and an old man came in, crying for Makareta. It was all strange to me.

Before the arrival of these visitors Sonny had been out to buy food, and he'd helped me to unpack dishes, cutlery and pots and to organise the kitchen and dining room so that people could be fed. While the visitors were in the room with Makareta, I did the best I could, setting up the table with the best cutlery and dishes.

I sliced meat and made salads and sandwiches, cooked a tray of sausage rolls and a tray of scones. It's one thing I know how to do.

The man called Ben, father of Makareta's cousins, came out into the lounge with Sonny, who did the ringing up for him. Soon there were other people, including a doctor, a policeman and the men from the undertakers, coming in.

It was late afternoon before everyone was ready for the lunch that I'd prepared. The undertakers had taken Makareta away.

After everyone had eaten, most of the people went away to get a change of clothes. Sonny and I put mattresses into the lounge room, unpacked the bedding and made up beds for the cousins when they returned, and for the people coming from 'back home', who would arrive at midnight. We prepared food for their arrival.

'So you found a cousin,' Sonny said. I had never told him about my mother's family and had always said that I didn't have any relatives.

'I met my mother's family once,' I said, 'but I never heard from them again, so I pretended they didn't exist.'

'How come you found this one?'

'One day she rode past me in a bus. We saw and recognised each other.' That's all I told him.

He asked me if I wanted him to come with me the next day so I would know what to do.

'Where? Come where?' I asked.

'To take Makareta back.' He paused, I suppose at the puzzled look that I gave him. 'You have to go,' he said. 'She's your cousin . . . like your sister. You were the one here when she died, now you've got to stay with her right through.' I couldn't say anything and after a while he said, 'I'd better come. I'll ring the job in the morning and go and get my stuff.' Then he said, 'What about you, your job?'

'I left it.'

'The house, some clothes?'

'I left there. I've got no clothes.'

'Money?'

'I left it for the Postbank to have.'

He looked at me and said nothing, and I sat there thinking how odd it must have sounded. So I told him all that had happened between Makareta and me in the weeks that I'd been there. After a while he started to laugh as though something was funny. 'Well, I better come with you,' he said.

The cousins came back. Other people came as well — many people, arriving in one group after another. Something was happening to me. I was being part of something and I wasn't used to it. I didn't know what all the people were doing, but I knew how to get the food ready and how to make the table look nice with all Makareta's beautiful things.

At midnight Aperehama, Girlie, Nonny and Win came. They cried for Makareta in a way that made me afraid. They all remembered me and cried over me too. I wasn't used to it and wanted to pull away from them but knew I shouldn't. I stood stiff and still while they held on to me, until at last I could go to the kitchen and make tea for them.

It was after two o'clock when they all settled down on the mattresses that Sonny and I had put down for them. I went to bed in the room that I had been sleeping in up until then, and lay awake thinking about all that had happened.

When I went out into the kitchen the next morning Sonny was already up and had been to the dairy for milk and bread. We started getting the breakfast and he told me that we would leave at eleven for the undertakers because they wouldn't release her before then, and that all the cars would go from there. I didn't understand everything he was saying.

It was just after eleven when we all left the house with our bags and bundles. I went in Sonny's car along with Pahe and Josie, the two old women that had come on that first day with him. Aperehama and Girlie took Makareta's car and her dog because it was the only car they could persuade Hipi to get into. Then all the cars drove together to the undertakers, where there was another line of vehicles ready to accompany us. I didn't understand at first that all these other cars were coming with us. I didn't know how all these people had found out about Makareta.

The hearse came out onto the road. Aperehama's car pulled

out to lead it and we all followed. I was only beginning to understand what was happening, starting to realise that I was now on
my way back to the place that I had spent a three-week holiday
in when I was ten, a place that had been in my mind for many
years afterwards, but that I had eventually put out of my mind,
pretending to myself that I had never been there.

It was a six-hour drive. The railway station where I'd got off
the train all those years ago looked so small, but it was the same
station. The white, dusty road that I'd walked along with Aunty
Gloria had been widened and tarsealed. Our group of cars travelled slowly along it, but even so, what had seemed a long way
then took a few minutes only. There was the place where the
creek ran close to the road where we'd climbed through the fence
with the suitcase. We rounded a corner and the old house was still
there.

There were several new houses as well. We climbed slowly
for a short distance, rounded a bend and then looked down to
where the meeting house stood. I had not been to the meeting
house, or even close to it, when I had visited there as a child, but
I remembered seeing it one day when we were going over the hill
to the creek. To me then it was just an old deserted building,
standing alone on a rough square of ground. This was a renewed
house with lawns and gardens round it. There was another large
building beside it and there were people about.

Our cars drove slowly down the long drive and stopped outside the gateway. When we were out of the car Sonny said to me,
'You have to go to the front with Pahe and Josie. You have to
lead the way, or that's how I've seen it done.'

'I'll come with you,' I said.

'I might be needed to carry her,' he said, 'And anyway, you
have to go with them.'

He was whispering to me in an urgent way. 'You have to
know it's your place. Not anyone else here, only you. Like you
told me your mother is the oldest of her family and you're her
only child. That means it's you. You're the one closest. You're the
tuakana — in one way, even if she's older than you. You got to
be there right through. It'll be big, this tangi, hundreds of people
will come tomorrow and the days after, for someone so well

known all over the country.' I didn't know what Sonny was talking about.

The undertaker was opening the back of the car. He stood there and waited. Aperehama came up to Sonny, and Sonny nodded but neither of them said a word. Other people have ways of knowing things that I don't know, but I could feel something happening to me. Sonny took my arm and led me to where the two old women stood. He spoke to them in their language.

'It's quite right, dear,' Pahe said. 'You got to come right along with your sister. It's your own sister there. Us two old kuia, we come along to help your family. This dear daughter here, she's not ours. We only come to help bring her home because we feel sorry for your family. Your family's got no old people in the big town there to help you.' They were patting me, stroking my arm. I didn't understand what they were saying. 'We're going to clear the way, and we're taking you along. Now, dear, it won't be just you on your own. It'll be us and all your tipuna with you, all your ancestors.'

The men had taken the casket from the car. There was Aperehama and Ben, Ben's son, his son-in-law, Sonny and the undertaker. The others, including Makareta's Hipi, were forming up around and behind them. But the two old women held me, one by each arm, and we stood at the head of the casket. We seemed to be waiting.

Then I heard the strange calling. I stood shocked and still, but only for a moment because something was happening to me. The old women were urging me forward, so I walked.

We made our way slowly through the gateway. All the people were waiting there in front of the house and they were calling out and crying. The older ones were dressed mainly in black. The women wore green leaves in their hair and held greenery in their hands. There were younger people in an array of clothing — skirts and blouses, T-shirts and jeans, bush shirts and boots, caps bearing messages, track tops, track pants, sports shoes, jandals. There were mats laid out on the ground.

I could see Aunty Gloria, Manny, Missy, Chum and other faces that I remembered. They were holding each other and crying. Something was happening. Beside me Pahe started to call, and then Josie, as we kept on our slow walk forward.

Something was happening, because suddenly the place became more and more crowded. Suddenly there were people sitting by where the mats had been lain, where at first there had been nobody. There were men and women with marked chins and faces who belonged to an older time. They had my own face some of them, Makareta's and mine.

The verandah of the house filled with more people too — these people from an older time. Some of them were soldiers in uniform. One of them was Keita, who seemed to be both herself and Aunty Gloria at once, yet there were two of them.

And then I saw a woman standing forward of the others, looking only at me. It was Anihera.

I had waited. For years I had waited. For years I had wanted. Now that I had decided that I would not want or wait, and would have only what I had already,, my mother had come to me.

Around us, walking with us, there were more people. Walking right by the casket was Makareta's own Kui Hinemate with fantails in her hair. Her hand rested on the wood.

In the middle of the big lawn we all stopped. Pahe and Josie started to weep with high sounds and tears were running down their faces. The people waiting began to cry more loudly. Something was happening to me. Something.

My eyes were filling. Water was running from my eyes. Streams of water. Water was running from my nose and dropping onto the ground, streams of water. I had never cried before in all my life and now I felt that I would never stop. We all wept for a long time there. All my tears were falling and I was just letting them run. I had never cried before. Years of tears. And I heard the sounds come out of me, the crying sounds, just like the sounds of the women around me.

Gradually our crying lessened and we began moving forward again. The men put the casket down onto the mats and women came and sat around it, touching and stroking the wood. I was led to some seating then, and everyone in our group sat down. One after the other, men stood to speak, and there were sad droning songs that went on and on. When all the talking was over we moved forward again. I didn't know what was happening to me, but there was nothing that made me afraid.

The people, Aunty Gloria and the others, were forming a line. The other people, Anihera and the ones who had come crowding in, had moved back, become shadowy, except for Makareta's Kui Hinemate, whom I could see plainly, seated by the casket. Our group went forward and the people were putting their noses together and beginning to weep again. I didn't know how to do it but I wasn't afraid. I followed on after Pahe and Josie, trying to do what they did. When I came to the women they held on to me for a long time and wept and wailed over me and I felt my tears rushing out again. Something was happening to me.

Then I saw Makareta's Kui Hinemate walking into the house. I didn't know if I was the only one who could see her, didn't know if I was the only one who could see the other shadow people, but I know that it didn't seem strange to me, just as it hadn't seemed strange when I'd gone into the room full of people the night Makareta died.

The men picked Makareta up and we all went into the house, and the casket was put down in a place that had been made ready. The undertaker began undoing the screws, but I didn't realise at first that he was removing the lid, didn't know that I was going to look at the dead Makareta again. The crying and wailing began again, and when I looked down at Makareta I felt my tears pour out once more. I wasn't sure that my tears, or any of the crying that I had done that day, were for Makareta. They seemed to come from an unfound place, from years.

I was taken by Missy to sit with her on the mattresses, she on one side of Makareta, I on the other.

There we were the three of us.

Aunty Gloria was unwrapping photographs and Bub was arranging them about the casket. I took my photograph out of my pocket and gave it to Bub to put there too.

Men were getting up and speaking. I think they were talking to Makareta. People were settling themselves and there was nothing to make me afraid. I looked about for those others. I looked for Anihera. I looked for Kui Hinemate. They seemed to be there even though I couldn't see them any more, but I knew I would see them again.